WOLF OF SIGHT

THE GYPSY HEALER SERIES, BOOK 5

QUINN LOFTIS

Published by

Quinn Loftis Books, LLC

Little Rock, Arkansas

© 2019 Quinn Loftis Books LLC

United States of America

1st Edition

All rights reserved. No part of this publication may be reproduced, distributed, or transmitted in any form or by any means, including photocopying, recording, or other electronic or mechanical methods, without the prior written permission of the publisher

This book is licensed for your personal enjoyment only. This book (whether in electronic or physical form) may not be re-sold or given away to other people. If you would like to share this book with another person, please loan it through the appropriate channels or purchase an additional copy for each recipient. If you're reading this book and did not purchase it, or it was not purchased for your use only, then please return it, and purchase your own copy. Copyright infringement is a serious crime punishable by law. Thank you for respecting the hard work of this author.

Quinn Loftis Books, LLC

PO Box 1308

Benton, AR 72018

lovetoread@quinnloftisbooks.com

Photography and Cover Design: KKeeton Designs

❃ Created with Vellum

For Bo. Because you put up with me and no one else would.

PROLOGUE

"I have always thought the ability to see was overrated. I have met too many nasty people in this world. If they are *that* ugly in spirit, I cannot imagine what their physical appearance must be like."
~Heather

Fifteen years ago ...

"Mama, what's it like to see?" Five-year-old Heather Banks asked as she and her mother sat on the front porch swing. It was late November, and autumn had finally decided to make an appearance in the small town of Shady Grove, Texas. A slight breeze rustled the leaves covering their front yard. Heather could smell the crisp scent of the pine trees that stubbornly held on to their needles. The girl only knew it was the pine she was smelling because her daddy had, on several occasions, walked her around the whole of their property. Heather would touch and smell the different plants and trees so she could learn about them in a way she would understand. Her father often told her she shouldn't view her blindness as missing sight, but regard it as an opportunity to "see" the world in a way that those with sight never would.

"Some days, sight is wonderful," her mama said. "There are many fantastic things to see: vibrant colors, interesting animals, stunning lightning, freshly fallen snow, or the smile on a child's face. These are all amazing things to witness. However, there are days when sight is a curse. There are many things I wish I couldn't see. The hateful look of a person whose heart is full of malcontent, the daily pictures of bloodshed and violence on the evening news, the aftermath of a natural disaster, or watching a loved one waste away from an illness that has no cure. I suppose it is a blessing and a curse, just like our other senses."

"I wish I could see," Heather said. She rarely voiced this feeling. The girl didn't want to disappoint her parents and, somehow, even at that tender age, she knew it did. But every now and then, her heart would grow sad because she knew she was missing out on wonderful things.

"I know you do, honey," her mom said gently. "And I don't judge you for that. Don't ever be afraid to express your true feelings. Keeping them all bottled up inside stops you from dealing with your emotions in a healthy way. They become infected, like an unclean wound. You will grow bitter because of your disappointment. Before you know it, life has passed you by, and you've missed incredible blessings because you were too busy crying over things you can't change."

"Daddy says I am blessed because I can see the world the way others can't."

"That is true. Your daddy has always had the ability to find the good in circumstances that often seem only bad. Tell me this, little Tumbleweed, what do you hear right now?"

Heather focused on her surroundings and let her ears take in the sounds. "I hear the wind ... and the sound of something scampering on the ground. I hear five, no, six different types of birds. I hear the hum of the air conditioner, the tumbling of the dryer, and the clinking of the ice in your glass as it melts."

Her mama chuckled. "I hear very little of that. I hear the birds, but not all the different ones, and I hear the wind. But my ears are easily distracted by my sight, so I miss out on the other things. I know the strength of your other senses might be a poor consolation prize for your lack of sight, but don't miss out on what having those acute senses offer you that others will never experience."

LATER THAT NIGHT, Heather lay in her bed. Her parents were asleep, and she could hear the soft snores of her father. The house creaked and groaned in its usual fashion, as if it, too, was getting settled in for good night's rest. But as the world around Heather quieted, the little girl couldn't sleep.

The words from her conversation with her mama repeated in her mind. Heather knew she didn't want to live her life missing out on things because she was too busy wishing she wasn't blind. After all, Heather was actually five and a half, which was nearly six. She'd be in double digits before she knew it.

"Don't go wasting the opportunities the good Lord gave you, Heather Banks," she whispered to herself. It was something one of the old ladies in her church had said to her recently. Heather hadn't known what it meant at the time, but now, she thought maybe she did.

She took a deep breath noting the familiar smells of her home. The leftover scent of the cinnamon candles her mama liked to burn, the pipe her father smoked every evening after dinner, and the dryer sheets from the freshly laundered towels that filled her bathroom cabinets. These were scents that would forever be burned into her mind and would always fill her with warmth and joy. She smiled as she heard one of the dogs outside howl, causing the neighbor's dog down the road to answer. She heard the rustle of the willow tree that grew just outside her window and the hoot of an owl. It was as if the world around her was telling her good night because it knew she alone would hear them.

It was then and there, sitting on her bed at five and a half years old, but really nearly six, that Heather Banks made a decision. She wouldn't miss a single thing in life. She would wake up thankful to be a part of the world, knowing God made her for a reason. Therefore, she needed to get on living so she could find out what that reason was.

Finally, at peace with herself, she scooted underneath the blankets. The warm flannel sheets felt good against her chilled skin as she snuggled herself down. Heather fell asleep with a smile on her face as she realized she was excited about her future or, as her daddy called it, the adventure that was life. Hers would be a grand adventure because she would make it so. She would find the joy in every minute and hold tight to it like she did her tire swing rope as it flew her through the air. She would smile and laugh and joke and laugh some more. There would be no room for bitterness or disappointment. "Good night, world," she whispered and she swore she could hear the whisper of a woman's voice answer back, "Good night, little healer."

1

"Damn these wolves. They just don't know what it's like. *Their* mates are of age. *They* can perform the Blood Rites whenever they want. *They* don't have to feel like some sort of weirdo creeper every time they lay eyes on their mates. This is going to be the longest year of my life. If I could stand to be apart from her for longer than a few minutes, I'd go on a yearlong hunting trip in the middle of nowhere." ~Nick

"WE'RE JUST SUPPOSED to sit back and do nothing while our mates become witches?" Nick asked as he danced out of the way of a kick Kale had just aimed at his head. The pair had been sparring most of the morning. Their mates hadn't woken, and the men looked like idiots sitting in the hall across from their door so Ciro suggested they work off some excess energy with a little extra training. With the threat of a fight with Volcan looming, they could use all the training they could get. A few minutes into the sparring session, Kale and Nick, panting and dripping with sweat, had pulled off their shirts and thrown each other around the yard several times. Ciro stood close by, encouraging and commenting on their techniques.

"I dare you to forbid Kara from doing it." Kale chuckled. He bounced on the balls of his feet and sidestepped Nick's punch. Nick got him when he spun back around and backhanded Kale's chest.

"I would advise against that," Ciro said. "Keep an eye out for that backhand, Kale. Crouch lower the next time you sidestep and then spring forward." The Alpha's voice was measured and calm, as usual.

"I'm not an idiot," Nick huffed. "I know she'd probably kick me in my jewels if I attempted to forbid her from doing anything. But I'm not above engaging in other tactics to try and get my way."

"What other tactics?" asked Kale between panted breaths.

"Seduction," replied Nick, grinning.

Kale smiled. "Now that's a plan I could get on board with."

Nick circled the Irish beta, watching for the tell he'd picked up on the last time the two had sparred. As soon as Kale dropped his chin just a fraction, Nick dodged and swept his leg out. Kale jumped and narrowly avoided being put on his rear end.

"What do you think the girls will say when we tell them that *we* are the sacrifice?" Nick asked.

"They will fight us tooth and nail," Ciro said. "These women are strong. They've had to fight to survive their childhoods, relying on no one but themselves. Out of that milieu come women who are fiercely independent. Our mates are not used to anyone giving them anything. They will not accept the gift of a mate who sacrifices himself so they may live."

"We can't avoid them all day," Nick said, not that he would want to avoid Kara. Quite the opposite. "Eventually, they'll wake up and we'll have to face them."

Kale glanced up at the window of the girls' room. He grinned and waved. "They're awake. We have an audience."

"If I would have known that, I might've tried a little harder," said Nick. He glanced up but it was too late. All he saw was a ruffling of the curtains. *Damn*. He wished he could speak to Kara through their bond.

"Ha," replied Kale. "*I* only held back in case someone was watching. I didn't want to embarrass you in front of your mate."

"Right. Whatever you have to tell yourself, Irishman," Nick muttered as he wiped the sweat from his brow.

They looked at one another and grinned. Seconds earlier, their sparring for the day had been all but complete. Now, the two wolves attacked each other with a renewed ferocity. Though they'd already been at it the better part of an hour, their movements quickened. They struck with more force, each wanting to prove his dominance in front of his mate. They lunged, punched, and blocked, throwing their entire effort into each movement. They wrestled each other to the ground, rolling around like a couple of pigs in slop until they were covered from head to toe with sweat and grime.

Ciro tried to offer instruction, but his words were lost on Nick. All Nick could think of was showing off for Kara. Was it ridiculous for him to feel that it was necessary to show off for her? Probably. Did that change his behavior? Now way.

After a particularly nasty strike to the side of Kale's head, Nick stepped back and roared, flexing his muscles like a professional wrestler and staring up at the window.

"You two are behaving like idiots," said Ciro, though Nick could hear the humor in the Alpha's voice.

While Nick was staring at the window, Kale rose and plowed into the wolf, sending him sprawling. Now, it was Kale's turn to preen. Facing the window, he struck a pose, flexing his huge biceps.

"You are being especially dense, Kale," said Ciro. "Have you forgotten your mate can't even see you?"

Kale deflated, a crestfallen look on his face. "Aye." But then he perked back up. "I'm sure da other females will describe to Heather what I'm doing to Nick. Heather will be the queen healer because of her mate's strength. It will put the other healers ta shame probably."

Ciro rolled his eyes. "That might be so if that's what was happening," said Nick. He hit Kale like an out-of-control bus, and the two males were again rolling around in the dirt. Ciro let the males go on for a few more minutes. Neither was able to get the upper hand.

"Enough, you two peacocks. Put away your tail feathers, and let's go get this over with."

The other wolves didn't acknowledge him. Kale held Nick in a chokehold from behind. Nick worked himself up to his feet. He jumped into the air, lifting all of his and Kale's weight in the process. Nick threw himself backward, purposely falling to the ground as he did so. He landed squarely on top of Kale, who let out an *oomph* but held fast.

"Enough," yelled Ciro. This time he put a little of his Alpha power into the command. The wolves froze momentarily and Kale released his grip. "Please, gentlemen, that's enough."

"We're just having a bit of fun, Ciro," said Nick as he rose from the ground.

"Aye," agreed Kale. "No hard feelings. It's all in good fun."

"I don't doubt that. But now is not the time for juvenile shows of strength. The strength our mates need from us now isn't physical."

"True enough," said Nick as he extended a hand to Kale. The other wolf took it, and Nick pulled him to his feet. The Canadian Beta turned to the house and sighed. "This little fight is nothing compared to the one we are about to be in with our mates." He picked up their shirts from the ground and tossed Kale his, who caught it and flung it over his shoulder.

"What are the chances it could end up as a wrestling match?" Kale asked as they walked toward Peri's house. "I could go another round."

Ciro chuckled and Nick noticed Ciro's previous ire fled as quickly as it had come.

Nick glanced out of the corner of his eye. "Me, too. Do you think we can somehow get Jell-O involved?"

"What is it about finding our mates that has turned you two into adolescent pups?" Ciro asked.

"I don't know, but isn't it great?" Nick said. "I feel exactly like I did on my first hunt. I just want to sink my teeth into something." He smiled and squeezed his hands into fists.

"And I bet I've got an idea on what that might be ... or should I say *who* that might be," said Kale, clapping Nick on the back.

"You got that right, brother," said Nick grinning.

Ciro rolled his eyes. "I hope you two understand what all being a mate entails. Yes, you are Betas. But the responsibilities you have to your pack are great. And one never knows when his status will change from Beta to Alpha. It can happen in an instant. Leading a pack is one thing. But doing so while worrying about protecting your mate, well, that's something else entirely."

"Don't you think our duties will be easier now that we've found our mates? Won't they give us the strength to be the leaders we need to be? Not to mention, keep the darkness from growing. That's what I've always believed would happen," said Nick.

"Indeed, your strength will increase. And right along with it, so will your responsibilities. You cannot have one without the other," said Ciro. "You must think of your mate's needs first, as well as your pack's. It is a delicate balance and a heavy burden to carry."

"A burden I will happily bear as long as I have Kara by my side."

"Aye, and me, as well, as long as I have Heather," said Kale.

"Just remember, this isn't all fun and games," said Ciro, his brow drawing into a deep 'V.' "Enjoy your newly discovered mates, yes, but remember not to lose your head. Which, ahem, I can see from that last little display you two are prone to do."

"I'm going to go enjoy my mate right now," said Kale, practically hopping on the balls of his feet. "Too bad yours is still underage, mate." He punched Nick in the shoulder and bounded ahead.

"Not so fast, Kale," said Ciro. "Remember what Peri said. Our women have to be pure of heart for the spell to work. I know we haven't decided anything yet, but don't go corrupting Heather before she has a chance to make up her mind about the spell."

"Seems like a good way to get out of this mess," he replied.

Nick nodded his agreement but forced himself not to indulge any thoughts of corrupting his mate, no matter how much he wanted to. And bloody hell did he want to.

"Yeah, until Peri finds out and makes you into a wolf-skin rug," Ciro chided, his frown turning into a smirk.

Kale practically purred. "As long as Heather is the one laying on me in front of the fire, I might risk it."

Nick didn't respond to the other wolf's goading. He was too busy pondering what Ciro said. Nick wasn't delusional enough to think they weren't in store for some dark times. But now that he had Kara, he could face anything. What troubled him, however, was that he *didn't* actually have her. She was underage so they couldn't perform the Blood Rites, and their mental bond wasn't yet formed. This would leave them both vulnerable until she turned eighteen. It worried Nick more than anything else. He wouldn't be able to bear it if he lost his mate so soon after finding her. Such a thing would spell the end of him, even if they weren't yet bonded.

Would the opposite be true? If the spell was successful, he might be the one who died. That would leave Kara all alone in this new life she was just beginning to come to terms with. He growled in frustration. It simply wasn't fair. Kara was far too young to have to deal with these things. And she shouldn't be left without him. The males would just have to find some way to sacrifice themselves ... and not die. What could be easier?

2

"Flying around with a penis for a nose is bad enough. But it's really bad when the organ works as intended. Imagine my embarrassment when a hot woman walks by. All of a sudden, I'm like a pixie Pinocchio. And sneezing is an experience I'd never like to repeat." ~Ciesel

Ciesel shuffled his feet. He was stalling. Plain and simple. The pixie took two steps forward, then one step backward. Clenching and unclench his fists, he jumped into the air and spun in a circle a couple of times, then landed again. He kicked at a stone and sent it rocketing forward. It crossed effortlessly into the fae realm. Ciesel was loathe to follow, though he knew he must.

When Ciesel had first been commanded by Volcan to spy on the healers, he'd been happy to do it. After all, the dark fae had fixed his nose. That was worth quite a bit, especially a little bit of snooping. It was the perfect way to get back at them for refusing to change his nose back to a non-phallic shape. He subconsciously placed his hand upon his proboscis, silently thanking his gods Volcan had been able to return it to its regular form. Now, however, the full weight of what he was about to do descended upon him. If Perizada of the fae caught him, she would kill him ... quickly. He was certain of that.

But if he didn't do what the dark fae asked, Volcan would also kill him. And Ciesel was sure Volcan *wouldn't* do it quickly. Ciesel shuddered. He didn't want to die screaming in agony. The only way to survive this was to do what Volcan asked. He'd just have to be careful not to get caught.

He cast every cloaking spell he knew on himself. Then, the pixie stepped slowly forward and passed into the fae realm. No alarms sounded announcing his presence. *So far, so good.*

Now, Ciesel just had to make his way to Peri's home undetected. He went slowly, skipping from one branch to another, pausing and listening carefully at each tree before moving to another. Volcan had commanded the pixie to hurry, but he liked being alive and was in no particular rush to get caught. Volcan might be irritated if Ciesel took his time, but he'd be a lot angrier if Ciesel got caught and didn't come back at all.

Hours later, Ciesel finally spied Peri's home through the foliage. He took a breath. Now came the tricky part. He had to sneak up without alerting anyone. Ciesel flitted to the ground and found a rotting log covered with moss. Rolling it over, he dug out some of the soft dirt underneath and spat on it. Working the mixture over in his hands, Ciesel created a sticky mud paste and then covered his entire body with it. He also mixed in some of the moss to the concoction. Ciesel knew there were *Canis lupus* present, and he wasn't going to take any chances. After he was sure he wouldn't be detected, at least by scent, the pixie climbed back into the trees and sat to watch. The sun was high in the sky, the worst possible time to try and sneak up on one as powerful as Perizada, but it couldn't be helped. An hour passed and Ciesel saw no one come or go.

Growing impatient, the pixie decided to make his move. Being of royal pixie blood he was able to sprout wings at a whim. He began flying from tree to tree, slowly closing in on Peri's home. He wished there was a tree right up against the house, but the closest was about ten yards away, a towering oak. Lucky for Ciesel, the foliage was dense. He rested on a thick branch close to the top. It wasn't perfect cover, but someone would have to look almost directly up to see him. Even then, they'd have to see through his cloaking spells. While he was confident Peri could see through them as easily as breathing, he figured the magic would fool wolves. Again, the pixie sat, watched, and waited. Another half-hour passed and still no one emerged. Ciesel rose to a crouch. He was just about to make his riskiest maneuver yet—a quick flight to the roof of the house—when the front door to Peri's home swung open, and three wolves in their human form emerged.

Ciesel sucked in a breath. That was almost disastrous. Had he jumped, they might have heard him or seen an unnatural shaking of the tree branches. Then they'd have surely called the cavalry, which would include a high fae with a penchant for vaporizing beings that got on her nerves. Something told Ciesel that spies were *definitely* something that got on Peri's nerves.

The pixie watched as the wolves walked to a clearing. Two of the wolves began sparring. The other looked on, calling out to them periodically. The ones who were fighting were also speaking to one another. They must have been joking because their faces continually switched from laughter to concentration and back to laughter again.

The pixie plucked a leaf from one of the trees. He whispered some words over the leaf, casting one of his favorite spells. He rolled the leaf into a tube shape and held it up to his ear, pointing it in the direction of the three men. Their words came to him on the wind, and Ciesel could hear them as if they were up in the tree next to him. What they were saying didn't make a lot of sense, but he was sure it was exactly the kind of information Volcan had sent him to gather. The wolves were talking about some spell their mates wanted to perform and bemoaning the fact that because of the spell, they couldn't perform the Blood Rites ceremony. Ciesel wasn't completely familiar with the Blood Rites, but he knew it was some kind of *Canis lupus* mating ritual. There was also talk of a sacrifice, and each of the wolves declared they would be the sacrifice for their respective mates.

Ciesel guessed the mates in question must be somewhere in the house. He needed to try and find them so he could determine if they, too, had any important information Volcan might want. The wolves were some distance away and probably wouldn't see him leave his perch and fly to the house, but still, Ciesel couldn't take any chances. Clutching his enchanted leaf, the pixie waited until one of them landed a particularly nasty blow and sent the other sprawling, which earned a catcall from the wolf watching. As quietly and quickly as he could, Ciesel leaped into the air and flew to the other side of the house, shielding himself from the wolves' view. He landed deftly, sure that no one within would have heard him. He crept quietly to the apex of the roof and peered over, checking to see if he'd drawn the attention of the three wolves. Apparently, they hadn't noticed him as they were still punching and kicking one another.

Retreating back down the roof a few steps, Ciesel saw that there were two gables, one on each side of him. He crept to one of them and slowly peered around it into the window. There was an empty bedroom. *Curses.* He flitted to the other gable and looked into it. *Jackpot.* Three female humans sat on a bed speaking to one another. He could just make them out through the curtains. Two of them rose and went to the opposite side of the room, turning their backs to him. A window there faced out into the front lawn and they stared out of it, apparently watching the wolves spar. The third woman stayed put. Ciesel pulled his head back out of sight, took his leaf, and held it against the roof. They were a bit muffled, but Ciesel could hear the words the women were saying.

"Look at those idiots out there, fighting like a bunch of children," said one of the women.

"Not your mate," said another. "He's watching. Probably telling them what they're doing wrong."

"Fighting? Oh, I wish I could see it. Describe every detail," said the third woman. "Do they have their shirts off?"

Ciesel scratched his head. *Why would she need the scene described to her?* Then he remembered one of the healers had no vision. This must be the blind one.

"I'm afraid they do," said the second woman. The third one groaned.

"And they're sweaty," said the first woman. "Glistening."

"Don't say glistening. I've never *seen* something glisten. I can't even begin to imagine what that means, but it sounds sexy as hell."

"It is," assured the first healer.

Ciesel furrowed his brow. This was ridiculous. Did Volcan really need these women?

"Ooh," came the second healer.

"What happened?" asked the third.

"Nick just knocked your man on his ass," said the first woman.

The third one gasped. "No! Is he okay?"

"Yep, he's back up," said the second healer. "Oh, he just tackled Nick. Now, they're rolling around and hitting each other. Ouch!"

There were several more *oohs* and *ahhs* from the first two girls and more growls from the third and a declaration that the universe was a cruel bitch because it caused her to be born blind and miss this fight.

All of a sudden, the first two girls burst out into a fit of giggling. "What? What?" asked the third.

"Nick just knocked Kale down," said the first woman. "Now, he's actually flexing his muscles at the window."

"You're kidding," said Heather. "Are they impressive?"

The second healer made a sound halfway between a moan and squeak. "Kara says yes, they are definitely impressive." Ciesel rolled his eyes and looked down at his own diminutive body. *Stupid wolves.*

"Oh, wait," said the first woman. "Now, your mate has knocked down Nick. You've got to be joking!"

"What?" yelled the blind woman.

"Kale is flexing now." Kara laughed. "This is too much."

"How does he look?" asked the third girl. "Lie to me if you have to."

"Well," said the first healer, "if you like broad shoulders, large arms, and washboard abs, then I'd say he looks pretty good."

"Are those things good? Do I like those things?"

"Let me put it to you this way," said the first woman. "You see with your hands. I don't think you're ever going to get tired of exploring the chiseled parts of that poor boy's body."

"Ooh," said the blind one. Though Ciesel couldn't see it, he could imagine the woman shuddering as she made the noise.

"And they're back to fighting again," said the second healer.

"C'mon, ladies," said the first healer. "Let's go downstairs and get some coffee. If they don't come inside soon, we may have to go out and drag them in."

"I'm all for that," said the third healer. "The quicker Kale gets in here, the quicker I can start exploring."

Ciesel heard the girls exit the room. The pixie shook his head. He'd gotten nothing useful out of the healers. He crept back down to the eave of the roof and pointed himself toward the closest spot of dense forest. Without looking back, he launched himself into the air and flew quickly into the cover of the trees, anxious to get back to Volcan and report what he'd learned and the fact he'd not seen Perizada of the fae anywhere on the premises.

∼

KALE DID FEEL like an adolescent pup. He hadn't felt this good in decades, and it was all because of a sharp-tongued little female. She was beyond anything he could have imagined for his mate, and he was thankful the Great Luna had blessed him so profoundly.

Heedless of the mixture of dirt and sweat he was leaving on Peri's sitting room floor, Kale stepped lightly into the room, followed by Nick and Ciro. The three females they had just been discussing were sitting, dressed, each drinking coffee and staring at them. Well, his mate was simply looking in the direction of the door, as she couldn't actually see him. But the looks on all the girls' faces made it clear they, too, had been discussing their mates. Unlike the males, however, it was obvious the females' discussion wasn't so positive.

"You're looking lovely, lass," Kale said to Heather, a slight growl of appreciation in his voice as his wolf took in their mate's beautiful form.

"And you *smell* anything but. You all smell like you've been rolling in a field of manure. And if you think flattery is going to get you out of trouble, pal, you've got another thing coming," she said.

"She's right," added Stella. "I don't even have her super-nose and I can smell you three."

"Make that two," said Ciro gesturing to the shirtless, dirt-covered Nick and Kale. "As you can see, I didn't engage with these two pups."

"Guilt by association," said Stella.

"Trubul?" Kale asked Heather loudly. His eyebrows rose to the top of his head. He let his accent thicken. He rarely spoke this way anymore, but he could lapse into the old tongue at any time, and he thought his mate might get a kick out it. "What ya mean, mot? I've only been tinkin' about how tha lilies of the field cannut compare to your beauty."

Heather made a gagging sound in her throat. "I don't know what a mot is, but you can stow the pretty words, Irishman. You're going to tell me right now why you've had our bond closed down tight all morning if you want to get back into my good graces. That or your mouth is going to have to do a lot more to me than talking."

The girls laughed. Nick coughed and Ciro cleared his throat.

Kale blanched for a second, then recovered himself, grinning. "You might not want to draw that particular line in the sand just yet, mot. Not unless you're ready for me to cross it."

"You keep calling me that," said Heather. "What does it mean?"

"Mot is an old Dublin word," interjected Ciro. "Originally derived from the word *maith*, meaning good. It's morphed into an endearment meaning girlfriend."

Everyone turned to give Ciro a questioning look. He shrugged. "What? You live as long as I have, you pick up on a few things. I've hunted with the Irish pack several times over the centuries. I've become familiar with their vernacular."

"Aye, what he said," said Kale, jerking his head at Ciro.

"Regardless," said Heather, "pet names will not excuse you. I want answers or I want action. Now. Give it up, wolf. And I mean that however you want to take it."

Kale's wolf practically jumped out in response to her teasing. It was all Kale could do to contain the beast. Heather did something to him he didn't think possible. She made him lose all control. Ciro was right. It was going to be hard not to lose his head around her. A high-pitched sound escaped his throat before he stifled his wolf and tried to cover the noise with a cough.

"Did he just yip?" asked Stella.

Kale tried to plaster a look of dignified offense on his face. "I did no such thing." He'd wanted to tease his mate, to make her uncomfortable in front of the others. His wolf had wanted to play with her, to watch her squirm. Instead, she'd instantly turned the tables on him. And that playfulness was just one of the reasons why he adored her so much.

"He did," said Heather, smiling. "He just yipped. I made my wolf yip."

"I didn't—" Kale began.

"I've never heard one of them yip before," said Kara.

"That was so cute," crooned Stella. She turned to Ciro. "Are you going to yip for me?"

Now it was Ciro's turn to look affronted. "I do not yip. Only pups yip." He gave Kale a pointed look and Kale quickly looked away. "I am an Alpha. I am a *Canis lupus*. I may growl. I may snarl. I may even bark on occasion. But I will never, ever yip."

"Yep, he'll yip for you, Stella," said Heather. "I can tell by his voice. He might act all serious now, but get him alone and he'll roll over and yip as much as you want him to."

Ciro cleared his throat and ignored the comment. "Ladies, if you would allow us fifteen minutes to get cleaned up, then we can discuss matters," His calm, diplomatic manner had returned. Kale had to admit he admired the way Ciro handled himself. Kale's temperament was a bit more volatile. The fieriness of his temper was matched only by the color of his hair.

"By all means," Heather said. "Wash off the stench so we can focus on more important things ... like your hot accents ... I mean ... whatever important matters are weighing on your minds."

Stella sighed. "How did you become the spokesperson for us today?"

Kale's mate shrugged. "I'm just going with what feels right. I'm doing me. Isn't that the modern-day lingo of being yourself? Be a unicorn and all that jazz?"

Stella groaned. "Please, for the love of all things ridiculous, don't latch on to the unicorn fad. I've had all the sparkling farts and rainbow manes I can handle."

"You're just a little ball of sunshine." Kara laughed.

As Kale walked past her, he paused next to Heather and leaned down. "Good morning, love," he said and then pressed a kiss to her neck just below her ear. She sighed and tilted her head to the side, giving him better access to her throat. Kale chuckled. *"Are you trying to tell me something?"* he asked through their bond, letting go of the tight reign he'd had on it while he'd been talking with the other two males.

"I just don't want the rest of my neck to feel neglected. If you're going to kiss my neck, then you need to be an equal-opportunity neck kisser," she replied.

Kale pressed another kiss to her neck and then another. Then he whispered in her ear, "I'll have to take care of the rest of your neck at a later time."

"I suppose I can wait." She sighed. Kale could feel her mirth coming through their bond, though she was doing her best to sound disappointed. "Go wash your stink off," she added, making him want to kiss that smart mouth of hers. Kale stood up and continued past her. He needed to get away before he swept her up in his arms and took her somewhere more private. Damn Peri for declaring the Blood Rites off-limits. The ceremony needed to be performed now.

Ciro couldn't take his eyes off of Stella. She was simply a vision to him. Her skin was a lovely shade of brown that reminded him of smooth, melted chocolate. It was flawless. Her eyes were light brown, crystal clear, and turned up slightly at the outer points, giving her an exotic look. She had full, plump, lips and high cheekbones.

"I could take a picture of her for you," Kara said, breaking into Ciro's thoughts.

Ciro smiled as he watched Stella nudge Kara and mutter something along the lines of 'Shut it, little healer.' "I appreciate the offer, but I don't plan to have her out of my sight much so I don't think a picture will be necessary." Ciro didn't want to intimidate or scare Stella by being too forward, but he wouldn't lie to her. Now that he'd found her, he'd be as patient as she needed him to be, but that didn't mean he planned on allowing any distance between them.

Stella met his stare, and there was more curiosity in her eyes than anything else. "Good to know," she said with a small smile.

"Will you ladies please remain inside while we clean up?" Ciro asked.

All three of them saluted him. He couldn't help but laugh.

"What?" Heather asked. "What happened?"

"You three seem to be very in sync with one another," Ciro said.

"We all did the smart-ass salute," Stella said.

Heather put a fist in the air. "Healer solidarity. It's how we roll."

Ciro's brow drew down. "I'm going to have to learn a new language." Half of what the girls said made no sense to him, but he wasn't about to admit that out loud.

"That you will," Heather agreed. "Or just pretend to understand. I'm pretty sure that's what the other males do."

"Yep," Kara agreed.

As Ciro walked past Stella, he paused and held his hand out to her. He waited several heartbeats until she finally set her hand in his. Ciro leaned down and gently pressed a light kiss to the back of it. "I look forward to spending more time with you today," he said. Ciro was trying to be cautious in his pursuit of his mate, but he also wanted to make it clear he had every intention of getting to know her and giving her time to get to know him.

Stella gave him a small smile. "I'm not going to lie," she said. "I don't envy the position you're in. I'm not going to be an easy conquest."

He chuckled and shook his head. "My dear, I have no desire to conquer you. Quite the opposite really. I want to see you soar and be there for you to give you a gentle push when you need it. I also want to be at your side should you come into trouble and need my help or protection. I simply want to be your partner, your equal." Ciro released her hand and then headed upstairs to get cleaned up. He hoped his words would give her something to think about and that he'd planted seeds of hope in her heart.

"THE LOOK on your face right now is creeping me out," Stella said to Heather.

"I have to agree with her," Kara said.

"And I might care if I wasn't floating on a cloud of Irish hotness." Heather sighed. Her mind was filled with thoughts of Kale. He was intense. She'd never experienced with anyone else the kind of connection she felt to him. Not that she'd dated much in her short life. But she'd also never thought she'd meet someone like Kale. Both of her friends sputtered as they laughed at her words.

"A cloud of Irish hotness?" Stella said slowly. "And how exactly does that feel?"

"Yes, please do tell," Kara added with a playful eagerness to her voice.

"I'm not sure you gals really want me to go there. Not

unless you're really okay with hearing me say things like tingling in my core and moisture flooding my—" Heather rubbed the palms of her hands down the arms of her chair letting her fingers curl over the edge.

"Whoa!"

"Stop!"

Stella and Kara both shouted at the same time, the cacophony of their mingled voices startled her. Heather bit her lip to keep from laughing.

"I don't want to know what your two filthy minds were thinking. I was going to say moisture flooding my mouth with the need of his kiss. Y'all really need to get your minds out of the gutter."

"Psht, please." Stella huffed her Bronx accent magnified in her sarcasm. "Your mind is nothing but a system of interlocking gutters and sewer pipes. Your thoughts run through one gutter only to flow into a culvert, then drain into a ditch, which eventually makes its way to a swamp."

"Just tell me this," Heather said leaning forward. "Does he look as sexy as his accent sounds? I mean, do I have a reason to have tingling cores and flooding mouths? Lie to me if you have to."

"He is," said Kara breathed deeply and Heather wondered if it was to find the right words for the lie or because she was swooning. "Probably even better than you can imagine."

Heather groaned as she slid down her chair in a melted version of a slouch.

"We don't have to lie, honey," said Stella. "He's the real deal. But it's not just yours. Every one of them is so..." Heather tilted her head to hear how she would describe them. Without sight, Stella's words would have to be conjured in either descriptions of sounds, smells, or mouthwatering gutter talk. Stella already knew which way Heather preferred.

"Out-of-this-world, off-the-charts, so-smoking-hot-they-make-your-eyes-hurt good looking?" asked Kara. Heather squeezed her eyes shut to elicit a pain of just how good looking that could be. *Maybe if she poked her eye...*

"Not exactly how I was going to put it but, yes, he *is* as hot as his accent and so are the rest of them." Stella's affable tone underlined by mentioning Kale's Irish accent shot Heather into a straight sitting position with excitement.

"I knew it." Heather shivered. For the first time in a long time, she really wished she could see.

"Knew what?" Kale's voice filled the room as his scent hit her. The night air right before the storm awakened her more than their gutter talk, but it was masked with smells of dirt, sweat, and a foreign body odor she assumed was Nick's from their fight. Tackling would do that to a man.

Was it ridiculous that she wanted to throw herself into his arms and gush about how much she'd missed him in the past fifteen or so minutes that he was gone? *Yes, yes, that was ridiculous,* Heather thought to herself. She'd never imagined she would be one of those clingy women. But here she was, giving serious consideration to just climbing on his back and making him haul her around like some freaky, human backpack just so she wouldn't have to spend a second away from him.

"That you're a stud muffin," she answered. Heather thought for about five seconds that perhaps she should be embarrassed by her frankness, but then she remembered the dangers they were facing. Her amazing new life could very well be coming to an end in the not-too-distant future. She wasn't about to waste the time she had left by being proper or self-conscious. If she had to spend that time as a human backpack, so be it. As long as she was wrapped around Kale, she'd be just fine.

"Does the muffin part of the statement have anything to do with why you've got flooding moisture in your mouth?" Kale asked her.

Heather self-consciously licked her lips.

"You heard that, did you?" Heather asked, feeling her face grow warm. Then she felt a finger brush across her cheek.

"You make my mouth water, too, lass. Never be embarrassed by what you feel for me," Kale said, using their bond to speak to her. "And I'm sure we could work something out in regard to you climbing onto my back. I'm really never going to be opposed to the idea of you climbing on me in any way."

Of course, he'd been listening to her inner dialog. "As long as you're just as upfront with me about your feelings then we're good," she said. "And feel free to share any ridiculous thoughts you might have. Then I won't feel so unhinged about my ludicrous thoughts about you."

"All right then, up you go," Kale said out loud as he suddenly scooped Heather up from her chair. A second later, she was sitting in his lap.

Reaching out to steady herself, her hands gripped his soft shirt away from a hard surface. Chasing the hardness outward was like dragging her hands of her family's dining table, smooth with rounded edges. Rolling her hands over rounded shoulders, and down the hills and valleys of his arms, Heather smiled. Kara was right. Being blind and mated to a chiseled male like this would never cease to enthrall her.

"Were there no other seats left?" she asked, smiling like a fool. Turning her back to him in relaxation, the heat of his body loosened up muscles she hadn't realized were bunched up with tension. Consumed by her favorite scent, his body was a contrast of hard and soft. As if she didn't know how small she was in comparison to the wolf, he rested his chin on the top of her head.

"There are plenty of seats, but none of them had you in them," he replied.

His chest vibrated with the rise and fall of his lyrical voice.

"Smooth, Romaine, smooth." Stella chuckled.

Heather could hear another set of footsteps and then another. The air shifted as two men, whom she assumed to be Nick and Ciro, passed.

"Now that we're all here," Kale began, "we have some things we need to discuss with you lasses."

"Please tell me this isn't an 'it's not you, it's me' kind of conversation," Stella said dryly.

"Isn't that the kind of talk you usually have in private?" Kara asked.

Her voice sounded from Heather's left, and she turned to be a part of the conversation.

"I have no clue," Stella answered. "I've never done the whole relationship thing."

Stella sounded farther than Kara but on the same side of the room.

"Then how do you know about that kind of conversation?" Heather asked as she raised her eyebrow.

"I watch TV."

"You shouldn't," Kara said. "It's just the government's way of brainwashing us." Her tone told Heather Kara expected them to fully understand her conspiracy theory. Heather blinked as if it would clear her vision enough to make the link between television and relationships. It didn't, but she blinked a few more times hoping it would help. Nope. Still dark.

"They're brainwashing us into having the 'it's not you, it's me' kind of conversations?" Stella asked.

"Broken relationships equal broken people. Broken people equal instability. Instability equals lack of commitment, which equals unsteady jobs, which equals dependency on government help," Kara explained.

"You're seven kinds of jaded for one so young," Heather said shaking her head.

"I grew up dependent on the government through the foster care system. Believe me, my best interest was the last thing they cared about."

The disgust and finality in Kara's tone elicited a growl from Nick who was on the right side of the room.

"Okay, no more TV," Stella announced. "From now on, we play board games."

"Board games? And we are going to play these board games in between dealing with Volcan and worrying about Jewel and Anna. Not to mention, we are planning on becoming witches ourselves, while at the same time not becoming mindless slaves of Volcan," Heather added.

Kale cleared his throat. "Speaking of witches, that's what we need to talk to you about."

3

"I spent hundreds of years trapped in the dark forest. I don't think I'm boasting when I say most other men wouldn't have survived it. It took all of my strength, cunning, and patience. I had to fight countless creatures that would have torn lesser beings to pieces. After all, they don't call it the dark forest for nothing. Who would have thought a creature outside of the dark forest would end up slaying me? And who would've guessed it'd be my own mate?" ~**Lucian**

Peri and Lucian sat alone in their bedroom. Well, Lucian sat while Peri paced and muttered to herself.

"How can I help you, my love?" he asked, sending visions of himself covering her with kisses through their bond. Propping himself up on his elbow in the center of the bed, he patted the space in front of him with a seductive smile.

"You can stop trying to distract me, for a start," she

replied as she turned from the alluring sight of her mate. She knew it was unfair to take her irritation out on Lucian, but unfortunately for him, he was the only person in her immediate vicinity and a myriad of problems weighed heavily on her mind.

"I'm not trying to distract you. I'm simply showing you what I'd like to do to you. If that somehow distracts you, well, that's on you. I can't be held responsible for everything that distracts you."

His deep voice climbed up her spine like a living thing, burning every nerve ending with the very thing she couldn't abide. Distraction.

"I'll hold you responsible for the lives of those five girls if you don't quit." Narrowing her eyes at him, she pointed toward the door as if the five girls were pressing their ears against the wood to listen in.

"That's a bit harsh," he replied.

A taste of hurt leaked through their bond, and Peri stopped pacing. For a brief moment, she thought about telling him how harsh she *could* be, but then realized with a sigh how unfair she was being to her mate. "I'm sorry," she said. "I'm just so frustrated. I was tasked with keeping these healers safe and I muffed it from the start. It seems like Volcan is always one step ahead of us. He's put our Jewel in an impossible situation and dragged Anna along with her."

"As always, beloved, you focus on the wrong things." Lucian's voice was deep, rich, and maddeningly calm. He sat up from his prone position.

Peri pinched the bridge of her nose. "Meaning?"

"Like the fact you saved three healers from his clutches. Imagine what would've happened if your sister had gotten to them before we did."

Lorelle's face appeared in her mind, a bedraggled

zombie rising from the dead with the desire to feast on Peri's flesh. It shouldn't have brought Peri comfort when Dalton ripped her sister's head from her body, but having one less enemy to worry about certainly lightened the load. "Ugh, don't mention that gutter-tramp to me."

"That's your own flesh and blood, Peri." Lucian's cautious chiding didn't comfort her. Instead, it stoked the anger that hovered just below the surface of her mind. Peri's hands formed into fists.

"No," she pointed at him, "she stopped being my sister when she chose to betray the council and serve Volcan. She got what was coming to her." Peri pictured Lorelle's head rolling on the ground in a tangle of dull blonde hair.

"Guard your heart, Perizada." Low and gentle, her mate broke the memory's hold on her. Lucian's eyes glowed with his wolf, visible protection for an invisible enemy.

"What's that supposed to mean?" she snapped.

Lucian rose from the bed with feline grace and placed his hands on her waist. The wolf continued to make his presence known, but he didn't take the man's voice yet. "It means you've fought the darkness for far too long."

"And?"

"And I worry about you," he pressed his forehead against hers and breathed in deeply of her scent. The simple press of skin-on-skin comforted her soul just as much as it did him. "I wonder how much the great Perizada can take before she, too, loses her way."

"You think I'd turn evil?" Perizada whispered. Lucian's admiration of her mind and heart poured through the bond as he squeezed her closer. As he nuzzled her neck, his awe at her strength filled up the corners where her quiet doubts lived. Pulling back, she looked into his silver eyes.

"Not at all," he stroked her jaw. "But you might become

too hardened against the evil you're fighting to recognize the goodness in front of you." *He thought so highly of her, but still didn't rely on the strength he was attracted to?* With a scoff, she pulled out of his arms. He sighed and released her.

"It's a chance I'm willing to take," she said with a flex of power flowing through her veins. "But don't worry. I've bested Volcan before. Have you forgotten I'm the one who imprisoned him in the dark forest?" Smirking at her man, her confidence died on her lips at the look in his eyes.

Lucian grunted. "How could I? You trapped me in there, too, in case *you've* forgotten."

Unnatural darkness filtered through the bond. Taking a liberty she wouldn't normally take, she peeked to into his mind. Black trees rose from scorched earth like claws digging from their graves. The heavy weight of unrest crept through the landscape, a mist of unnamed fear. Something rustled the dead brittle branches to her right. Peri closed her eyes and forced away the vision of the dark forest. It took several minutes for her breathing to return to normal.

"A mistake I will eternally regret, Lucian. You have every right to hate me for it."

Running a hand through his hair, he leaned into the touch, forcing her nails to scratch his scalp. She poured love through the bond.

"I could never hate my beloved. You had no way of knowing what you were doing. If I held any bitterness, I'd have mentioned it long ago. I'm just saying it's different this time. Volcan has had more time to prepare. He's laid traps. Set up surprises. Forced you into a corner. Again and again, Peri, you've been called upon to sacrifice yourself to save your friends. That kind of thing wears on a person. I don't want you to fall into one of Volcan's traps because you're too exhausted to see it coming."

Comfort and strength lightened the burden on her mind, but no amount of Lucian's love could take away the doom looming over them. Pushing away from him, she hardened herself against him and closed down the bond. He could still feel her in the back of his mind, but he couldn't influence her emotions. Lucian growled but didn't follow her as she resumed pacing.

"Well, who else will do it? Who else *can* do it?"

"That decision may have been taken out of your hands. It appears that Volcan's going to require our gypsy healers pay the price this time."

His words were a slap to the face. "And I'll be damned if I'm going to let them pay it," she replied.

"Which brings me to the elephant in the room."

Peri was surprised Lucian's wolf wasn't speaking in guttural tones with how affected the man was. They were unified in their thoughts, the wolf willing for the man to maintain his interrogation of her. It spoke of Lucian's strength, maturity, and power. If she wasn't so annoyed by his words, she'd be proud.

"What do you mean?"

"I mean the fact that you told everyone you were going to sacrifice yourself for Jewel."

"And?" She raised her eyebrows. Lucian rarely showed any frustration with her, but when he did, his reasoning was fair. He wasn't one to complain without cause, so Peri made sure she gave him all of her attention.

"And don't you think that's something you should have discussed with me before you made the declaration? After all, we're bonded. It's not just your life you are sacrificing."

Peri interlaced their fingers and sighed. "I didn't think I had to discuss it with you. I know you, Lucian, and I know you'd lay down your life for any one of those girls, especially Jewel, after what she's been through."

"That may be, but we are a team, Perizada. Even after all this time, you still refuse to allow my help."

A sting of separation echoed in the bond. Everything a wolf was, and designed to be, was unified. The function of the man and his wolf, the wolf and the pack, and the wolf and his mate, was meant for unification. Loyalty and dependence upon a pack were encoded onto the spirit of the Canis Lupus. The fae weren't made like that.

Peri sighed. "I know. I know. But thousands of years of independence don't magically disappear overnight. Cut me some slack."

"I can do that," he said, "if you promise you'll *try* to at least remember to consult me on decisions before you make them, especially when they involve the word sacrifice."

While the fae weren't created to be co-dependent, she could bend for her mate.

"I'm consulting with you now," she said. "What do you think we should do?"

"Before or after we play out that little vision I sent you earlier?" he asked.

With the trace of betrayal gone, desire flooded their mate bond, causing her skin to flush.

"Don't change the subject. As a matter of fact,"—she pulled away from him and stuck her chin up in the air—"I don't think you should be touching me at all."

"Perizada." He growled. "What are you talking about?"

She shouldn't push his buttons. Really. She shouldn't. But if she could hold back, she wouldn't be the woman he fell in love with, right?

"Well," she said, "the healers and their mates can't perform the Blood Rites, otherwise the sacrifice will kill them both. *And* I've forbidden them to touch so they all remain pure so the spell to save them will have a chance at success. And Dalton and Jewel can't touch each other anyway or the darkness inside him grows."

"Your point?" He hissed in a completely un-Lucian way as his head tilted in a wolf-like manner.

Keeping her face as serious as she could, she shrugged one shoulder. "You've heard of leading by example, Lucian. It's only right that if the wolves can't touch their mates, then their fearless leader should abstain as well."

"You're joking."

There was nothing sexier than her mate with glowing eyes looking like he wanted to teach her a physical lesson. He was mouthwatering when he was calm, but he was pure temptation when he was so close to the edge of sanity, and the epitome of passion when he went over the edge.

One more push ought to do it.

"I'm not joking." She raised her chin even higher and turned away. "It would be a nice show of solidarity from you. Restraint will be good for me, too. Like I said before, I don't need any distractions right now."

"Peri, you know me as a patient man ..." His breath was on the back of her throat, sending her heart racing.

"The most patient, which is why you shouldn't have a problem fighting off your carnal desires for a while, at least until this all blows over."

The breath on her neck was gone.

"So, you want me to keep my carnal thoughts to myself?" he said from a distance. "And keep them from flowing to you through our bond?"

Turning, she found him across the room. Keeping the distance as she'd asked. Peri frowned. "Yes." She breathed.

The curve of his lips told her she was the bunny to this

wolf, the prey to the predator. Her muscles tightened in anticipation.

"And if I begin thinking about running my fingers through your silky, white hair, then I should just keep that thought to myself?"

She thought about his large hands and the strands of her hair entwined between them. A semblance of the experience grazed through her white hair. "My hair *is* silky, isn't it?"

"The silkiest," he said before sending her an image of himself running a brush through her locks as they sat together in front of a fireplace, her naked skin glowing under the warm flames.

Her own moan broke through the evoked romantic atmosphere, snapping her out of the image. "Definitely keep such thoughts to yourself," she snapped.

"And if I begin to imagine myself slowly placing my lips on your ruby red ones, I shouldn't share that either?"

A ghost of his lips rubbed over hers. His breath mingled with hers. Snapping her eyes to his, he still stood on the other side of the room looking too innocent for her liking.

"Nope," she said flatly.

He sent her an image of them sitting on a blanket under a starlit sky, their lips a fraction of an inch apart.

"Stop it," she said. "I know what you are trying to do." His silver eyes swam in her mind's eye, staring deep into her own as she imagined him putting his lips on hers. The pressure of his soft mouth had her trembling.

"And if I were to think about placing my hand ... just here ..." He reached out and placed his hand on the back of her neck and gently turned her to face him. How he crossed the room so quickly was lost on her. "And my other hand ... I don't know ... here?" He placed his free hand on the small of her back and pulled her closer. "I shouldn't let you know where I want to put my hands."

"Keep your hands and your thoughts to yourself." Her protest held no strength as he dug into her flesh with a grip promising pleasure.

"So, I should let you go right now, then?" he asked and then leaned forward, placing a small kiss on the crease of her neck above the collarbone. Peri shivered in spite of herself. She needed to pull away but her mate wasn't playing fair. "Lucian," she whispered as her head fell to the side, fully exposing her neck. He growled as his teeth latched onto her flesh.

LUCIAN UNDERSTOOD his mate's need to join the healers in their separation from their mates and he would allow her that ... after. The fact of the matter was that he and Peri *were* mated. Their bond was complete and the need to reinforce the bond, to re-establish the bite on her skin, was as fundamental to him as breathing. He pulled her closer, angled her throat a little lower, and then sunk his teeth deep into her throat. Lucian heard her gasp and felt her arms wrap around him as she pressed closer.

"You are mine, female." He growled into her mind. *"And I am yours. I have need of you and, whether you want to admit it or not, you have need of me."* Her warm blood coated his mouth and his throat as he drank in her essence, loving that her scent was mingled with his own. He pulled back and licked the wound. Peri's eyes were hazy with desire, and Lucian wanted to howl in victory as he stared at her. She was breathtaking in her passion. "Your turn, mate," he said as he pulled her face toward his neck. "I need you, Perizada. And you need me."

"Yes," she whispered as she kissed his throat in the spot where she'd bitten him so many times before. A few seconds later, Lucian felt her teeth pierce his flesh, and he was lost in the euphoria of her bite. He could feel the warmth of her magic flowing over both of them, and her hands were everywhere even though he knew they were actually only wrapped around his neck. She was using her power to overwhelm his senses.

Lucian's hands had a mind of their own as they began tugging at her clothes. He heard the fabric rip, but as soon as his hands hit bare skin, he didn't care about the damage to her clothes. The only thing he could think about was feeling *all* of her. His wolf was just as desperate as the man to be flesh-on-flesh with their mate. He finally had her all to himself, and he wasn't about to give that time up without a fight, even if he had to fight dirty.

"Lucian." Peri breathed out as she lifted her head from his neck.

"You don't want me to stop," he said as he picked her up and carried her to their bed. Lucian laid her down and continued pulling her clothes off until she was finally bare. His body immediately covered her own, and he didn't give her time to protest. His lips followed his hands as he touched every inch of skin, reveling in the sounds she made because of him. No other could ever make her feel the way he did. No other would ever be able to satisfy her as he would, and he wasn't about to lie and say he didn't take great pride in those facts.

"You're doing an awful lot of thinking for a man who is attempting to seduce his mate," Peri said as she tugged at his clothes. A moment later, Lucian was completely naked. It made him chuckle anytime she used her magic to take her own clothes off or his. His mate was impatient and she was giving in.

"I would say *attempting* isn't the correct description. I would say, lovely female, that I have succeeded in seducing my mate."

"Less talk, wolf." She growled. "Less talk, more touch."

"As my lady wishes," Lucian said as he focused his full attention on her body. He couldn't stop the grin that spread across his face as she pushed his hands where she wanted them. So demanding, his mate, but he wouldn't change her. And he was happy to let her think she was in control, for now.

Minutes turned into an hour, and an hour turned into two as he indulged his mate's every thought and desire. Lucian left no inch of Peri's body un-worshipped, and when she was convinced she'd had enough, he proved her wrong by teasing her until she was begging him for more. When Lucian was done loving his mate, she was going to be pissed because she was going to be too exhausted to truly be angry at him and too sated to regret it. When he gave her one last deep kiss and breathed in her satisfied sigh, Lucian decided she'd had enough.

"Maybe it is you who has had enough," Peri purred at him. Her fingers drew lazy circles across his chest and his wolf rumbled with contentment.

Lucian chuckled as he tucked her against him. "I could never get enough of you. But I worry if we keep going, then you will be completely worthless to your charges. My goal was to recharge us both, not put us both into carnal stupors."

Peri raised up on her elbows, giving him a tantalizing view of the tops of her breasts. "Carnal stupors? Really?"

"What would you call it?" he asked, raising his eyes from her chest to her annoyed gaze.

"Sex coma?"

Lucian pursed his lips as he cupped her jaw. "That is crass."

She laughed as she pulled away from his hold. "It is accurate and a very real risk. And you are correct. I am pissed that I am not angry with you. I'm also irritated you were right. I needed you. Thank you." Kissing a line down his bare chest, she stopped at the sheet.

"That was hard for you, wasn't it?" he asked.

Peri picked up her head to look at him. "What? Admitting you were right?" Her eyebrow rose in a sarcastic challenge he wanted to meet with a bite to her white skin.

"Admitting you were wrong," he corrected.

She shook her head. "I never admitted I was wrong. I just admitted you were more right. There's a difference."

"Of course there is," he said, shaking his head.

"I need to get back to Jezebel's to check on Jewel and Anna, then I'll see how our friends at the veil are getting on. Hopefully, they've managed to crack Volcan's spell and open the damn thing," she said as she crawled from their bed. He didn't have time to enjoy the view of her glorious body because she was dressed by the time she was standing. *Damn fae magic.*

"Then, I've got to figure out how we are going to get out of this mess for good. Thad needs to de-spell those pages for us, and translate them. But it's up to us to perform the spell and keep everyone alive. I need to be sure all the details are worked out before the ritual begins. Which is going to require a blood sacrifice, something important, but also not kill anyone. You figure that out for me and then we can continue attempting to drive ourselves into that carnal stupor thing, as you called it."

Lucian groaned. "Don't worry, my love. You have a centuries-old djinn helping you, Jezebel, and a gypsy genius. Between the four of you, you'll be able to come up with something. And I will hold you to that promise. You owe me a carnal stupor."

"You better hope we can figure it out. Otherwise, this fantasy carnal stupor will be something you will be pursuing on your own with pruny fingers from all your cold showers." With a wink of her pale green eyes, a stream of cold air glided over his skin, causing goosebumps to appear.

"You are a cruel, cruel woman who needs to be spanked." Lucian dragged the covers up to his neck to ward off the magic.

"You like it."

"Spanking you? I'm beginning to think it is definitely something I could find pleasure in." His eyes followed the dips of her curves with a renewed hunger.

"Watch it, wolf. I might not turn you into anything unsavory because I like your hands too much, but that doesn't mean I can't find other ways to make you pay," she promised.

"Of that, I have no doubt, my love. Now be on your way and be safe. I love you." Using the bond, he placed a cracking slap on her sultry backside. With a jump, she rubbed the offended area with a laugh.

Peri's features softened. "I love you back. See you soon."

∼

"Before you try to talk us out of it, let me save you some time and breath," said Stella. She was staring daggers at

Ciro, Kale, and Nick. "We're doing it. Jewel and Anna need us. They've been out there this whole time without us. That shouldn't have happened. We're all in this together. They're witches, so we will be witches, too. I'm not abandoning those girls to any more of Volcan's torture."

"No, no," said Kale. "That's not what we're saying. We're not going to try and talk you out of performing the spell. Volcan has to have his witches. We get that. We know we couldn't stop you if we tried. Frankly, as gypsy healers, there is no way you could *not* help your friends, or anyone in need for that matter. It's in your nature."

"We just want you to understand what all it entails," added Ciro as he folded his hands in his lap, his elbows balanced on the arms of chair closest to Stella.

"And how would you all know what it entails?" asked Stella punctuating the challenge of her question with an eyebrow raise.

"Peri came and spoke with us about it."

"To you?" said Stella. "Why did she speak with you? We're the ones about to go all 'I'll get you, my pretty, and your little dog, too.'"

"Peace, mate," said Ciro and held up a hand. "Peri came to us because she thinks she has an idea of how to allow you all to become witches but *not* go all 'I'll get you, my pretty,' as you so eloquently put it."

"You mean we can let Jewel turn us into witches but not become evil?" asked Heather.

"Exactly," said Nick. "And we asked Peri to allow us to speak with you all about it."

"Then there must be a *big* catch. Otherwise, she'd be here and this would already be done." Heather snorted, which earned her a nip on the ear by Kale's sharp canines.

"Let us explain," Kale said after removing his teeth from her ear.

"Ouch," she said. "Do it again." He did and she giggled.

Stella studied her hands, avoiding the play between the other couple. Watching their level of intimacy was causing her to feel pressure to behave in the same manner with Ciro. The giggles. The touching. The PD-freaking-A. She'd never be comfortable with that in a million years.

Peace flowed through her bond with Ciro. "I would never require more than you are willing to give, Stellina. You are still the star that guides us."

Turning her gaze on him, she saw his dark eyes boring tenderly into hers. She trusted him, of course, but some walls weren't easily toppled.

Ciro cleared his throat. "There's always a catch when Peri is involved. Jewel and Anna have found out what it takes to become a witch. We know, now, why their attempts have failed."

Stella shook her head, trying to clear it of the insecurity that was so pervasive a moment before.

"How?" said Kara.

"Finding out was easy, apparently. They just asked Anna's mom," Kale said, taking his mouth from Heather's ear. All eyes, save Heather's, turned to Kale, who only had eyes for his mate.

"Huh?" said Heather.

"Yeah, news flash," added Nick. "Anna's mother is a witch, and Anna didn't even know." Kara covered her mouth in shock, but Nick kept hold of the other hand.

"Ouch," said Stella. "And I thought my family had issues."

"Jezebel, that's Anna's mom, has always been aware of the supernatural world and how dangerous it is. So, she kept

Wolf Of Sight

her true identity from Anna to keep her safe. I guess it didn't work out like she planned," continued Nick.

"The dangers of the supernatural world found her in a big way," said Heather with a sad shake of her head.

"Regardless," said Ciro, "Jezebel knew, not only why Jewel and Anna's attempts at making witches have failed, but also, and maybe more importantly for our purposes, how a person might become a witch without turning evil."

"And that's where we come in," Heather interjected.

"Aye," agreed Kale.

"Well, go ahead, spill it," said Stella rolling her hand for him to go on. It would have been easier getting tips dancing at the bar on a Monday afternoon than getting information from this crowd. Ciro growled in her mind, and she realized she couldn't let that kind of sarcasm fly if she didn't shut down the mental link first.

"Apparently, it can't just be any lass or the spell to create a witch won't work. The new witch needs to have specific qualities."

"Okay," said Stella. "Apparently it has nothing to do with the darkness in the soul or any of that nonsense. Jewel and Anna are about as far from evil as the North Pole is from the South."

"You're correct. It doesn't necessarily have to do with the state of their morals. It has to do with their familial ties to the witch attempting to change them," Kale said. "The witch doing the changing has to have a connection to the person they are attempting to change."

"So, a person could change their mother or daughter?" Kara asked.

"Exactly," replied Kale. "But it doesn't necessarily mean a blood relation. Family, after all, can come in many forms."

Stella could sense there was more to Kale's words.

"There's something else, I can tell. What aren't you telling us?"

"Kale?" Heather prompted.

Kale frowned, a pained expression showing Stella he didn't want to be the bearer of bad news. Heather touched his face to get him to talk. "Uh..."

"The spell requires a sacrifice," offered Nick with a hesitant look at Kara.

"What kind of sacrifice?" Stella asked. "Like slaughtering a goat or giving up sugar for Lent, that kind of thing?"

"That part isn't exactly clear," said Ciro. Hope leapt in Stella's chest. "Apparently it can vary from person to person. The only thing that *is* certain is that there must be some kind of shedding of blood." Stella took in the seriousness hiding in the depths of his light brown eyes.

"Okay, no big deal, a little scratch, a little drop of blood, then boom, instant good witch. Sounds easy enough," said Heather with a shrug.

"Um, yes ... but no," said Kale. He shook his head, and Stella wondered if he forgot his mate couldn't see the gesture.

"Yes, but no?" she asked. "What's that supposed to mean, Romaine?"

"The last woman who performed the spell to create a witch died. It was a fae named Metea."

"But the sacrifice might *not* die," said Nick quickly. "Jezebel says the sacrifice doesn't always die." Kara pulled back from Nick, her shoulder bumping Stella's in the process.

"Wait, wait, wait. Hold up." Stella stood and raised her palms as she leaned forward. "You're saying we have to find a woman that has some kind of family ties to us, then find someone else who's willing to sacrifice themselves, and this *sacrifice* may or may not die in the process?"

If these wolves would quit speaking in riddles, she'd be able to wrap her mind around everything. If their mates thought it was easier listening to gobble-de-gook from them instead of Peri, they were wrong.

"No, the women are taken care of, obviously," said Heather. "That's us. We have familial ties. We are part of a pack now. Jewel can do the witch-creation thing on us, no problem, I bet. Just like she did with Anna."

"We assume that to be true, yes," said Ciro.

"And the sacrifices are taken care of, too," said Kara quietly.

Stella turned to face her. "What are you talking about?" she asked, her voice sharp.

"Why do you think the males wanted to be the ones to speak to us? They plan on sacrificing themselves."

~

THE SHUFFLING of feet followed by the grating of the iron bars of Evanora's cell awoke her. Both were noises she'd come to dread. She had been languishing in this dungeon for so long, time had no meaning for her anymore. She had no idea if she was about to be fed, or fed *upon*. Always a thin person, she was now gaunt as a result of the vampire's persistent use of her as his favorite midnight snack.

Laying on her cot, she opened her eyes and rolled toward the door of her cell. It was the vampire Morfran, as he called himself. Who else would it be? Evanora had long ago given up hope of rescue. For a while, every time she heard a noise, she prayed it was her mate, Sly, storming the castle to rescue her. But every time it was the vampire.

He wasn't carrying food or drink. That meant it was his turn to eat, not hers. The woman lay there motionless and squeezed her eyes shut, imagining she was anywhere else in the world. Evanora wasn't going to resist him. That only made it worse. But she wasn't going to offer herself up willingly, either.

A few moments of silence passed, but the vampire didn't move. She reopened her eyes and looked up, curious. Morfran wasn't patient and he didn't play games. He fed, spoke only when necessary, and then left. To see him staring at her now was unnerving.

"What?" she rasped, her voice rough from lack of use.

"Come," he beckoned.

Without conscious thought, Evanora slowly slid her legs over the edge of the cot and rose to her feet. Morfran turned his back and walked away. She knew better than to do anything but obey, so she purposefully shuffled after him. As she walked behind him, it didn't even cross her mind to try to escape or attack the vampire. The first day or so, she might have thought about something like that. But she'd learned how foolish those types of thoughts were.

They reached a set of stone steps, and the vampire ascended. Evanora's legs were already burning from the short walk. She didn't know how she'd make it up them, but she knew she must. One after another, she climbed. By the time she reached the top, her breath was coming in labored gasps.

The staircase opened to a hallway that led to a set of double doors. Beyond that, she could see Volcan's moldering throne room. Evanora had only been there once, when the man had told her her life depended upon the success of her mate and her brother's ability to accomplish a task he'd set for them.

The stone around her was broken. In several places, light filtered through holes in the roof or walls. Moss and mold grew everywhere. The vampire needlessly grabbed her arm and forced her into the throne room. Again, she didn't resist.

By the time she reached the throne, Evanora's legs were trembling. Whether this was from fear or simply from the exertion after such a long period of lack of use, she couldn't say. The throne sat upon a dais, and the fae sat upon it, looking down at her. She had no trouble kneeling when he commanded it. She could have hardly stood there any longer anyway. She kept her eyes on the ground in front of her.

"My usefulness for you has come to an end," said the fae.

Evanora had no clue how to respond so she didn't.

"The task I set for your mate and your brother is nearing completion. And though it might sadden Morfran, I see no compelling reason to keep you among the living."

She lifted her eyes from the stone floor and faced him. "So, it ends now, then?" Her voice sounded tiny, distant, to her own ears.

Volcan didn't answer right away. He pursed his lips and appeared to be thinking as he surveyed her closely.

"I'm going to leave that decision up to you. I could kill you now. Or, I could let Morfran have his way with you, drinking you dry until you're nothing but a husk until you have no more blood to sustain him."

Evanora shuddered. "Just kill me, ple—"

"Or..." Volcan cut her off and held up a finger. "You can join me."

"What do you mean join you?"

"I've been in a very experimental mood lately. I've already created a being of incredible power by mixing my blood with that of a gypsy healer. I've never tried to turn a warlock into a witch before. You could be the first. I don't expect you to match my gypsy witches in power, as they are something special. But you could still be great. You can join my army and help me conquer all the known realms. I've done plenty of damage in the past with simple human witches. I can do so again with a warlock turned into a witch. And a loyal employee is so hard to find these days."

"What makes you think I'll be loyal to you?" she said. "After how you've treated me?"

Stop asking questions, Evanora. She mentally berated herself. This life doesn't matter anymore. Your mate... Your brother... They're gone. Just give up and die already. Quit engaging the bastard who tortured you with questions that don't matter.

Volcan shook his head. "It's always the same with you people. *Why should I serve you? You're so mean,*" he said in a whiny voice. "You all never understand until afterward how good it feels to have true power. It's better than anything, trust me."

"I'll take your word for it." Evanora rolled her eyes. Even that effort tired out her frail body.

"Don't you ever wish you could conjure fire out of midair? Don't you ever desire the power to turn water into wine? Open locks without a key? Bind people from speaking?" The passionate light in Volcan's eyes blinked out as he frowned. "Tell me, what do you do with your power? Do you do parlor tricks to entertain children? Perhaps you use it to provide for your people? Pathetic. Don't you think there's more to magic? I'm offering you the chance of a lifetime."

Evanora pictured her home under the base of the mountain. She remembered her parents showing her and Z how to anchor themselves to the energy of the earth. Finding the ley lines and combining them with earth's elements, Evanora had discovered she favored water rather than metals like her kin. Sly's own affinity for air enhanced the power of her water magic as they tended the woods around their mountain home. They were the mages of the forest, the keepers of the land. Parlor tricks were not a warlock's specialty.

"Truth be told, you're really lucky to have been captured by me." Volcan's hand pressed against his chest as his eyebrows brushed his hair line. A look of pure self-aggrandizing pride graced his ugly face.

She'd been working a storm over the Carpathian Mountains to refill the rivers and streams evaporating in the worst heat wave they'd had in twenty years. Sly had received orders to move toward the northwest to push the hurricane away from the shores where another coven of warlocks lived. A normal life serving their people.

Camping close to human civilization, she had to cloak her presence as well as her looks. Being over six-feet with dark hair, pointed ears, and yellow cat-like eyes would draw undue attention. If her magic hadn't been so strained from dragging water away from the Carpathian's snowy peaks into something natural and keeping her existence a secret, she would have noticed when the wards around her tents failed.

She would have been alerted to the vampire lurking in the middle of the night.

"Better than winning the lottery," she replied, eliciting a chuckle from the fae.

"That's nothing compared to what I offer, Nora."

"Don't call me that," she hissed. Volcan did more than chuckle now. He laughed heartily, the sound echoing in the cavernous throne room.

"Nora, Nora, Nora, I can make all your dreams come true. The choice is yours."

"You're giving me the choice between becoming a witch and serving you, or being tortured to death by your pet vampire?" Her breath strained with the last of her words. *It's not worth arguing with the psychopath. Just let them kill you already. What the hell are you fighting for?*

"That's such a crude way of putting it, but I think you've worked it out. It seems like a pretty easy decision to make if you ask me."

"You're right about that," she said and rose to her feet. "Terribly simple." Evanora spread her arms and turned to Morfran. "Do your worst. Kill me now," she yelled, and her voice cracked under the strain. The vampire didn't move though he held a look of hatred on his face that said he wanted nothing better than to take the woman up on her offer.

Volcan laughed even harder now, his voice maniacal. When the laughter subsided, he spoke. "I thought you might say that. But only because you don't understand what you're turning down." He put his palms together and smiled. "I'm doing this for your own good, Nora. Morfran, take her to the altar. We shall begin the ritual shortly. Evanora, welcome to my army."

4

"What's worse? Knowing there is someone in the world created specifically for you and you might go mad and have to be put down before you meet her? Or finding her for a brief moment before she's ripped away from you and twisted into something ... evil? Is there still any good left inside my beloved?" ~Dalton

"I don't think so, pal. We were given a job to do, and we're going to do it. My mate's life depends upon it," said Sly.

Dalton growled as he stared at the warlock glaring back at him, refusing to drop his gaze. Dalton had to respect the man. The warlock was either very strong or very stupid. Dalton didn't know and he didn't care. He was tired of these two males hanging around Jewel and Anna. It was bad enough the girls had been alone with them for weeks. He trusted Jewel implicitly, but the thought of another male with her made Dalton's wolf restless.

"And my sister's life, as well," said Z. "You have no idea what Volcan is capable of, wolf. If you think we're going back to him without some witches in tow, you're crazy." The warlock's yellow eyes flashed in resignation and determination.

"That's exactly what he is," said Gustavo stepped in line with Dalton. "And I'm a bit *loco* myself. So why don't you do as we ask before we show you two whelps just how crazy we are?" Like a striking snake, Gustavo's hand darted out and clamped around Z's neck. There was a loud pop and a burning smell. Just as quickly, Gustavo yanked his hand back and yelped.

Dalton heard Anna gasp from somewhere behind him. Dalton's eyes widened. "What was that?" He snarled at Z. The warlock reached under his shirt and pulled out a glowing amulet.

"We're not exactly defenseless, cur," he replied, tucking the amulet back under his shirt. "Warlocks, remember? Now, would you like to know what other tricks I have up my sleeve?"

"It's going to take a little more than that to keep you from getting ripped to pieces," said Dalton. He felt his teeth elongate and knew his eyes must be glowing as well. He'd been itching for a fight the last two decades as the darkness clawed through him for footing, and for the sake of his pack, he'd always held back. But the moment for patience and hesitation was over.

"I don't remember wolves being this stupid." Jezebel's voice rose above the sound of his growling from the backroom of the shop.

Peri answered and it only spurred Dalton on. "I've yet to meet a smart one. But this one *is* particularly dumb."

"Go ahead, wolf," said Sly, rolled his shoulders and cracked his neck. "Let's see if that fur is fireproof."

"Dalton..." Jewel's voice was a warning, piercing through the haze of fury as only a mate could.

"You don't understand, Little Dove." Dalton's growl was gone for her, but his eyes tracked the slightest movements the warlocks made, his body on a hair-trigger.

"No, *you* don't understand, Dalton," she replied, her tone sharp like a cracking whip. "These guys protected us."

The words flowed over Dalton like sand blasted across a cactus in the desert. *He* was the one meant to protect his mate, not these strange warlocks. The fact that Jewel endured so much, and he'd just sat around powerless while these two men spent so much time with her, traveled with her, ate with her, talked with her... It was more than Dalton could take. He couldn't help himself. One second, he wanted to phase and rip the warlock to pieces. The next, it was happening. The third second, he was frozen in place, his jaws held open, slavering. The warlocks yelled and jumped backward, both holding up hands filled with magical fireballs. Peri took a step forward. Her power made everyone freeze.

"Enough, you testosterone-filled mutts," she said to the room. "I am sick and tired of having to force you impulsive wolves to play nice. If I'd have known when the Great Luna came to me all those centuries ago that my job as ambassador was going to consist entirely of babysitting a bunch of hairy toddlers who can't keep themselves from having temper tantrums, I would have told the goddess to go pound sand!" She stepped in front of Dalton. Gustavo growled from his position next to Dalton, but he didn't phase. Peri's eyebrows raised, and she transfixed him with her gaze. "Oh, I'm sorry, Gustavo. Did you have something to say?"

Gustavo's mouth opened but nothing came out. Dalton watched from his frozen state in his wolf form. He could see the confusion in Gustavo's eyes as the man struggled to speak.

"No?" said Peri with a smirk. "That's what I thought." She turned her attention to the warlocks. "You two, listen closely. Usually, these wolves are honorable men who protect the innocent. Unfortunately, when it comes to their females, they don't think clearly and they become very foolish. They are unable to recognize that you behaved honorably in protecting their women. But I recognize it, and I thank you on their behalf. I understand Volcan has put you both in a terrible position." She sucked in a deep breath and let it out slowly. Dalton could see the weight of the world pass across the fae's face. "I shouldn't do this," she appeared to say to herself. "I shouldn't freaking do this. Sly, Z, I promise you this. For the service you've performed in the protection of these healers, a task to which I was originally assigned, I promise to do everything in my power to help you rescue this woman who is your sister, Z, and your mate, Sly. Apparently, I don't have enough to do already."

"Evanora," Sly practically whispered. "Her name is Evanora."

"Evanora," Peri said. "I promise to help you rescue your mate, Evanora."

The fireballs disappeared from their hands. "Thank you, Perizada of the fae," said Z. "We, in turn, shall continue to aid you in the protection of the healers and the defeat of Volcan."

"To the best of our ability if it doesn't put Evanora in danger," said Sly.

"Very good," said Peri. "Now, to put this issue to rest once and for all." She turned to the frozen wolf who was now slobbering all over the floor. "Dalton Black, you have to be the dumbest dum-dum of all the furry dum-dums in the entire pack. I understand that you have endured much when it comes to Jewel. But, I'm tired of dealing with you. I've already had to put you in your place once. Apparently, the message wasn't received. This one *will* be." The fae rolled her shoulders and stretched her neck from side to side. She rotated her right arm in its socket, and her fist began to glow. Dalton felt his wolf eyes grow wide. He began to shake violently but couldn't break free. He would have growled if his mouth wasn't fixed in a snarl. Peri reared her fist back and smashed it straight into the wolf's snout. Dalton squealed then flew across the backroom of the Little Shop of Horrors. He hit the wall but didn't stop. There was an explosion of drywall and lumber as he flew out into the alley behind the building.

Dalton landed in a heap, unable to move. From his position on the ground, he could only stare back at the giant hole his body had left in the building. He began to hear something happening in the room he'd just come flying out of, such as things crashing around and Peri yelling, "Jewel, stop!" A few moments later, he heard Gustavo scream, "Anna, what are you doing?"

Then, with a blinding flash, Jewel and Anna came flying backward out of the building to land next to him.

"DALTON..." Jewel's voice was a warning.

"You don't understand, Little Dove." His growl softened to a rasp.

"No, you don't understand, Dalton," she replied, her tone sharp. "These guys protected us."

"Dalton's right." The oily voice whispered in Jewel's

mind. "Those warlocks never had your best interest at heart. They were just trying to gain your trust, waiting for the right opportunity to strike."

Jewel frowned and shook her. "No," she muttered as her hands balled into tight fists. "That's not true. Get out of my head." She looked back at Dalton, who, along with Gustavo, had Sly and Z pinned up against the wall.

Her resistance to Volcan's magic crumbled a little. A breach in her hull, and Jewel's heart picked up speed when she saw her mental walls spring a leak.

"And your mate's just the same." Instead of a hint of his voice, it was as if he spoke right in her ear, low and sultry.

"Stop." Jewel tensed her muscles to reinforce her mental walls. Volcan had been too close for comfort in her mind, but like a crack in a vessel, his magic was trickling into her. "Leave him out of this."

"You think he really wants you?" Volcan's ghostly hands rubbed down her arms as she flicked her eyes to her mate. Her mind forced the memory of last night through the gelatin of Volcan's power. Whispering those very words while she lay in Dalton's tight grasp, she had slept like the dead.

"He does," she replied.

"Maybe once, but not now. Not now that he knows what you've done. Not now that he knows you belong to me. That I've marked you." A breath shuddered in her ear. "We are one, Jewel. How would you feel if he was united to a woman the way you and I are connected?"

Jewel pushed her hands against her temples and growled. His magic pooled around her knees, stroking up her legs. The ship of her sanity was sinking, and no one was coming to rescue her.

"And do you really want him?" Ruby viscous fluid flowed

over her hips. She couldn't run from Volcan now if she wanted to.

"Yes." She whimpered. Fear held her shaking as her arms dipped into the blood magic. Warmth spread over her body, but without comfort, like a French fry in a vat of boiling oil.

"He's a murderer, Jewel. A predator. He cannot change. Once a killer, always a killer. Is that who you really want to be with? With me, you can have knowledge, power. With him, you'll probably be dead before your next birthday. Or worse."

Her breaths raced in and out of her chest as the warmth traveled up. Tilting her face up, she gritted her teeth. "Shut up," Jewel said out loud. She trembled as she watched Peri speaking with the warlocks.

"Very good." Peri's voice caught her attention. "Now, to put this issue to rest once and for all." She watched Peri approach Dalton and speak to him. The fae began stretching her limbs.

"She's going to kill your mate," said the slimy voice in Jewel's head. Fear sputtered into anger as the sanguine liquid lapped the underside of her jaw, begging for entrance.

"She won't," said Jewel. "Peri is our protector."

The voice in Jewel's head cackled. "Protector? Perizada of the fae cares about protecting only one thing, her own ego. You don't get to be that powerful by protecting others. You get that powerful by seizing opportunities when they arise. And that's exactly what she's doing with you healers." His magic seeped into her mouth, choking out of her voice, galvanizing her anger. "I won't subjugate you like Peri will, Jewel. I will rule alongside you." Power boiled the liquid into her very bones as the idea of being squished under the boot heel of the pale fae solidified in her mind. "Now, you should probably stop Peri before she kills your mate. Or don't. It would probably be for the best anyway. I don't think you're safe with him."

The last thing Jewel saw before her vision went red was Peri striking Dalton in the face and her mate flying through a wall. The fae stood with her back to Jewel, facing the newly created hole in the back of the Little Shop of Horrors. Then, the witch-healer simply reacted. Jewel leaped toward Peri, swinging her fist at the fae with all her might.

ANNA WATCHED Dalton and Gustavo accost Sly and Z. She needed to intervene, but she didn't want to say anything to make matters worse. Gustavo had already proven he'd go to the ends of the earth, even into the pixie realm, to be with her. She had no doubt he would kill the warlocks if he thought anything inappropriate had happened between her and them. It hadn't, though she and Jewel had been through quite a bit with the warlocks. Anna wasn't sure anything she would say would calm Gustavo, so she stayed silent. Anna tried to look at the situation from her mate's point of view. How would she feel if he was somewhere far away with two strange women? The thought made her stomach churn.

She considered reaching her mate through their bond when a voice entered her mind. It wasn't Gustavo's. Instead, it was a voice with which she was all too familiar. A voice that made her skin crawl. *"You'll never be alone again, Anna."* The voice was low and sinister, wrapping around her stomach like a slithering bandage.

"I know," Anna replied defiantly. *"I have Gustavo now. He will always be with me."* Despite her irritation at the renewal of the fight with the warlocks, Gustavo's strong profile capti-

vated her. He didn't hesitate to stand between her and danger.

"Always, mi amor," Gustavo responded in his neverending patience. "I will take care of you. I will treasure you. But who are you talking to?"

The mate bond shut down like a muscle with a cramp before she could alert Gustavo. She shivered in response.

The voice laughed. "*No, foolish girl. He will not. He will betray you. Men always betray.*" The fleece slithered around her chest, not constricting, but with warmth.

"But he's diff—"

"Don't be an idiot," said the voice. "When has a man ever been faithful to you? Faithful to your mother?"

"*But...*" The softness of the fleece worked under her arms and angled over her shoulders trapping any words of descent to rise. Her fight, like a sleepy child, was lulled by soft warmth.

"*Jewel is faithful,*" said the voice. The material slid around her upper arms.

"*Jewel is my friend,*" replied Anna. "*Of course, she is faithful.*" The warmth relaxed her in the confidence of her words.

"*What's going on, Anna?*" came Gustavo's muffled voice. The relaxed state of her mind opened the bond a tad, but the fleece tightened around her body swaddling her like a child. "*You're pushing me away.*" With another small painless squeeze, the fleece closed the bond in the process.

"*She's more than a friend,*" said the evil voice. The comfortable warmth increased in temperature as if the fleece blanket was electric and someone plugged it in. "*She's your sister. You and Jewel share a bond that Gustavo will never understand.*"

Anna didn't respond. She knew the voice was right, but she didn't know what it wanted from her.

"Your sister needs you," said the voice, answering her unasked question. The fleece wrapped its red material around her throat, triggering her heart to beat out of her chest. Squeezing slowly, the wave of heat seeped into her mouth and down her throat.

"What do you mean?" Anna asked. Her voice sounded muffled to her own ears as the red material started to cover her eyes.

"Look for yourself."

Anna looked up to see a huge wolf flying through the back wall of her mother's store. Peri, faintly glowing with power, stared after it. The fae took a step toward the opening in the wall and looked outward. Then a redheaded blur smashed into Peri with the force of a speeding dump truck. Jewel attacked the fae with a ferocity of which Anna didn't know the healer was capable. She was punching Peri like a professional fighter, and her fists were connecting. The blows weren't just bouncing off, which is what Anna would have expected to happen when anyone tried to hit the powerful fae. Instead, they were connecting with force, and Peri was being battered. It looked as if the fae was already bleeding from a cut cheek.

"Jewel, stop!" Anna heard Peri yell. Anna didn't have time to process what was happening, and she didn't need to. She could feel the rage burning inside Jewel as if Anna was feeling it herself. Anna knew only one thing. She had to help her friend kill the fae called Perizada.

PERI SIGHED as she watched Dalton fly through the back wall of Jezebel's shop. She hoped this would teach the wolf once and for all. They didn't have time for petty jealousies. The stakes were just too high now. If he didn't learn his lesson, well ... Peri didn't want to think about what would happen next. She was just about to walk out to the alley and give the wolf a lecture when she felt something she hadn't felt in a very, very long time—pain. Something that felt like an iron bar struck the back of her head.

Lucian's voice slammed into in her mind with a growl. *"Peri, what's going on? Why are you in pain?"*

"Not now, babe," she grunted back at him.

Peri stumbled forward before righting herself and spinning, ready to end some poor fool's life for good, but she had no idea who would have been dumb enough to attack her from behind. What she saw was not what she expected.

Jewel was screaming an unintelligible battle cry and charging directly at her. The healer's eyes were entirely blood red. No sign of a pupil or their normal emerald green could be seen. The healer was slavering at the mouth as she ran, bringing a fist back and launching it at Peri's face. Peri brought up a hand to block the strike, but it was too late. Jewel moved with a supernatural speed Peri had never before seen. The blow connected with Peri's cheek, and she went down on one knee.

What the—? The thought was cut off as Jewel came crashing down on top of her, her hands reaching for Peri's neck. Peri threw all her weight backward and brought her knees up under Jewel, thrusting upward. The healer's momentum threw her forward, and she went crashing into a shelf full of plastic shrunken heads.

"Peri!" Lucian's voice was a panicky howl in her mind. Pushing his alpha power through the bond, he searched her for signs of injury.

"Don't distract me right now, Lucian," she mentally yelled back. He didn't respond, but she could still feel his fear coming through the bond.

Peri rose to her feet and faced the healer who was doing the same.

"Jewel, stop!" she commanded with her hand raised. But the girl did not stop. Jewel didn't even acknowledge the fae's words as she charged. Perizada raised the other hand to freeze Jewel mid-motion, but the healer plowed through the simple spell with all of the finesse of a bull through a matador. Jewel was in front of her before she could conjure a shield, so she did the only thing she could think of.

She punched Jewel square in the face.

The high fae still understood that Jewel was in her care and it was Peri's job to protect her, no matter what was happening at the moment. Because of this, Peri didn't put all of her force into the blow. Had she done so, Jewel would have made a hole in the opposite wall of the store to match her mate's as she flew out into the alley. But Peri only struck Jewel at half strength, which she knew would still be enough to incapacitate the healer.

Had Perizada been thinking clearly, she might have simply cast a spell to stop Jewel or placed a shield around herself. Instead, she was still too stunned at what was happening. So, Perizada did the only thing she could think of. But Peri wasn't so shocked as to forget she didn't want to seriously injure the girl.

She was wrong.

Peri's hand bounced off Jewel's face as if the fae had struck an oncoming car. Jewel continued on and barreled straight into Peri, tackling the fae like a linebacker smashing a defenseless quarterback. Peri went down with Jewel on top of her once again. Jewel straddled Peri's chest and began raining down punches. Peri placed her hands up to defend herself as Jewel brought blow after blow down upon her. Peri managed to get hold of Jewel's long red locks and she wrenched her head back, slowing the healer's onslaught somewhat as she tried to strike Jewel with her free hand. At the same time, Peri kicked with her legs, trying to shake the witch/healer off. Then something even more surprising happened. Peri felt Anna jump on top of her. She was adding her weight to Jewel's, helping the healer pin Peri in place.

"Anna, what are you doing?" Peri heard Gustavo scream. The male grabbed Anna around the waist, but stopped when she hissed at him like a cat. Taking a couple of steps back, Gustavo stared dumfounded.

"Get off me," Peri yelled at them. But the two healers kept attacking.

The fae realized she wasn't going to be able to fight them off with supernatural strength alone. Again, trying not to injure the two healers, Peri drew in her power and released it. With a flash of light, the two healers went flying through the air, zooming out the hole in the wall made by Dalton.

Before they could recover, Peri scrambled to her feet and ran out after them. She threw her hands out, and the girls froze as they were trying to rise, but a force pushed against her power. The strain of energy going in two different directions whipped the women's hair around their faces and fluttered their clothes. Both Jewel and Anna were hissing and snarling, fighting against Peri's power, hell-bent on tearing the fae limb from limb.

Peri's eyes widened as Jewel took a step toward her. It was a small step, just a couple of inches, but it shouldn't have been possible.

Peri's blood ran cold as she realized what was happening. Volcan had taken over both healers' minds. Lucian's surprise radiated over hers through the bond. With a growl he pushed his alpha power to fortify her strength.

Gustavo sped past Peri toward his mate only to skid to a stop right in front of Anna. Red-eyed and snarling, Anna's growl sounded unearthly.

"Gustavo," yelled Peri. "I need your help, bud." She turned to the wolf and saw panic in his eyes.

"What's going on?" he asked her frantically.

"It's Volcan." She growled through gritted teeth. "He's controlling them. He must be using the blood connection, pouring his power into them. I don't know how much longer I can hold them." Using the mate bond, she could feel Lucian standing at her back to brace her and keep her upright. Leaning into his strength, an idea sparked in her mind.

"Lucian." She grunted through the bond.

"Yes." His voice sounded strained, but Peri didn't have time to reassure him.

"You're about to feel a big drain through the pack bonds, Lucian. It's Gustavo. I need you to respond to it. Send him all the Alpha power you've got."

"I can't risk diverting any from you," he replied.

"No," she snapped. "It has to be Gustavo. He needs it to help Anna."

"Will do," Lucian replied. She could tell he wasn't about it, but she could feel his trust of her coming through the bond.

"What can I do?" Gustavo asked, tearing at his hair.

"You've got to get through to Anna. Use the bond to help her fight Volcan's influence. If we can get her back, she can help us stop Jewel." With a growl worthy of a lioness, Jewel flexed her shoulders. The surge of power was miniscule but enough to jerk Peri's hands. Exerting the limits of her control, Peri's face turned red, and she knew the vein Lucian teased her about was poking out of the center of her forehead.

"How?" Gustavo asked.

I don't know," Peri said.

"Just do something!"

G‍USTAVO REACHED for his mate's mind and immediately recoiled. Gone was his lovely, sweet *Criña*. Gone was the kindness, and gone was her soft spirit. In its place was only anguish. He barely recognized her voice as he heard it hissing. *"Kill the fae! Kill the fae!"*

"Anna, it's me," he said through their bond. Gustavo felt as if his words rebounded off a chain-link fence. The fence gave way for a second, only to throw his mind backward through the bond. It was as if he could see his Anna on the other side of that fence, straining in rage and pain like she couldn't breathe, but he couldn't get to her.

"She's blocking me," he yelled to Peri.

"Well, make her unblock you," she replied.

Gustavo stared at his mate. Every day he had a chance to look at her he was blessed, but the blood-red eyes stabbed into the old wound. Even by his side, he still couldn't protect his mate. Snarling the wolf lunged toward its mate and the unseen enemy torturing her. *My mate.* The man barely leashed the animal as he renewed his purpose. *Our mate,* Gustavo agreed.

Gustavo went at Anna's mind again. *"Anna, please, let me in."* Again, the fence repelled him. He pressed his forehead against the invisible barrier to better see her. The once hazel eyes, now red with power that wasn't her own, met his and the fear and pain in them tore at his heart. Her dark hair lashed around in an emphasized and pained shake of her head, denying him. Anna's pain could only have one response from him. He couldn't leave her to face this on her own. He wouldn't.

"Criña, it's your Gustavo. You must let me in. Let me hold you. Let me be there for you. Let me love you. I can take this pain away."

Her mouth opened as if she was struggling to breathe and his heart tore. Lucian's commanding strength poured over the pack bond and into him, an alpha power Gustavo hadn't felt since he was a pup. Safety and assurance whispered to the wolf. He was not alone in bringing his mate back. His pack was there to help him.

Gustavo used the power to press against the walls of Anna's mind as hard as he could. This time, he heard a growled response. *"You'll just leave me, too, just like my father. I never knew him. And I don't know you."*

"Criña, no! I would never leave you." In his mind, Gustavo pictured himself grabbing the chain-link fence and yanking as hard as he could, ripping and tearing with all his might. It gave a little, then held fast.

"Yes, you will. Especially now that you know what Volcan has done to me. He's marked me, Gustavo. I'm his now."

His response in her mind was a roar of defiance filled with pain, but also with a determination to break through to her.

Outside of their bond, Gustavo approached his mate. She was held motionless by Peri's spell. Vaguely, he noticed that Jewel had moved a few more inches toward the fae, and Dalton, still in his wolf form, lay still on his side. Gustavo wondered what the other wolf was thinking. Gustavo could feel anger and pain pouring through the bond from his Anna. Dalton wouldn't be feeling the same thing since he and Jewel's bond was broken. Dalton could only see what was happening in front of him, and he probably had no clue what was going on.

Adrenaline mixed with fear and despair as Gustavo looked into Anna's eyes. They were shining red, almost glowing. Behind them, he saw no hint of his *Criña*. He reached out and placed a hand on Anna's arm. Though nothing physically happened because of Peri's spell, Gustavo felt Anna recoil through their bond. His heart quailed at her reaction.

"*Criña, please don't shut me out. I'd do anything to be with you.*" Gustavo poured everything he had through the bond. Every emotion, every ounce of love he felt for her, every instinct of protectiveness, his unrelenting dedication, showing her that he would never leave her, not while he could draw breath.

For a brief second, Gustavo saw his *Criña*. The beautiful hazel eyes returned before they slipped back to blood red.

"*Yes, yes, Anna, it's true. Everything I've said is true. Let me in!*" In his mind, Gustavo pictured himself straining against the fence. Combining the power Lucian was feeding him into his own power, he ripped and tore with all his might.

A hiss escaped Anna's lips, and Gustavo redoubled his efforts. Finally, the metal gave way, forming a small hole. He let his wolf claws come out just enough to tear at the hole, widening it. It ripped some more, leaving jagged bits of chain-link metal surrounding the opening. Gustavo didn't care. He forced himself through it. The metal ripped at his flesh, tearing at his mind, leaving bloody gashes in his imagined flesh.

He ran straight to Anna, wrapping her in his arms, saying her name over and over.

"Let her go, Perizada! You can let her go!" Gustavo yelled

with his arms out to catch his mate. Back in the alley, Peri released the spell, and the physical Anna fell into Gustavo's arms.

He sat gently on the ground and cradled her in his arms, looking down in her soft hazel eyes.

"Do you promise?" she asked, her voice a whisper.

His wolf settled with the feel of his mate in his arms. "I promise, *Criña*, with everything I am. I'll never leave you."

"Thank you," she said.

"But right now, we have to help Jewel. I don't think Peri can hold her off much longer."

"*Yes, yes, kill her,*" the voice in Jewel's mind implored. She no longer resisted it, now.

"Yes," Jewel agreed. "I'll kill Peri. Then no one will be able to stop us, Volcan. I know the secret now. I can create the witches."

"Very good," Volcan purred. *"Break through her defenses. You can do it. With my help, you are stronger than Peri!"* Her hands glowed with a pink tinge, and the scars on her stomach burned with sweetness against her skin. Licking her lips, she could almost taste the power of Peri's blood on her tongue.

"Yes," Jewel confirmed, as Volcan's bloody essence sent tingles through every scar on her skin. *"I am stronger!"* She pushed with all her might and felt Peri's spell give way just a little. Jewel moved forward another step. Even though her eyes were gritty and her throat was parched, her body had never felt more alive.

She looked at Peri and saw fear in the fae's eyes. Jewel could tell Peri knew Jewel's strength was greater than her own. It was only a matter of time now. With Perizada's death, she would prove to Volcan and the world she was worthy to be his queen. She would be the epitome of his power and might and she hoped it came with a crown.

Jewel was vaguely aware of Anna's mate running to her. *Fool.* Anna was her sister, part of her family now, part of *Volcan's* family. A family of witches, a sisterhood destined to take over the world. No one would stand in their way. Anna would cast the cur aside just as Jewel would do with Dalton.

"Very good, my queen." Jewel burned hot with his words slithering into her mind. "You've almost broken Peri. One more push. Force all of your power into it. All of my power."

Jewel sucked in a deep breath, closed her eyes, and ground her teeth together. Preparing for one final push. Preparing for her destiny to be fulfilled.

"Jewel, stop. What are you doing?" Another voice entered Jewel's mind. It wasn't the dark oily hiss to which she'd become so accustomed. Nor was it the strong voice of her mate that she missed so much. This was her friend, her sister, Anna.

"I'm going to kill Peri. What do you think I'm doing? Why aren't you helping me?" The distraction of Anna not standing with her caused Jewel to blink once.

"Jewel, this is madness. We can't kill Peri. She's our friend. She's the only one who can stop Volcan." The warm glow of Anna's voice chased the pink glow from her hands.

Then Jewel heard a sinister laugh in her mind, and the oily voice returned. The warm light dimmed with Volcan's laugh and Jewel knew Anna heard the voice as well. *"Stop me. Poor, poor, Anna. No one can stop me."*

"Yes, she can." The strength in Anna's glowing presence took the authority out of Volcan's statement. "We all can. Jewel, we just have to work together. We need each other's strength. But right now, it's up to you. You have to resist him.

I'll help you. Gustavo and I will lend you our power. But you must fight his influence."

"Shut up, you foolish child," came Volcan's voice, and it sounded like a hiss. A punch of Volcan's power took over her body, blotting out the light. The sweet burn of every knife cut slid against her skin ending in the deep 'V' of Volcan's mark on her stomach.

For several moments, no one said anything. They just strained against one another—Anna, Gustavo, Peri, Jewel, and Volcan all pushing their own respective powers in different directions. Jewel felt as if she were caught in a web with a spider at each corner. Every time she tried to take a step toward one of them, another pulled her backward.

She knew Volcan was right. After all, he'd made her. She wouldn't even be a witch if it weren't for him. She could feel his magic pulsing through her veins, willing her on. It would be so easy to simply accept her fate and bow to his will. To be his queen, to share their power and flex it onto the world, what could be worth more than that?

But wasn't Anna her new sister? A bond Jewel herself had created. More importantly, wasn't Anna her friend? Why would she be resisting Volcan, the figurehead of their family?

"Peanuts are one of the ingredients in dynamite," said Jewel.

"What?" Volcan spat. "What are you talking about?"

"Yes!" said Anna. "Peanuts! What about dynamite? When was dynamite invented?"

"Dynamite was invented in 1867 by Swedish chemist Alfred Nobel. And if that name sounds familiar, yes, it is the same Alfred Nobel who established the five original Nobel prizes."

"Of course, it is," said Anna. "And for what are the five Nobel prizes given?"

"Physics, Chemistry, Peace, Physiology or Medicine, and Literature. Though the prizes have been expanded since to include Economic Sciences."

Volcan roared in their minds. "What is this nonsense? Stop it, now, Jewel! Kill the fae!"

"I know you're scared, Jewel," said Anna, ignoring Volcan's outburst. "I know you think Dalton won't want you, but it's not true."

"Shut up, girl," screamed Volcan.

"He will. You're his true mate. He cannot reject you." In her mind, Jewel saw Dalton's dark hair. She heard his steady voice. She felt the hold of his arms.

"He doesn't love you," yelled Volcan. His voice was weaker this time.

Jewel's head began to throb. She wanted both of the voices out of her mind. The desire to destroy Peri was beginning to fade. Yet she could still feel Volcan's power straining against her, spurring her on.

"A shark is the only fish that can blink with both eyes," Jewel said.

"Ooh, yes, that's a good one," said Anna. "Here's one I know. Did you know shark embryos attack one another?"

There was a long silence. "I didn't know that, Anna," said Jewel. "That's very interesting. Did you know that sharks kill, on average, less than one person a year, but hippopotami kill more than 500?"

Anna laughed in Jewel's mind. The sound was a balm for her brain. So different from the dark, oily voice of Volcan. Anna's voice was filled with light, goodness, and purity. Though even through that laugh, Jewel sensed Volcan's dark influence on her friend. She could sense it and she hated it. She loathed Volcan for what he'd done to both of them, what he was still doing.

"Of course, I didn't know that, Jewel," said Anna. "Only Jewel Stone, resident gypsy healer of the Colorado Pack, genius extraordinaire, would know such a random fact. I didn't even know the plural of the hippopotamus was hippopotami."

"Shut up!" Volcan hissed again. *"Don't listen to her."* His voice sounded farther away.

Healer of the Colorado pack? Is that what she was? The thought seemed strange to Jewel. She'd never belonged to a pack before. She'd never belonged anywhere. Volcan had given her somewhere to belong. But so had Dalton, Peri, and Anna.

Jewel remembered the first time she'd seen Anna. She remembered walking through the forest with Anna, lost, while Jewel spouted one random fact after another. She remembered Jewel feeling Anna must think she was a complete nut job. And she remembered Anna didn't think that at all. Instead, she accepted her unconditionally. In an instant, it was like a dark veil lifted from her eyes. She heard Volcan's voice inside her begin to scream. *"No!"* The word went on and on, but its strength faded. Eventually, the sound of Volcan's voice became background noise. It wasn't gone completely, but it no longer controlled her.

"Okay, Peri," Anna's voice echoed somewhere outside of her body. "Let her go!"

Jewel collapsed to the ground as Peri lifted the spell on her and Dalton. In an instant, the wolf phased back to a man. He lifted Jewel and cradled her in his arms. She shivered and he pulled her closer. Her skin was pale and clammy, and she was more exhausted than before.

Jewel's head swam. Her arms and legs felt like as if she'd

just run a marathon holding a bag of sand. "Dalton," she whispered, staring up at him.

"I'm here, Little Dove," he whispered. "I'm here and I'm never leaving you."

Thankfully, Peri had enough strength left to conjure up some pants for the naked man before she, too, fell to the ground, exhausted.

5

"Volcan is smart. But he's not as smart as me." ~Peri

Peri watched as Dalton gently lowered himself to the ground. She could tell he was careful not to jostle Jewel, who was lying in a daze.

She could see the two warlocks watching, wide-eyed and slack-jawed, from the hole in the back of Jezebel's shop. Jezebel had run out into the alley and knelt next to Anna and Gustavo.

"Peri." Dalton's voice was guttural. "Would you like to tell me what the hell just happened?" Glowing eyes stared back her.

"I'd kind of like to know that myself," said Jezebel as she side-stepped once away from the disgruntled alpha.

Peri drew in a deep breath but said nothing. She put a hand to her head, feeling the blood that matted her hair. Her clothes were ripped, and her body was cut and scraped. She could only imagine she looked like ... well, she looked like she'd been in a back-alley brawl against two witches.

All of a sudden, the fae began to giggle. Then the giggle rose to a laugh. The rest of the people in the alley stared at her. It was clear they thought the fae had lost it. Peri rose to her feet. The laughter slowly subsided, and she began to brush herself off.

"That ... was awesome." Peri grinned.

"Not exactly the word I'd use, Peri," said Anna. Her head leaned back against Gustavo, her hair every bit as disheveled as Peri's.

"Because you've never been immortal before," replied the fae. "It gets boring, after a while, you know? Knowing nothing and no one can ever threaten your safety. Sometimes, believe it or not, I relish the idea of a fight I might actually lose. It has been a long time." Lucian's growl in her mind reminded her she was no longer alone in the fight.

"I'd prefer it, Beloved, if you would let me fight your battles for you."

"What? And let you have all of the fun? No way," she replied.

"You're nuts," said Sly as he shook his head.

"Bonkers," agreed Z. They stood shoulder to shoulder looking more like brothers than brothers-in-law.

"You want to know what happened, Dalton?" asked Peri. She smirked at him.

"As would I," came Lucian's voice in her mind. "Are you okay?"

"I'm fine, babe. You can check me over thoroughly for injuries when I get back home. Now, listen through the bond."

Dalton nodded, his eyes wide. "Uh, yeah, Peri. Please, enlighten us."

"Well, for starters, your mate almost killed me." The others continued to stare and Jezebel gasped, but Peri ignored them. She waved her hands around her body and muttered. Her skin began to shimmer, and the cuts and scrapes started to disappear. "And *she* tried to help." Peri pointed to Anna.

"Sorry," muttered Anna weakly. "I couldn't help myself."

Jewel remained silent in Dalton's arms.

"I know," said Peri.

"How is that possible?" asked Sly. "I thought Perizada of the fae was a total badass. I was under the assumption you could mop the floor with anyone."

"Oh, I am and I can," she replied. "If I wasn't, I'd be dead. There's no doubt. And I think that was Volcan's plan, but he made a crucial error."

"Explain," said Dalton.

"Keep your fur on, wolf," said Peri. "I'm getting to it. It's been a few centuries since I've crossed swords with Volcan. When I sealed him in the dark forest centuries ago, he was one of the most powerful high fae to ever exist, almost as powerful as me ... *almost*. But in a straight-up fight, I could take him ten times out of ten.

"Now, though, we know he's added his blood to Jewel's body. This has given her incredible power. He's basically mixed the blood of the most powerful dark fae to ever exist with a gypsy/witch—a creature that has *never* existed before. I wasn't sure how that would work. He probably wasn't either, for that matter. But now we know. As much as I hate to admit it, Volcan has created something more powerful than me. Unfortunately, that blood bond works both ways. Just as she has gained power from the exchange, so will he have increased his own strength by taking her blood."

"That ... is ... terrifying," said Z.

"True dat," agreed the fae. "Terrifying indeed. But, as usual, in its lust for power, evil has moved too soon and made a crucial error."

"What's that?" asked Gustavo.

"Volcan has tipped his hand. Now, I know his true plan. He wants to use Jewel to eliminate me. When I'm gone, the good guys lose their leader, and there's nothing standing in his way. With Jewel's power, not only will he have his army of witches, he'll personally be unstoppable. That can't happen."

"If Jewel is more powerful than you, how were you able to stop her?" asked Jezebel.

"That's the big question, isn't it?" said Peri. "And the only advantage we have against Volcan. The answer lies with those two." Peri pointed to Gustavo and Anna. "And with my mate, and with all the wolves, really."

"We used our bond," said Anna.

"Exactly," said Peri. "*I* didn't stop her. Anna did. I assume she convinced Jewel that she was still a good guy. And Anna was only able to do that by using the power given to her by her bond with Gustavo, which comes from being *Canis lupus*, from being part of a pack. It's pack magic. A force that Volcan doesn't understand. He thinks he does, but he doesn't."

"Wow," said Jezebel.

"Wow, indeed," agreed Peri. "What exactly Anna said or did to bring Jewel back from the brink, I have no idea."

"I distracted her with facts," said Anna.

"You did what?" asked Dalton.

"Maybe distract isn't the right word. Jewel's a genius, you know. And everyone who knows Jewel, or at least knows her well—her friends—knows she spouts random facts when she is scared, nervous, and can't make a decision. When I heard her spout a random fact about dynamite, I knew she was trying to fight Volcan's influence. She just needed to be reminded she *does* belong somewhere, and it isn't as the leader of an army of witches, no matter what she has done. Somehow, I knew if I kept asking about random facts the real Jewel, the genius Jewel, the Jewel we all know and love, would eventually come out. Luckily, she did."

"I belong here," came a weak voice from Dalton's arms. "With my family, with my pack." Dalton bent down and kissed Jewel on the forehead.

"Damn right you do," said Peri. "Now, we just have to figure out a way to keep you from killing me in my sleep."

"Put me down, love," Jewel said to Dalton. Some of the color was returning to her skin.

"Well, how do we do that?" asked Gustavo.

"The first thing we do is keep that big idiot as close to Jewel as possible," the fae replied, pointing at Dalton. "Even though their bond is no longer intact, there is still magic between true mates. His presence will help her fight the darkness growing inside her. But because the bond is broken, it won't work if he isn't physically near her."

"Something tells me that won't be a problem," said Jewel.

"That's ironic. It's usually the other way around. The females are supposed to fight back the darkness in us," said Gustavo.

"Now the shoe is on the other foot. Get used to it, because the same goes for you two. Anna isn't as powerful as Jewel since she was only created by Jewel instead of by Volcan himself, but she's still damn dangerous. And she's also susceptible to his influence."

"Great," groaned Anna.

"Just be vigilant," said Peri. "You've already proven you

can fight off his mental attacks. Let that give you confidence. I wouldn't be surprised if the time comes when Jewel needs your strength again to bring her back from the edge. God help us all if she goes over."

"You aren't being very encouraging, Peri," said Sly.

"Look on the bright side," she replied. "At least now we know what we are up against."

"There's just one problem," said Z.

"What's that?" asked Peri.

"The All-Powerful-Super-Wheeler still has to make witches." The pet name earned a growl from Dalton, but he didn't move from where he stood behind Jewel, his arms around her waist. Z continued without acknowledging the large wolf. "And I'm just a wee bit afraid if she succeeds, they may come out just like her and—I don't know—kill us all ... violently, which is exactly what Volcan wants." Z's voice rose as he spoke, and he threw his hands in the air.

"Can I ask a question here, Peri?" said Anna.

"By all means, Wheeler, ask away."

"Not you, too," said Jewel, rolling her eyes.

"Hey, I thought it was dumb at first, too, but if the nickname fits..."

"Anyway," said Anna, "I'm just wondering why we really even *need* to make the witches. What if we just tell Volcan to stuff it and we all go ... I don't know, somewhere ... somewhere safe?"

"Did anything about what just happened seem safe to you?" asked Sly. "You more than anyone should know what Volcan is capable of after he kept you in a dungeon for three months and carved you up like a fish." The statement drew a snarl from Gustavo.

"Peace, wolf," said Peri. "The warlock is not wrong. To answer your question, Anna, Volcan isn't simply going to go away if we don't do what he wants. There is no place safe. He will continue creeping into your mind and into Jewel's until you no longer have any power to resist him, no matter what kind of strength you're able to garner from your respective mates and packs. Just look at what Jewel did before coming here. Six women died in one night because of Volcan's influence."

"I'm sorry," whispered Jewel. Dalton wrapped his arms around her and began kissing her softly and whispering into her ear. The words were too soft for the others to hear because they were meant only for his mate. She needed him. She needed to know she wasn't responsible for the things Volcan had forced her to do. Dalton would remind her every day for the rest of his existence if that's what it took.

"Don't worry about it now, Jewel. It's water under the fridge at this point."

"Don't you mean water under the bridge?" asked Z.

Peri looked at him and raised an eyebrow. "No, that doesn't make any sense. Water is supposed to flow under a bridge. Who cares if water goes under a bridge? But if ice falls under the refrigerator, then that's a giant pain in the ass. It becomes water, and you can't get under there to clean it up. It's a problem, but you can't do anything about it. Exactly what we have here."

"Ooookay," said Z with a shrug.

"There's another reason we must make the witches," continued Peri. "But I don't want to reveal it right now. I'm really not sure what Volcan can see and hear through the minds of his witches. It's probably best not to lay all my cards on the table right away. I'd like to keep a little something up my sleeve, just in case I need it later."

Now Dalton and Gustavo both growled. "Please don't

call our mates *his, Señora* Peri," said Gustavo. "They do *not* belong to him. I do not care what he has done."

"My apologies, Gustavo. Poor choice of words."

"Forgive me for continually being the wet blanket," said Z. "But we still don't know how to make witches that don't want to kill us all and take over the world."

"That's where the spell comes in," said Jezebel. "It should allow us to make non-evil witches, if the sacrifice is adequate, of course."

Z nodded. "Ah, yes, I must have forgotten the magical spell book we stole from the witch museum. That none of us can even read! It's been *so* helpful up until this point."

"Are all warlocks so whiny?" asked Peri. "I feel for Lilly having to be mated to one. It must be a constant headache."

"I'm not whiny. I'm just being realistic," said Z.

"There's a saying in my realm," said Peri. "Warlocks should be seen, not heard. Did you forget Jezebel and I are on a first-name basis with an all-knowing, all-powerful djinn who can read the book?"

"I don't think that's a real saying, Z," said Sly to his partner. Peri rolled her eyes.

"Well, then, Mrs. I-have-an-answer-for-everything, why doesn't this all-knowing, all-powerful djinn just zap 'ol Volcan right in his ass and be done with it if he's so powerful?" asked Z.

"Slow your roll, warlock," said Peri. "It's not like Thadrick can snap his fingers and all our problems are solved. It's more likely that he snaps his fingers and an entire city gets destroyed. That kind of power can't really be harnessed. If Thadrick confronted Volcan directly, then yes, Volcan would die. And so would everyone else."

"Then what good is he?" asked Anna.

"He can read ancient magical books, for a start," said Peri. "And he can ... assist and evaluate."

Sly blew out a breath. "Better than nothing, I guess."

"I'll go and fetch him shortly," said Peri. "It's past time you all met our resident djinn. I need to swing by my place to let the others know what's going on, so it might take me a few minutes."

"Where is he?" asked Jezebel.

"He and some others are trying to break down the door to the draheim realm. We're pretty sure that's where Volcan is holed up."

"Nasty ones, those draheim. I hope he hasn't convinced them to join his side," said Z.

"I'd be surprised if he hasn't," said Peri. "All the more reason we need our own witches. The more supernaturals we have to throw against Volcan, the better. Now, you all hang tight, I'll be right back. Keep a close eye on those two." She indicated Jewel and Anna. "Gustavo, if Anna starts to slip back into the darkness, you know how to bring her back. If Jewel starts to go, then it's all on you, Anna. If they both go at the same time before I get back, then I'd suggest the rest of you run as fast as you can.

"And, Jezebel, don't worry about this mess. I'll clean it up as soon as I get back."

"Peri," said Jezebel, holding up a hand and stopping the fae before she was able to flash away. "Can I speak to you privately a second before you go."

Dalton returned his attention to his mate. Nothing else mattered at the moment.

PERIZADA RAISED HER EYEBROWS. "SURE," she replied before

they walked into the front room of the Little Shop of Horrors. "What's going on?"

"There's something I think maybe I should tell you before you bring Thad back here," said Jezebel quietly.

"I'm all ears," said the fae.

Jezebel hesitated, picking at her fingernails. Peri raised her eyebrows. "What is it, woman? I don't have all day."

Finally, Jezebel spoke softly. "This is kind of hard to discuss."

"Find a way to power through it. I'm a bit pressed for time."

"Okay, okay, here goes nothing," said Jezebel before she drew in a large breath. "Peri, something happened after you, Thad, and I cast the spell and Metea sacrificed herself. Remember, it wasn't long afterward that I went into hiding and we all went our respective ways and lived our own respective lives?"

"Yeah?" said Peri.

"Well, Thad and I didn't exactly go our separate ways, at least not immediately."

Peri narrowed her eyes. "What are you trying to say?"

"We may or may not have had a ... relationship ... before I went into hiding."

Now, Peri felt her eyes go wide. She grabbed Jezebel's arm and spoke through gritted teeth. "Are you telling me you had a fling with an all-powerful djinn a hundred years ago and you never told me about it?" Several emotions threatened to explode from the fae. "I don't know whether to give you a high five or strangle you."

"Probably strangle would be more appropriate." Jezebel's face took on a look of shame.

"Oh no," said Peri. "What happened?"

"I may or may not have cheated on him..."

"No," said Peri, putting her hand on the bridge of her nose and squeezing her eyes shut.

"With a warlock..."

"No," repeated Peri.

"In Thadrick's bed."

Peri groaned. For several seconds, she said nothing. The fae just shook her head and tapped her foot. Finally, she said. "There's nothing to be done about it now, I guess. But it's about to get real awkward for you real fast. I just hope he doesn't hold your past transgressions against the rest of us. Have you spoken to him since?"

"Nope," Jezebel replied.

"You know Thadrick might be the most petty, stubborn, temperamental, unpredictable being in existence, don't you?"

"Yep."

"And now we're depending upon him to *not* hold a grudge against you so he will help us save five young women, one of which is your daughter, from becoming evil witches, right?"

"Yep."

Peri patted her on the shoulder. "Great, just so we're clear on exactly what's going on."

"I'm sorry," said Jezebel.

"No, no, no," Perizada replied. "I'm glad this happened. I really am. Before, this job was going to be way too easy. We might've been done with this whole messy business before lunchtime. That wouldn't have been any fun at all. Now, at least, it's going to be a challenge. I'd hate for anything to actually be easy for once. Who likes things to be easy? Certainly not me. I'M BEING SARCASTIC, IN CASE YOU COULDN'T TELL!" Peri stomped her foot.

"I ... I ... I got that," said Jezebel.

Peri paused for a second and then said as sweetly as possible, "Jezebel, I'm going to go now." She put her palms up and spread her fingers, then clenched her hands into fists. "Before I make good on that strangulation threat. When I return, I will have your ex-boyfriend with me. I'd suggest you start thinking about what you want to say to him so he will still help us and so he doesn't turn us all into little piles of ash. Goodbye." With that, the fae vanished.

6

"When I was taken from my home with virtually no explanation given and lead blindly (pun intended) into the supernatural world and told that I was destined to be mated to a werewolf and that I had secret healing powers, I thought I might have some time to ... you know ... practice or something. I didn't know I would be almost instantly turned into a witch and that my werewolf mate would have to die for me. And I thought being born blind was unfair." ~Heather

Ciesel flitted toward the crumbling castle in the draheim veil. The location Volcan was currently using as his lair was entirely too far into the draheim land for his liking. The pixie hated crossing into the draheim realm. With every second that passed, his fear grew. He just knew that one of the great beasts was going to leap out from behind a boulder and gobble him up. Ciesel was faster and much more agile in the air than the draheim so he was confident he could evade them *if* he saw them coming. But if one ambushed him ... Ciesel gulped. He could almost feel the massive teeth snapping his tiny bones.

So far, though, he'd seen no sign of the beasts since he'd entered their realm. Luckily, the draheim's ferociousness also made them few in number. They couldn't abide very many creatures, including their own species. Weaker draheim were quickly killed off by the stronger ones, acting as an automatic Darwinian population control, which Ciesel couldn't be happier about. He breathed a sigh of relief when he flew over the castle walls into the courtyard. He passed through a doorway—its wooden door long ago rotted and crumbled to dust—flew down a hallway, and stopped outside of Volcan's throne room. He didn't dare just rush in.

"Ahem, the pixie, Ciesel, here to request an audience with the almighty fae, Volcan," he yelled into the chamber.

"Enter," commanded a voice like sandpaper.

"The vampire..." squeaked Ciesel before hurrying in. He did so but froze a few paces in when he saw his first draheim of the day, which was languishing in a corner of the room. Volcan sat upon the throne staring down at him, but the pixie took no notice. He couldn't tear his eyes away from the huge purplish-green beast in the corner. Its eyes were closed, and its huge scaly tail was wrapped around itself, tucked under its chin. Ciesel could smell the thing from across the room, and it wasn't a pleasant experience.

"Never mind the draheim, Ciesel," said Volcan. "Approach."

Ciesel did so, slowly, as if he might awaken the beast if he moved too quickly.

"He won't hurt you, Ciesel. Unless I tell him to. I assure

you, pixie, the draheim isn't the most dangerous thing in this room. Now, stop wasting my time."

Ciesel gulped and hurried forward, kneeling before the fae. He wished he could deliver his report and get the hell out of the draheim realm. He had no clue where he'd go, just as long as it was as far as possible from the evil fae or the giant magical killing machines known as draheim.

Volcan stared down at the pixie that knelt, quivering on his knees. The little being had actually done quite well, but the dark fae wasn't about to let him know it. Volcan pursed his lips, narrowing his eyes. He was looking at the pixie, but his thoughts were far away with the goodie-two-shoes Perizada. *What was she up to?*

The three healers were planning to turn themselves into witches. That was good. It meant that his queen was doing her job. She was coming over to his side; there was no doubt about it. Soon, he would have his witch army. And the other three gypsy healer witches would be the first members. They would be his captains as his forces wreaked havoc on the world.

But what of the sacrifice the male wolves had spoken of? Why were they willing to sacrifice themselves, and what was this spell they had mentioned? The whole thing stunk of Perizada. He was sure the high fae had something up her sleeve, but he didn't know what. Volcan had hoped mixing his blood with Jewel's might have given him the power to see through her eyes. While it had indeed made him stronger, that particular trick eluded him.

And he was beyond frustrated his plan to kill the fae had failed. He was so close to taking her down. Had Anna and Jewel cornered Peri alone, the woman wouldn't have had a chance. *Curse those damn wolves.* Still, the effort wasn't a total failure. He now knew his witch queen was not only Peri's equal, but her better. When the time came, Jewel would eliminate the fae, he was certain of it. Unfortunately, now, his queen was going to be on her guard at all times. He'd have to a bit more subtle the next time he tried to take over Jewel's mind.

Until then, he would bide his time a little longer. The effort of imposing his will on Jewel and Anna from so far away had taken a lot of his energy. He was weakened, at least for the moment. But Volcan's power would replenish, so long as the healer's blood coursed through him. This made him chuckle. The healing power within the gypsies was amazing, and he'd been able to harness it for himself. Now, it acted as his own internal gypsy healer, involuntary mending his wounds. No one in history had ever done that.

"And that's all you heard from the three healers?" Volcan turned his attention back to Ciesel. "Giggling over their so-called mates?"

The pixie nodded vigorously. "I stayed as long as I dared, Volcan. The women didn't say anything else."

"I'd have hoped the other healers held a little more gravitas. If they're going to be commanders in my army, they'll have to learn there are more important things than foolish romance."

"Indeed," agreed Ciesel.

"Hush," snapped Volcan. "Don't speak unless spoken to."

"Yes, my lord," whimpered the pixie.

"And you're sure Perizada of the fae was not on the premises?"

"I didn't see her, and I couldn't sense any magic recently performed. I was honestly surprised the fae's house was so easy to infiltrate."

"She's probably had to drop some of the wards with all the individuals coming and going."

Volcan wished he could rush in and drive the high fae from her little perch right now. Much like she'd done to him so long ago when she'd banished him to the dark forest. The bitch would pay for that. But she wouldn't just be banished. She'd be destroyed. Volcan wanted to strip Peri of everything before he killed her. He wanted to take away her power, her friends, everything she loved. When Perizada knew that everything she'd ever held dear was lost, only then would he grant her the mercy of a very slow death.

If he'd been able to convince more of the draheim to join his cause, he might be able to attack Peri now. But he'd only persuaded two of the great beasts—a ruthless pair of brothers, huge monsters the size of city buses called Grus and Volaman. Regrettably, the evil beings' territorialism, hatred for one another, and a general lack of ambition kept them from aligning themselves with anybody. They were usually merciless with outsiders who entered their realm. But even the great draheim recognized Volcan wasn't someone with which they should trifle. And two would be enough when the time came, especially if he had his witch army at his back. He would destroy Perizada first, then the wolves, then move on to the rest of the supernaturals. It wouldn't take long to subjugate them all. They would serve or they would die. It was that simple.

Volcan smirked at Ciesel, who continually glanced at Volaman out the corner of his eye. The draheim was coiled into a ball, watching the pixie intently. Volcan wasn't sure where Grus was at the moment, surely off killing something. "Does my companion frighten you, Ciesel?"

"F-f-frighten? Of course not. I've just never seen one this closely before."

"Few people do and live to tell about it," came a scratchy voice from inside the draheim, though the thing's huge mouth never moved.

Ciesel squeaked from his kneeling position on the ground. "How'd it do that?"

Volcan laughed. "The draheim have many magical abilities few people understand or even know about. Volaman and his brother will be great allies in the battles to come."

"Yes, I'm sure," said Ciesel. "I look forward to hearing about your conquests."

Volcan laughed again. "Hearing about them? Why, my good pixie, you'll be seeing them firsthand. You don't plan on leaving my service anytime soon, do you, Ciesel?"

"Uh, of course not, my lord. But I'm not much of a fighter."

"You're not," agreed Volcan. "But you have certain skills, however minuscule, that might be of use, such as your penchant for moving about undetected."

"Okay."

"Now, back to my healers. What should we do with them?"

"I ... I ... I ... don't know, my lord."

"That was rhetorical, Ciesel," said Volcan.

"We could go eat them," came the draheim's voice from the corner.

"Not the healers," hissed Volcan. "Be patient, Volaman. You'll have plenty of wolves to eat soon enough."

Volcan considered for a moment calling Jewel and Anna back to him. He was sure he had just enough strength to force their return. But it didn't sound like that was necessary. Apparently, the women were doing their duty as he commanded, attempting to determine how to build his army, and it sounded like they'd succeeded. They would start with the other three healers first and then work from there. After he had those five under his thumb, he'd consider his options.

In fact, five witch/healers plus the two draheim might just be enough to take on Perizada and her band of merry wolves. Then again, he might need to bide his time just a little more and let Jewel and Anna continue to make witches. It should be easier for them going forward now that they'd apparently learned the secret. Though Volcan wanted his army as quickly as possible, and though he hated it, he was used to waiting. After all, he'd spent hundreds of years in the dark forest. He could wait a few more days to accomplish his goals.

Still, one thing niggled at the back of his mind. Why did Perizada not want the wolves to perform the Blood Rites ceremony? It must have something to do with that sacrifice. This much he was sure of. *But why?* Volcan couldn't guess. Though one thing was for sure. If Peri didn't want the wolves to perform the Blood Rites ceremony, then Volcan certainly did.

"Ciesel, get up," he commanded.

The pixie jumped to his feet so quickly he actually rose involuntarily a couple of feet from the ground. Quickly, he landed, a look of expectant terror on his face.

"I'm sending you back to Peri's abode," said Volcan, ignoring the pixie's antics. "And this time you won't just be observing."

Ciesel gulped. "Yes, my lord. What would you have of me?"

How fitting. I'm sending a tiny creature to fly around and make foolish people fall in love with each other. "Ciesel, you're going to be playing cupid. I hope you look good in a diaper."

"It's not happening. Ciro can just forget it. I'm not letting him sacrifice himself for me," said Stella.

"Same for me," said Kara. "I couldn't watch Nick die. It would end up killing me, too, even if this whole Blood Rites ceremony-thingie hasn't been performed."

They both looked at Heather, and though she couldn't see them, Heather could feel their stares and knew they anticipated she would echo their sentiments. Instead, she remained silent. After hearing the males intended on sacrificing themselves, Heather had called a powwow. The women had kicked the boys out into the hall so they could discuss what the males had said about the spell. Now, Stella and Heather held their bond closed tightly so their mates couldn't hear the discussion. Kara, of course, didn't have that problem since theirs hadn't yet developed due to her young age.

"Don't you have anything to say, Heather?" asked Stella. "Usually, we can't get you to shut up. Now, you want to go quiet on us?"

"I don't know what to say," Heather whispered finally. "There's just so many unknowns."

"Unknowns? What's unknown about it? You've been introduced to the man of your dreams. He's a werewolf. Now he's going to die for you. Only you can stop him. And you're actually thinking about letting him go through with it?"

Heather began, "Wow, when you say it like that it sounds so—"

"Romantic," interrupted Kara.

"Exactly," said Heather.

"Insane is the word I would use," said Stella.

"Of the three of us, I'm surprised you're the one having the biggest issues with this," said Heather.

"Why would you say that?"

"It just seems you and Ciro ... I don't know ... don't necessarily have the same connection that Kale and I have."

Stella shook her head. "Uh. Do not go there. Can you see in my mind? Do you know what Ciro and I have talked about? No. So, don't go thinking you know anything about our bond. I might have some baggage to work through, but that doesn't mean I'm any less enthralled with my man than you two are with yours."

Heather held up her hands. "You're right, you're right. I shouldn't have said that. It's just, I'm so confused."

"There's nothing to be confused about. No one is sacrificing themselves for me, especially not Ciro."

"But if they don't, then we become evil witches. Ciro isn't going to want you if you're an evil witch."

"I don't know that," replied Stella. "If you knew how patient he was, you might not think that. He'd want me if I was a three-headed cyclops. And I'm sure Kale feels the same way about you."

"What if they don't even have to die?" asked Kara. "You heard what they said. Sometimes the sacrifice doesn't die."

"You tell that to Mateo or Metata or whatever that chick's name was. She died. That means our mates could, too," said Stella. "I'm not willing to take that chance."

"What if we can't stop them?" asked Heather.

"What do you mean? They can't sacrifice themselves if we refuse to perform the spell," said Stella.

"So, you would allow yourself to be transformed into an evil witch if it means saving Ciro's life?" asked Heather.

"One hundred percent."

"I think I'm with Stella on this one," said Kara.

"There has to be another way," said Heather.

"I'd love to hear any ideas you might have."

Heather scratched her chin. "Maybe we should spend some more time with them. I know it seems we've been in this world our whole lives, at least it does for me. But it wasn't long ago we had no idea the supernatural world existed. We certainly don't understand the whole Blood Rites stuff. Maybe we should spend some time alone with our mates, get to know them better, help ourselves understand what it's like from their point of view."

"That sounds like a good idea," said Kara. "I definitely want to spend some more time with my biker. Then, we all decide as a group, the six of us. And it has to be unanimous. One for all, all for one, that type of thing."

"Exactly," said Heather.

"Bup, bup, bup, wait a second. You know what Peri said," offered Stella. "No touchie-touchie. We have to stay pure. And absolutely no bitie, bitie." She pointed to her neck.

"To be honest, I think this should be a decision made between us and our mates. I mean, I know Peri has our backs, but it's sort of personal." And for her it was extremely personal. Heather had lived her whole life in darkness and since meeting Kale, for the first time in her life, she felt as though she'd stepped into the light. She was terrified of losing it, of losing him. "And I'm not just saying that because I want my man's lips and teeth on me like I want my next breath," said Heather.

"I understand what you're saying, Helen, really I do. But we can't take our eyes off the bigger picture. We go off on our own and these guys start getting all, 'you're my true mate and blah, blah, blah.' The next thing you know, the fangs and claws come out and we're being ravished."

"I can't see *any* pictures, bigger or smaller. And ravished sounds exactly what I want to be by Kale," said Heather.

"And Peri finds out and turns us all into toads or cockroaches or something," said Stella. "Not to mention, now we've got completed bonds, and if one of us dies then our mate dies."

"Being a cockroach would suck. It would put a damper on the whole mating thing," said Kara.

"Or make it even better," offered Heather.

Stella made a retching sound. "Eww. I cannot believe you just said that."

"You never know," said Heather. "Frogs and cockroaches have, like, a million eggs. They must enjoy mating quite a bit."

"Please stop," said Stella.

"How about this?" asked Kara. "We each agree that if things get too heavy, we find one another and then regroup. This will be our HQ. That way, we can spend time with our mates—it still feels weird to call them that—and we have our girls to protect us if the claws and fangs come out."

"Perfect," said Heather. "This will be the AWBDL headquarters."

"AWBDL?" asked Stella.

"Anti-werewolf Bite Defense League, obviously," answered Heather.

"Can't believe I didn't get that," said Stella deadpan.

"Whaddya say?" asked Kara.

"Okay, I'll do it," said Stella, "but only because I love you two goofy white girls, and I don't want you to turn evil. Nothing worse than more EWWs running around."

"EWWs?" asked Heather.

"Evil White Witches."

"Touché," she replied.

"Is there a reason you two are speaking in abbreviations?" asked Kara. "I feel like I'm the uncool kid being left out of the club."

"Naw." Heather waved her off. "We'd never let you be left out. Besides, just being near us makes you cool. Stella and I seem to be on the same wavelength today."

Stella blanched. "Says the girl who thinks being turned into a cockroach will make sex better. No, we are not even close to being on the same wavelength. I'm only speaking in abbreviations because it seems to be a language you understand."

"Whatevs," said Heather. "Miss out on the best insect sex of your life. See if I care."

"I know I've said this already, but eww," said Stella.

"Okay, okay," said Kara. "How about we agree, no more abbreviations and no more insect sex talk."

"Please," said Stella.

"Fine," agreed Heather.

"Alright then," said Kara "I'm all for getting my wolf time on. Let's do this."

"Better yet, let's wait until the morning," said Stella. "I'm tired. I could use a good night's sleep before I face Ciro again."

"Excellent idea," said Heather.

"I doubt the guys are going anywhere," said Kara. "I'm pretty sure they're sitting just outside our door again."

"We are," came Nick's voice.

Kara's eyes went wide. "Do you think they've heard this entire conversation?"

"We have." This time it was Ciro's voice.

"Damn it," said Heather "We forgot about the wolf hearing. That one's on me. I should have thought of that."

"You should've, lass," said Kale loudly.

"Mind your own business, mutts," said Stella "Before we change our minds and decide to stay in this room for the rest of our lives."

"See you in the morning, love," said Ciro, ignoring her statement.

"Goodnight, Kara," said Nick.

"*Codladh sámh*, Heather," said Kale.

There was a moment of silence. "And a very pleasant coleslaw to you, too," she replied. She heard him chuckle through the doorway.

"It means sleep tight, love."

"Ah, well, then thank you. You too. See you tomorrow. I mean ... I won't *see* you, see you, but ... you know what I mean."

He laughed again. "Hopefully, I'll see you before then, in my dreams tonight. And I pray you won't be a cockroach."

"Sounds more like a nightmare," said Stella.

"I was only kidding about that," she yelled at Kale. "Don't imagine me as a cockroach. I'm all girl. And you're all boy. Dream about that."

"But he's actually not all boy... He's a werewolf," said Kara.

"Oh, yeah," said Heather. "On second thought, if you want to go all furry during the dream, I'm cool with that, too," she said loudly to the door. "Just take good notes. I want a full recap in the morning."

"As you wish, lass," he replied.

"You know there is something seriously wrong with you, don't you?" said Stella to Heather. "I mean, not just a little wrong, but seriously, seriously wrong."

"What can I say," replied Heather, throwing up her hands. "The freaky heart wants what the freaky heart wants."

7

"They call me a *good* witch, whatever that means. Sure, maybe I've never killed anyone. And maybe I've never made a sacrifice to a denizen of the underworld. I've never cursed anyone ... but I'm far from good." ~Jezebel

"Gustavo, I'd like to speak to my mother," said Anna.

He touched her chin gently and lifted her face so she was looking at him. "I'll be right out here. If you need me, just call." Gustavo leaned down and pressed his lips to her forehead. She wanted to sink into his strength and warmth, but this talk was long overdue. She stepped away and walked past the two warlocks who'd begun picking up strewn debris left over from the fight and stacking it against the back wall of the Little Shop of Horrors. Anna entered the room and found Jezebel staring into space.

"Mom." Jezebel spun around, and Anna saw tears in her eyes. "What's going on?"

Jezebel quickly wiped the tears away and sniffed. "It's nothing, dear. I just had to tell Peri something about Thadrick."

"What about Thad?" Anna asked.

"It's nothing, dear. Really."

"Mom, don't give me that. I know that look. You're hiding something from me. You always used to get that same look in your eyes every time you were about to take off. Are you about to leave again?"

Fresh tears appeared in the witch's eyes. Jezebel shook her head. "No way. Never again."

"What does that mean?" asked Anna. "Does that mean you *don't* think evil spirits will be drawn to you if you don't stay in one place?"

"Something like that."

"No, Mom. That's not good enough. I want to know what's going on with you. You kept all of this from me, Mom." Anna held out her arms. "You kept an entire world from me. Werewolves, djinn, witches. I lived my whole life without knowing about any of this."

"I did it to keep you safe."

"And how'd that work out?"

"Anna—"

"No. Don't try to pacify me. I want to know everything that you've been hiding from me. You've explained your sister but not my father, and now, apparently, Thad too. What's going on?"

"Okay, okay," said Jezebel. "I'll tell you everything. You should probably take a seat."

∼

Dalton sat on the ground and pulled Jewel down to him. He held her in his lap and stared into her eyes, trying desperately to see what was behind them. Not for the first time, he wished the bond hadn't been broken. He wished so badly to be able to communicate with his Little Dove on a deeper level.

"Talk to me, Jewel."

"What do you want me to say, Dalton?"

"What are you thinking?"

"I'm thinking I almost killed Peri, and I couldn't help myself."

"It's okay, Little Dove."

"It's not okay, Dalton! None of this is okay." She wriggled out of his arms and sat up. "What am I going to do the next time he tries to use me to attack someone?"

"You'll fight him off again. Just like you did this time."

"And what if I can't?" she asked.

"You will."

Jewel just shook her head. Dalton ground his teeth. He wanted so badly to take the taint of Volcan from his mate's veins. He wanted to find the evil fae and rip him limb from limb. But he couldn't. All he could do was sit there, useless, powerless. Dalton hated feeling powerless. It reminded him of sitting chained in the dungeon all those years ago when his villagers had murdered his parents and kept him locked in a dungeon. But then he'd been alone.

Now, Dalton had his Little Dove with him. He had to be strong for her. If Dalton couldn't kill Volcan, at least he could try to be a good mate. If nothing else, he could do that.

"If it hadn't been for Anna, all would be lost now. Peri'd be gone, and there'd be no one to stop Volcan," Jewel continued.

Dalton looked at her and spoke. "Tell me about it, Jewel. What were you feeling? Why did you do it? Help me better understand, then maybe I can help you next time." He knew what she was going to say wouldn't be easy to hear. The thought of Volcan having any sort of control over his mate was almost unbearable.

Jewel's face contorted. "I don't know. It was like I was no longer in my own mind. Somehow, I was outside looking in. Volcan was there, directing my mind what to think and my body what to do. He was talking to me and I was responding to him, agreeing with everything he was saying. He was telling me Peri was trying to kill you and that I better kill her first."

A low growl came from Dalton's chest. "He used our relationship against you. First, he destroys our bond and now he does this?"

"I'm so sorry, Dalton." Jewel began to cry. She spoke through the sobs. "Another part of me was screaming at myself to stop, but I couldn't. I just couldn't, no matter how hard I tried."

He pulled her back into his arms. "Shh, female, no. It wasn't your fault. Don't be upset."

"What are we going to do, Dalton?" she said.

"Why did you come back to your senses?" he asked, calmly ignoring her statement.

"When I heard Anna speaking to me, some good part of me woke up. I think it was the gypsy healer part. According to everyone else, healers are supposed to be all light and goodness and stuff. I don't really feel that way about myself, but, apparently, something inside of me decided it would at least make an attempt to stand up to Volcan's darkness. I can't imagine what else it could be."

"I'm glad it did."

"Me, too," she agreed.

"If it makes you feel any better, I appreciate you coming to my defense."

She looked at him sideways and narrowed her eyes. "What do you mean?"

"You only attacked Peri because you thought she was trying to kill me. I appreciate that."

"But she wasn't trying to kill you," argued Jewel.

"Doesn't matter," said Dalton. "What matters is you *thought* she was. I've been alone for a long time, Jewel. To have someone jump in and fight for me when I'm laying on the ground helpless? Well, that's never happened before. It makes me feel ... many different things, I guess. Loved, most of all."

"I do love you," she said.

"I know. But seeing that love in action…" He shook his head as he tried to find the right words. "My wolf loves that you would go to battle for us. It tells us that despite the lack of the mate bond you are ours and ours alone. It angers us both that we couldn't protect you. We should have been the one fighting Peri, not you."

She smiled sweetly. "I guess that's what this is all about, helping one another in times of weakness. Even the mighty Dalton, a giant among *Canis lupus*, is helpless sometimes."

Dalton growled at the thought. "I can't be helpless. I *have* to protect you."

"I know what you've been through, my love," said Jewel, quieting him. "You've had to endure so much in your long life. And I thank you that you thought me special enough to share your past with, spending all that time with me when I was in a coma. But you have to learn from those experiences. Dillon was able to keep you in check for a long time, but he's not here anymore. And you're Beta of the Colorado pack, Dillon's representative. Despite how your instincts drive you when it comes to me, you have to start acting like it. You're powerful enough to be an Alpha in most any other pack if you wanted to."

"Power was never the issue."

"That's exactly what I'm saying," said Jewel. "I don't need Dalton, the powerful, though we may all need him before this whole messed-up situation is said and done. I need Dalton, the understanding, Dalton, the patient, Dalton, the thoughtful, Dalton, the lover of my soul."

Now, it was Dalton's turn to shed a few tears. He'd been such an idiot when it came to his Little Dove. He'd vowed to fight the darkness within Jewel and to keep all external threats away from her. But he'd forgotten that somewhere within that miasma of darkness inside Jewel, his mate was battered, bruised, and cut. She'd been tortured time and again by Volcan, both physically and mentally. Though in some ways, Jewel was tough as nails, deep inside, his mate was fragile. Dalton couldn't be the mate he needed to be unless he recognized that and started treating her like the delicate cargo she was. Whatever that took, he would do it. He had to. If he failed, his mate would end up being the most powerful evil witch the world had ever seen.

"I need to kiss you," he whispered as he pulled her into his arms. "I need five minutes alone with you to just feel you."

"We have to be careful, Dalton. The spell that Volcan put on us..."

"I haven't forgotten that I can't corrupt you." He chuckled. "This isn't about lust. It's about reassurance. Let me kiss you, Little Dove."

She sighed and then tilted her head up. Dalton didn't wait for her to change her mind. He took her lips as if he owned them, and perhaps, in his mind, he did. Just as she owned his. She owned all of him. Dalton cupped her face and tilted her head back, deepening the kiss. The instance their tongues touched and her taste filled him, he wanted nothing more than to take her somewhere private and reassure himself that more than just her mouth was fully functioning.

Dalton felt a sharp pain in his mind and the air pulled from his lungs. Jewel gasped and pulled away.

"What's wrong?" she asked, sounding as out of breath as he felt.

"I might have gotten a little carried away," he admitted as he pressed his hand to his chest. He could feel the darkness inside of him attempting to gain ground.

"Dalton!" She huffed as she smacked him in the stomach. "No lusting."

He grinned. "Is this a bad time to mention that your red hair is like gas to fire when it comes to my attraction for you?"

"Yes. It is a horrible time. Please, I don't want you hurt. I need you to be safe," she pleaded.

"Calm down, sweetheart," he said as he caressed her cheek in an effort to help her relax. "I'm fine. I'm under control. But, I don't regret it even a little. I am so hungry for you. All bets are off when this is all said and done. I'm finding the nearest church and marrying you, and then I'm going to sequester us away somewhere for a month."

Her brow rose. "A month? Feeling ambitious?"

He knew his smile was pure sin. "Oh no, baby, it's not ambition. It's pure fact. Once I have you, it's going to be a while until I work the edge off."

She visibly swallowed and Dalton took pleasure in the fact that he could see the desire in her eyes. She wanted him; she was just much better at hiding it than he was.

"Something to look forward to," she practically whispered.

"Damn straight, Little Dove. Damn straight."

∽

PERI STOOD in the hallway outside of the healers' room and watched the three wolves stomp away. She'd found them sitting in the hall across from the room where their mates slept. She wasn't sure if she was impressed or not that none of them, including the ancient Ciro, looked the least bit ashamed.

As they disappeared down the stairs, Peri sighed and tried to prepare herself to face the three healers who were bound and determined to try her patience until she finally just fell over and died. She was, perhaps, being dramatic but she had a feeling this was going to end badly. The fae knew it in her gut. Wolves, especially unmated ones, could not be trusted after they'd found their true mates. They were exceedingly stupid at the best of times. But during the period of time after they found their mates and the Blood Rites had yet to be performed, well, their stupidity graduated to an entirely new level. Peri had seen it so many times before. Hell, she'd even seen it in her own mate, and there wasn't a *Canis lupus* alive more mature or patient than Lucian. Ciro had a bit of sense. Perhaps he could keep his inner beast in check, but Nick and Kale? No chance.

Dammit. This was a bad idea.

If she couldn't count on the wolves to act responsibly,

then Peri would have to rely on the girls to keep the beasts in line. One girl was a blind nympho, one girl had been abused by her father, and one girl, with no family whatsoever, had been raised in foster care. And these three teenage healers, who'd never experienced genuine love before, had to repel three men who looked like Greek gods and continually declared their undying devotion for them at every turn. What could go wrong?

And if the girls can't control themselves, then the spell couldn't be performed because there would be no pure healers and no werewolf sacrifices, as the mate bond would kill the girls along with the males when they sacrificed themselves. And without good witches to oppose him, Volcan's evil army would take over the entire world. No biggie.

Dammit. This was a really bad idea.

Peri ground her teeth when she heard laughing and giggling coming from within the room. *The world is on the brink of destruction. What the hell could they possibly be giggling about?* Quickly, the fae pushed open the door. What she found reminded her so much of Jacque, Jen, and Sally, Peri's stomach dropped to her knees.

Heather stood at the mirror with Kara behind her, brandishing a blow dryer and a bottle of hair spray. "Hold still," she told the blind healer, which was met with a grunt from Heather. Stella stood next to them, carefully applying mascara. The perfume was so thick Peri didn't so much as inhale it as absorb it.

"I guess I had no reason to be concerned," she said coughing. "The males won't be able to get near you with all this perfume. They'll suffocate first."

All three girls turned to face her, and the three grins that met Peri's gaze were so wide they would have made the Cheshire cat jealous.

"That's Kara's fault," said Heather. "She trying to poison us. She wants all three males to herself."

"I can't help it if I wanted to smell nice for Nick."

"He's a biker," said Stella. "His idea of a nice smell is probably motor oil. If you really want to turn him on, you should spray transmission fluid all over yourself."

"Or antifreeze," said Heather. "That actually might work. Antifreeze smells really good. It's sweet."

"You've smelled antifreeze?" asked Stella.

"I smell everything. It's a blessing and a curse."

"I'm not rubbing any automotive fluids on my body. That's just gross," said Kara.

"No grosser than cockroach sex," said Stella.

Peri tilted her head. "Cockroach sex? What the heck are you talking about, Stella?"

"Ask her," she replied, indicating Heather. "She's the one who's been having fantasies about bumping antennae with Kale."

"Eww," said Kara, "I thought we agreed no cockroach talk."

"You know what?" said Peri. "I don't even want to know. Forget I asked. I can see, now, we have much bigger problems than I thought."

"What problems?" asked Heather.

"The problem of you three getting all gussied up like a bunch of junior high girls about to head off to winter formal. One of you is going to end up losing your virginity in the bed of a beat-up pickup truck parked behind the grocery store."

"There's a reason the trucks have *beds*, Peri. We'd just be using the bed for its intended purpose," said Heather.

"Good one, Heather," said Stella.

"And *gussied* is a bit strong, don't you think?" asked Kara.

"Not at all," said Peri. "There's definite gussying going on up in here."

"I don't think gussying is a word," said Stella.

"It is and it's exactly what you all are doing. Have you three forgotten what I told you about not allowing your wolves to bite or defile you in any way?"

"Ciro would never defile me," said Stella. "He respects me entirely too much. He's told me he will not push me to move forward in our relationship until I'm ready, and I believe him."

"Well, la-di-freaking-da," said Peri. "Aren't you two the picture of maturity?" Stella shrugged. "Just remember wolves run on instinct. His instinct is going to be to mark you. In his mind, it will mean you are protected."

"Kale *better* defile me, or why am I bothering to get all gussied up?" said Heather. "By the way, that reminds me, Peri, do you have a washing machine around here? I think I could stand to do a little laundry."

"No offense, Helen, but I'm not *just* dealing with you newly mated pairs, Volcan, healers turned witches, a sulking djinn, and a crazy pixie. I'm also dealing with the crap happening in America with a supernatural extremist group who want to enslave all of humanity and rule the world, and yadda, yadda, yadda. So, forgive me if I don't give a unicorn's butt hair about your clothes."

"All I asked was if you had a washer," Heather said dryly. "You haven't been around much to magic the clothes clean, and considering my sense of smell is nearly as good as a wolf's, I don't like my clothes to be more than a week worn."

"Actually," said Peri, "you're onto something there. A new wardrobe is exactly what all three of you need. Because your old clothes are covered with days and days worth of your scent. You don't have to be a wolf to notice that. Not even Kara's perfume can cover it up. And the stronger your scent is, the more the wolves within your mates are likely to try something stupid with no adult supervision around. I'll magic you up something."

"Oooh, a new wardrobe! That's so exciting," said Kara, clapping her hands and jumping up and down.

"Calm down, Little Orphan Annie. It's just clothes," said Peri.

"Do you know how many times I got new clothes living in foster care? Let me give you a hint. Never. Donations and hand-me-downs. And I wasn't supposed to get picked on at school wearing that garbage? Give me a break." She gave another little excited hop. "Being besties with a high fae is going to be awesome."

"We're not besties," said Peri. "I have no besties. Never say that again."

Kara's face fell. "Sorry. Who peed in your Cheerios?"

"It's not my Cheerios I'm worried about getting peed on. It's you three little fire hydrants. Now..." She tapped her chin. "We need something functional that you can move around in, in case you need to fight them off, but with many layers, so as to give you plenty of warning if they start trying to undress you."

"Don't you think you're taking this a little too seriously, Peri?" Heather asked. "We will only be sitting and talking. It's not like we're going to a hotel that rents by the hour."

"Says the girl who just said she wanted to be ravaged," offered Stella.

"In the bed of a pickup truck, no less," added Kara.

"I was only joking. I know how important this is, Peri.

We all do. Don't worry about us. As you said, you have tons more important things going on right now to worry about. We can take care of ourselves."

"We'll see. You all line up out in the bedroom. Kara, drop the hair spray. You've done enough damage."

"Line up?" asked Stella. "What is this? Some kind of inspection?"

"Kind of," replied Peri. "Just do it. Otherwise, I'll reinstate the spell Lucian put in place earlier, except in reverse. You'll be able to hear your mates but not talk to them." She scratched her chin. "Silent healers. That's not a bad idea."

"No, no," said Heather, holding up her hands. "We're cooperating. I'm already blind. I don't want to be mute, too."

With sour faces, the healers left the bathroom and lined up in the large bedroom. Peri stared at them for several seconds. She tilted her head this way and that. Then she snapped her fingers. "Got it." She waved her hands, and each of the girls flinched when the shorts and T-shirts they were wearing were replaced with thick, industrial safety coveralls, complete with reflective fluorescent stripes.

"You've got to be kidding me," said Stella.

Kara stamped a foot. "Peri, no! I wanted a biker chick look, black spaghetti strap top, ripped-up jeans, and a black leather jacket, not ... whatever this is." She motioned to the coveralls and glared at the material as though it had somehow personally offended her.

"Someone, please tell me what's going," said Heather. "I'm guessing by the sound of your voices Peri has placed us in something less than flattering."

"That's an understatement," said Stella. "She's decked us out in industrial blue coveralls ... complete with work boots."

"Not really sure what *blue* is, but I can tell by your tone we aren't the sexiest three chicks in the hen house. The material feels heavy." Heather tugged at the sleeve and rubbed it between her fingers. "Are we expecting some sort of chemical spill while we're spending time with our men? Or perhaps she really is concerned they will pee on us. Are these waterproof?"

"I look like I work for the highway department," said Kara.

"We look ridiculous," added Stella.

"Not at all," said Peri. "You look very responsible. Plus, I hear industrial safety garments are all the rage with the girls your age now. I think it's called occupational chic."

"Wait a second," said Stella. "What's underneath these terrible overalls?" She grabbed her front zipper and pulled it down. Underneath, she was wearing a black T-shirt with a pixelated picture of a castle. Above it, were the words" Your princess is in another castle."

"I don't get it," said Stella.

"What? You've never played Mario?" asked Kara.

"Like the video game?"

"Yeah."

"No, I don't play too many video games."

"Even in my foster homes, there was usually a Nintendo. Though sometimes they were old or broken. If you've never played, you wouldn't understand, I guess. After you beat the original Mario Brothers game, you find this little toadstool guy, and he says the princess Mario was trying to save wasn't even in the castle, and you have to start the whole game over again."

"Ooookay, and why the little joke, Peri?" Stella asked.

"Ciro, the Italian, needs to know what he's looking for isn't under those clothes."

Stella rolled her eyes. "Wasn't the video game guy a plumber?" asked Stella.

"I'm sure Ciro is going to love being compared to a plumber," said Kara.

"Just don't let him come in to inspect your main drain," said Heather.

"Good thinking, Heather. I've heard that can sometimes lead to them trying to lay pipe," added Kara.

"And he might need to use his ballcock valve," continued Heather.

"Occasionally, they have to break out their *caulk* guns," said Kara.

"Shut up," yelled Peri, holding up her hands. "No more plumber jokes."

"Thank you, Peri. What does yours say?" Stella grabbed Kara's zipper and yanked it down.

"Watch it," cried the younger girl. Underneath her clothes was another black T-shirt. This one had Jailbait emblazoned across it in large pink letters.

"Well, that's pretty self-explanatory," said Stella.

"What does it say?" asked Heather.

"Jailbait," Kara replied deadpan.

"Ah, too bad, Jailbait," said Heather. "Big, bad biker boy's gonna have to keep his hands off you or risk ending up being snared on *To Catch a Predator*. Read mine," she commanded, unzipping her own coveralls.

Neither of the girls said anything.

"What is it?" she asked, and Peri could hear the anticipation in her voice.

"Um ... it's just a bunch of dots," said Kara.

"Dots?" asked Heather.

"It's braille, you goobers," said Peri.

"Peri, why did you do that? They can't read it," said Heather.

Peri shrugged. "Not my problem. Figure it out."

Heather huffed. "Describe it to me, Stella."

"Okay, well, there looks to be two lines of dots. The first one has four ... letters, I think," said Stella.

"What's the first one look like?

"What's it ... *look* like?"

"Bad choice of words. Like, where are the dots positioned?" asked Heather.

"Um, one is at the bottom, then there's like a space, and then there's another—"

"Hold on," interrupted Heather. "Do you have any coins?"

"I've got some," said Kara, grabbing her purse.

"Dump them on the dresser and position them how they look on my shirt."

Kara put several coins on the top of the dresser and spread them out. "There's not enough to do it all, but here's the first line."

Heather placed her hands on the surface of the dresser and moved them gently across it. She felt three coins there. "First letter is k," she said. She moved to the second letter which was only one coin. "The second letter is a, then l then e. It says Kale. Must be a message for my mate. Exciting. Do the second line."

"Okay, hold still," said Stella. "I can't see the dots." Kara pulled Heather's T-shirt down and straightened it so Stella could see the second line. Stella arranged the coins on the desk. "I think that's it."

Heather ran her hands over the coins and called out the letters. "H-A-N-D-S."

"Hands," said Kara excitedly.

"Yes, Kara, we can spell," said Stella.

"O-F-F. And there's an exclamation point at the end," said Heather. "Hands off? Oh, come on, Peri!"

Peri, Kara, and Stella burst out laughing.

"That is *not* funny," said Heather. "Well, guess what, Peri? Kale doesn't even read braille, so joke's on you. He won't even get the message."

"Don't be so sure," replied the fae.

"What's that supposed to mean?" asked Heather.

"It means you all are using this time to get to know your mates. So, do that. They might have some surprises in store for you. But that is *all* this time is for. No touching, no kissing, and for the Great Luna's sake, do NOT let them bite you. No matter what happens."

"Biting, off-limits, we got it," said Kara.

Peri stood back and looked them over. They really did look ridiculous with their makeup, styled hair, and industrial coveralls. She knew what they were doing was important, but it scared the hell out of her. If something went wrong, the entire plan might collapse. Nothing to be done about it now. She'd just have to trust them.

"Great, now zip up your coveralls and get out there. Those males are going to be pacing back and forth outside, probably wearing a dirt path in my beautiful zoysia grass. Have fun."

"We will," said Kara.

"But not too much fun," added Peri.

"No promises," said Heather. She put a hand on Kara and followed her out of the room.

"Don't worry, Peri," said Stella. "I'll keep an eye on them."

Peri grunted. "Your mate said the same thing."

"See," said Stella, "I told you. We're the mature ones. We

are respectful of one another, and I'm not ready to move things along just yet. We'll be okay."

Stella walked out and Peri stared after her. "Somehow, I'm not reassured," said Peri after the healer had gone. "Oh, well, no rest for the weary. Now, I've got to go see a djinn about a witch." She flashed from the room.

8

"My brother thinks he takes care of me. He thinks he protects me from the world. In reality, though, it's just the opposite. You see, Derrick has never had a role model. All he's known is our father. And that's about as far from a positive male role model as you can get. But because Derrick has to continue to be my hero, he can reject the life our mother and father chose. He can be something better. This keeps him from walking the path of darkness the world offers." ~Stella

"We're supposed to spend the rest of our lives with these men, correct?" asked Kara.

"Yes," confirmed Heather.

"And apparently that life is going to be a lot longer than you thought, seeing as how we are some crazy supernatural healers and all," added Stella. "Why do you ask?"

"When I imagined dating my future husband, I certainly didn't picture myself wearing coveralls and a T-shirt underneath proclaiming me off-limits." The disdain was evident in her voice.

"The coveralls and ludicrous T-shirts are not the most bizarre things in this entire scenario," Stella quipped.

"No," Heather agreed. "I'd say the most ludicrous thing is a blind chick wearing a shirt with braille dots on it that can't be read by touch."

"Pretty sure Peri did that on purpose," Kara said.

"Exactly," said Stella. "We have no doubt if the braille dots were real, you'd be using the shirt to try and *teach*"—she made quotations with her fingers—"your mate how to read the braille when in reality he would be trying to cop a cheap feel and you'd be enjoying it."

"That is brilliant," exclaimed the blind healer. "And I have to say I am quite disappointed with myself for not even considering that."

"Of course, you are." Stella sighed.

"So, what's the plan to remain pure of wolf bite?" asked Kara. "I feel like there needs to be a plan in place. Being prepared is always the best policy."

"Is that years in the foster care system speaking?" Heather asked.

Kara thought back to her time in foster care and shuddered. Being prepared to move, run, or defend herself at a moment's notice had become a way of life. She'd learned very young that no one was going to look out for her best interest. That was her job, always had been. "You could say that," she finally answered.

"You okay?" Nick's deep voice was a soothing balm to her old wounds. Kara had been so lost in her thoughts she hadn't noticed the males approaching.

She looked up at him, his tough-guy exterior incongruent with the tender look in his eyes as he stared back, the concern evident on his face. She nodded. "I'm good," then corrected, "I'd be better if I wasn't wearing the fall fashion for *Mechanics Gone Tame*."

The three males all chuckled.

"Might I inquire as to why you three are wearing such out-of-character attire?" Ciro asked.

"I love how you make it sound so reasonable," Stella said. "As if it's not completely and utterly side-splittingly laugh-worthy we are dressed in matching, full-body coveralls that leave only our hands and faces exposed."

"Would this happen to be the work of a certain eccentric fae, hell-bent on making sure that you lasses remain unbonded?" asked Kale.

"Sharp as always," Heather said, pointing in the direction of her mate's voice. "And as determined as she is, I find it curious she actually put such cute sayings on the T-shirts underneath. She knew we'd want to unzip these things to show you all."

"She's slipping in her old age," Kara joked.

Nick leaned forward and pressed his lips to her ear. "Mate, could you please refrain from talking about removing clothing? I would greatly appreciate it if I could remain a gentleman and intact of all my parts. That fae who dressed you three has already threatened to do irreparable harm if I even breathed in your direction in an inappropriate way."

Kara's lips turned up in a slow smile. "Then you're going to love what she put on the front of my shirt."

Nick groaned, causing the others to laugh.

"And on that note, if you four don't mind, I'd like to have a look-see at this underclothing my mate has so kindly pointed out," Kale said as he took Heather's hand and tucked it in his elbow.

"Pretty sure that is exactly the opposite of what she wants," Stella called out as they began to walk off. "We haven't made our anti-bite plan, Helen!"

Heather held up a hand and waved at them over her shoulder. "Don't worry, Stells. I'll make sure my beast of a mate keeps his canines to himself."

"What about his hands?" asked Kara.

"I'll be keeping close track of those as well," she assured them.

Kara glanced at Stella. "Did you notice she didn't say she'd be making sure that he kept his hands to himself, just that she'd be keeping track of them?"

"I did," said Stella. "Oh well, we just have to trust her at this point."

Nick grabbed Kara's hand. "Let's go before there is more discussion about clothing removal. I swear you three are trying to get my pelt turned into a rug."

"You do have beautiful fur," Kara said with a grin. "But it would be a shame to put it on the floor where people could step on it. I'll make sure she turns you into something like a coat. That way, I can wear you out and pet you wherever I go."

"How considerate of you, my mate," Nick deadpanned. "So glad you find my demise humorous."

"I don't find it humorous. I do, however, find it irritating that you and Peri insist on regulating my choices about my relationship with you, my supposed soul mate," Kara said.

Nick gave her hand a gentle squeeze but didn't say anything, which only irritated her more.

"Nick—" Kara began but he cut her off.

"We will talk about it once we're in private. Let's just get farther away from the others. Okay?"

This appeased her for the moment, but she wasn't about

to let it go. Kara may only have been seventeen, but she'd been grown in many ways, for a very long time. High fae or not, mate or not, she wasn't going to be told how to live her life. She was free of the hell she'd lived in for so long, and her choices would be her own.

~

CIESEL FLITTED through the tops of the trees watching the couple walk along below them. It was the last of the three, the youngest. He'd already cast mind-influencing spells upon the other two, pushing them, increasing their lustful feelings. Or tried to anyway. The Irishman and the blind healer were almost too easy. He hadn't stuck around to see the completion of the Blood Rites. Listening to them whisper sweet nothings to each other had almost been enough to make him vomit. Watching a werewolf mating ceremony might just push him over the edge.

The other couple, an ancient wolf named Ciro and his mate, had been more difficult … actually, impossible. He'd tried to breach their minds to cast the spell but couldn't make any headway with either of them. The wolf was simply too old and too strong. Trying to cast the influencing spell on him was like tossing a bucket of water onto a brick wall. No effect. If he'd have tried any harder, he'd surely have alerted the wolf to his presence. The girl was much the same. Despite her young age, she had a maturity of someone far more experienced. Her mind was like an impenetrable fortress. Ciesel realized right away he wasn't going to influence her either, so he'd moved on to these two. Volcan would just have to get over it. Ciesel had the feeling that when this was all over, Volcan would be in such a good mood from defeating Peri, he wouldn't be concerned about one little failure.

As the pixie hovered over the final couple, he knew influencing them would be a cakewalk. They were both young for their respective species, especially the girl. She wasn't even what the humans would consider an adult. Now, listening to her drone on and on about not being told what to do by Peri, Ciesel almost laughed. In his experience, if someone had to tell you how mature they were, then you knew they weren't. Ciesel extended a hand and muttered several words in an ancient pixie language. An invisible bolt of magic flew toward the man and landed on his head like a gentle wind. It was then the man increased his advances toward the woman. He pulled her close and, with a quick motion, had her resting on her back with him leaning down on top of her. She didn't object.

The girl, Kara, clung to her man and leaned her head back when he began kissing her neck. Ciesel rolled his eyes. The couple was whispering to one another. Ciesel couldn't hear their words. All of a sudden, the girl pushed back.

Uh oh.

The man, still under the spell, continued his advances. The girl turned her head. She opened her eyes and...

Double uh oh. She locked eyes with Ciesel.

She's seen me. Nothing to be done about it now. Might as well have some fun. Ciesel gave her a sinister grin and winked at her. The girl responded by increasing her efforts to fight off the necking werewolf. The pixie laughed as he turned away, flitting through the trees. He'd be long gone before they untangled themselves and gave chase.

9

"It's strange being among the first werewolves mated to a fae. All my life, which has spanned hundreds of years, I had dreamed about her. Of course, all that time, I had imagined her as a wolf. I had pictured us in our wolf forms, hunting together, striding side by side through the forest, feeling the wind in our fur and the dirt beneath our paws. I'll never have that. And as I look at my beautiful fae mate, I realize I'll never need it. Elle has taken my expectations and blown them out of the water. Now, I feel sorry for those poor wolves who *are* mated to *Canis lupus*. They'll never get to experience having a mate that is so utterly and completely ... magical. Sad, really."
~Sorin

Sorin watched as Thadrick, Adam, Adira, and his mate, Elle, all struggled against the invisible barrier to the draheim realm. The other wolves—Drayden, Bannan, Antonio, Aimo, and his packmate, Crina—stood around looking just as useless as he felt. Sorin could feel his mate's anguish through their bond. She was lending her strength to Thadrick to help him fight against Volcan's magic, and the effort was draining her energy, which, in turn, drained his own. He could also feel the dark magic seeping through the veil. It felt like an oily film, covering every inch of his skin.

Sorin didn't understand why the djinn was having so much trouble. Wasn't this guy supposed to be all-powerful? Sure, Volcan was a high fae, perhaps the strongest of all the high fae, but Thadrick's power was supposed to be otherworldly. So far, all the djinn had done was stand around, muttering some unintelligible words, wave his arms a bit, and look constipated. Not for the first time, Sorin was glad he didn't have to bother with silly magic and foolish spells. If he wanted something done, he just phased and used his teeth and claws to make it happen.

"By all means, love, rip the invisible wall to the draheim veil open with your fangs. I'd love to see that." Elle's strained voice came through their bond.

"You heard that thought, did you?" Sorin asked Elle.

"It's hard not to. Your frustration is coming through loud and clear."

"Sorry, love. I'm just sick of sitting idle. I've fought evil fae before. They run and hide and scheme. They never fight fair. When you can't see them, that's when they're most dangerous. I'm ready to find this bastard and sink my teeth into him."

"Maybe you will if we can figure out how to get this damn veil open. Until then, the only one you're going to be sinking your teeth into is me."

"I think I can make that work."

"Enough!" Thad's loud voice pulled Sorin from his

conversation with his mate. "These efforts are futile." Immediately, Sorin felt Elle relax as she stopped pushing against the dark magic keeping the veil closed.

"This guy has a certain flair for the obvious," said Bannan, throwing his hands in the air.

Thad fixed his dark eyes on the wolf. "Hush, pup," he said. "I'm thinking."

"Pup?" replied Bannan. "I'll show you pup."

"No, you won't," said Drayden. "He'd wipe the floor with you in a second, and I'd have to explain to your Alpha why his third is laying in pieces outside the draheim veil. Just let the djinn think."

With a dark look, Bannan muttered something under his breath but then went quiet.

"How long will this thinking take?" asked Sorin. "We can't exactly kill the big bad high fae if we can't get to him. And every second that ticks by, the likelihood that Volcan is successful in creating his witch army increases."

Thad ran his hands through his long, stark-white hair and blew out a breath. "Thirteen thousand, three hundred and forty-seven."

"Excuse me?" asked Adira. "Thirteen thousand, three hundred and forty-seven what?"

"Years." With a confused expression, Thad looked at the pixie. "That's how many years of archives I must search through." He pointed at his temple. "And I must search within all those years for a particular spell. The process may take several minutes."

"Wait a second," said Antonio. "Are you saying the beginning of time started Thirteen thousand, three hundred and forty-seven years ago?"

"What?" asked Thad, the confused look on his face deepening. "No. I don't know when time began. I'm not a god. Thirteen thousand, three hundred and forty-seven years is how long I've been keeping the history of the supernatural races. I don't have records as to what happened in the world before my assignment began. That would be silly."

"Of course, makes perfect sense," said Sorin with a shrug.

Thad walked over to a large rock and sat down. Sorin and the others watched him closely. His face twitched rapidly, and his eyebrows kept raising up and down. Several times it appeared he was going to speak, but each time he went quiet. Finally, he stood up.

"Aha!" The djinn held up a hand.

"Aha, what?" asked Adira.

He sat back down. "Nope. Never mind, that's not it." There was a collective groan from the group. More minutes went by. Everyone stayed quiet, and Sorin guessed they all felt any noise would distract the djinn from the exhaustive search through his own brain. Just when Sorin was going to suggest to Elle that their presence wasn't entirely necessary to this operation and they should sneak off behind a cluster of nearby bushes, the djinn let out a groan of his own.

"What?" Sorin asked.

Thad got up again and walked back over to the veil. He placed a hand on it, resting it there for several minutes. He closed his eyes and bowed his head. Finally, he raised his head, looked at the wolves, and nodded. The gravity in the look on the djinn's face made Sorin shudder. "It's you all," he said, indicating Sorin, Bannan, Drayden, Antonio, Aimo, and Crina.

"What about us?" asked Crina.

"It's pack magic. He's using it against you."

"That's not possible," said Sorin. "Fae can't use pack magic."

"No, they can't," agreed Thad. "Unless, of course, they're part of the pack themselves."

"Is that true?" Drayden asked, looking from Elle to Adam. "You two are the only fae I know who would technically be considered part of any pack."

Both of the fae shrugged. "I'm not sure," said Adam. "We've not been part of the pack for long, and I've not really thought to test something like that."

"Me either," said Elle. "Although..."

"What?" asked Sorin.

"When Vasile gives Alpha commands, I do feel them. And not just through our bond, Sorin. I mean I actually feel them as if he's giving the command to me. I guess that means I am connected to the pack's magic somehow."

"What difference does it make?" asked Bannan. "Volcan isn't a part of our pack. It still shouldn't be possible."

"You are correct, pup," said Thad. "*Volcan* isn't a pack member. But the blood of one who *is* a member of the Colorado pack runs through his veins. This gives him a direct connection to the pack. He's figured out a way to exploit it."

"Jewel." Adira breathed.

"Exactly," said Thad.

"What does that mean?" asked Crina.

"It means that only wolves are going to be able to break down this barrier."

"Wait a second, djinn," said Sorin. "I thought you were some colossus. I thought you could move mountains. Are you telling me you cannot remove the spell by yourself?"

"Not at all," said Thadrick. "I could easily remove the spell. But the power it would take to open the veil in that manner would be catastrophic. It would blow a hole in reality itself, likely destroying this world and possibly the draheim veil as well. None of us would survive."

"That's just..." began Elle.

"A giant bundle of sunshine and unicorn poop." Peri's voice caused all of their heads to turn.

"Perizada," said Thad. "So nice of you to join us. I was just explaining to the wolves how Volcan has played a nasty trick upon us."

"I heard," she said.

"Then you know we're screwed," said Adira.

"Not exactly," said Peri. "The wolves have proven themselves capable time and again. I'm sure they can handle this. How can they open the veil, Thad?"

"Quite simple," replied the djinn. "They just have to cross the In-Between."

∼

"I'M GOING to go out on a limb here and say that you lasses had nothing to do with the clothes you're wearing," said Kale, his deep voice causing chills to run down Heather's spine.

"It turns out our friendly neighborhood fae has a true fear of you males being unable to control yourselves around us."

"She's right to have that fear," he admitted. "Peri has been around the wolves for a very long time. She'll know how strongly we wolves feel the need to mark and claim our lasses."

Heather wasn't worried about his declaration. Instead of saying anything about his remark, she placed her hand on his arm and then wrapped hers around his elbow. "Where are we headed?"

Kale tilted his head back and took a deep breath. "I can smell the direction the other males have gone with your friends. Nick and Kara have wandered off, and Stella and Ciro are still at the house. We'll go to a different spot." He began walking and Heather fell into step beside him. They were both silent, but it wasn't at all uncomfortable. "You're so easy to be around," he finally said. "It feels as though we've been together for years instead of weeks. I can't imagine what it'll be like when we've been together for decades."

"Me too," said Heather clutching him tighter and trying to contain the warm fuzzies that were exploding in her belly.

After walking for a few minutes, Kale paused. "There's a bench next to a little pond," he said. He led his mate to it. "The bench is directly behind you. If you take a couple of steps backward you will feel it on the back of your knees."

She followed his instructions, and once she was seated, Kale took the empty spot next to her. The air was crisp but not so cold that it was uncomfortable.

"How are you feeling?

"Just in general ... or is there something specific you're looking for?"

"Both."

Heather contemplated how she'd respond. There was so much going on inside, she didn't know where to start. Two big worries constantly vied for her attention. One was her relationship with him. The other was the situation with Jewel and Anna.

After a few moments, she figured she'd deal with the Jewel and Anna situation first. After all, much like he had said, it felt as if she and Kale had been together forever, and Heather felt so comfortable with him. She knew their relationship was solid. And as exciting as this new relationship was, the thought of being transformed into a witch was taking center stage in her mind. "Even though it's super scary, I'm probably *not* as concerned about the whole 'turning into a witch' thing as I should be."

"Why is that?" asked Kale as he brushed some strands of hair from her face.

She felt Kale's rough fingertips against her cheek and wanted to lean into his touch, but she had promised Peri she would behave and Heather didn't take promises lightly.

"Heather, why aren't you more concerned?" Kale asked her again, and she realized she'd been so busy thinking about his touch that she hadn't answered his question.

She let out a resigned sigh as she said, "I don't want you to think I'm keeping anything from you. I'm not. But I can't tell the reason." Heather didn't like giving him such a cryptic answer but, again, she'd given her word.

"That doesn't make much sense," he responded.

"I know, but it's something that involves all the healers, and we cannot share it. You will have to trust me on this one, mate." Heather's mind wandered back to the dream she'd had the night before, a dream that included her fellow healers.

Heather blinked several times and took a deep breath. She could smell the sweet scent of flowers and hear the sound of trickling water. She knew she was asleep, and yet her senses were telling her that wherever she was, it was just as real as the room in which her body slept.

"Where are we?" Stella's voice joined the sound of the water.

"Stella?" Heather said.

"Yep and Kara's here too."

"Are we dreaming?" asked Kara. "Because it doesn't feel like a dream."

"Unless Peri whisked us away while we were sleeping, I don't see how this couldn't be a dream," Heather said.

"But why are we all aware it's a dream and we are all in it together?" asked Stella.

Heather felt a sudden warmth on her face and skin. It wasn't hot, just a slight jump in temperature.

"You are here because I willed it," said a voice as clear and crisp as a winter morning.

"Great Luna," Heather heard Kara whisper.

Heather's heart started beating painfully in her chest as she realized she was in the presence of the goddess. Was she supposed to curtsey or bow? Did she need to get on her knees and touch her nose to the ground? What exactly was goddess etiquette, and why hadn't Peri explained that etiquette to them?

"We are waiting on the others," the Great Luna said. "There is much I need to share with all of you."

Heather leaned in the direction from which Stella and Kara's voices had emanated. "Psst," she whispered. "Are you two kneeling or bowing? Am I the only idiot standing in front of a goddess?"

"We're kneeling," Stella answered. "I thought that was kind of a given."

Heather huffed. "You two heifers let me stand here looking like a disrespectable blind ass instead of telling me to kneel?"

"She's a goddess, Heather," Stella said, sounding exasperated as if she were talking to a child. "Why wouldn't you kneel?"

"It's not like I go around hanging out with goddesses any

time I please," Heather said. "I'm not all up on the goddess do's and don'ts. How could I know?"

"I don't know what you do in your spare time," Stella shot back. "For all I know, you're out gallivanting with the goddess every night in your dreams."

"Don't you think I would have told you?" Heather's voice had risen with her ire.

"We leave you three alone for a few weeks and you're already at each other's throats." Jewel's voice suddenly joined Anna's and Stella's.

Heather's head whipped around at the sound, and then she moved forward until her outstretched hand was met with another. She pulled Jewel, whose scent she knew as well as the other healers, into a tight hug. "Are you alright? Is Anna here?"

"I'm here, Helen," Anna said, and Heather grinned at the nickname.

She reached out her other hand as she released Jewel, and then Anna's arms were wrapped around her. "We've missed you both," whispered Heather.

"We've missed you three as well, even your bickering," Anna chuckled.

Heather let go of Anna and listened as the two girls said their hellos to Stella and Kara. When their voices died down, she heard the Great Luna's once again.

"Please, rise," the goddess said. "What I have to tell you healers is vital. It is something you must think on but never speak of it again once you awaken. You must not even speak of it with each other, with your mates, or any other persons."

Heather felt something inside of her shift, and she tried to prepare herself for whatever it was that the Great Luna was about to reveal.

"The spell you must cast in order to fool Volcan, yet keep

your light intact, will take great sacrifice. I know your mates plan to stand in the gap for you. They cannot. The sacrifice will have to come from each one of you. You have been told the sacrifice must be one of blood. This is true. But do not be misled. Sometimes, blood comes from our bodies. Other times, it comes from somewhere else. This is a mystery you must ponder. The sacrifice you must make will not be one you can make easily.

"The road you healers must travel in this life is long and perilous. At some points, the journey will be rewarding. At other times, it will feel as if you do not have the strength to take a single step. Through it all, I am with you. I walk every step you walk. I feel every pain you feel. I cry every tear you cry. And I rejoice with every victory you have. If you need me, all you must do is ask."

Heather was struggling to breathe as the goddess's words penetrated her soul. She could feel the Great Luna's love for them and the depth of that love. It was hard for her human mind to even comprehend it.

"How will we know what our sacrifice must be?" Anna asked.

"Despite the pain it will cause you emotionally and physically, you will have peace about your decision," the Great Luna answered. "It will not be an easy decision to make, but you will know in your soul it is the right one.

"I will leave you here together until you awaken naturally so you may take some time to share in each other's comfort and friendship, but remember my command. What I have told you here today is to remain in each of your hearts and minds. It is a covenant between us, that as sure as you make your sacrifices for the greater good, so I will bless you in equal measure. For I always see what is in your heart and know the motives behind your choices. Let the light you shine be bright, my healers. Don't grow dim even in absolute darkness."

"Of course, I trust you," came Kale's deep voice. There was silence. "Heather?" Kale's voice broke the hold the memory of the dream had on her. She felt his hand on her chin as he turned her face and then felt his warm breath on her cheek.

"Where'd you go just now?" he asked. "You blocked the bond."

She shook off the remnants of the memory and smiled. "Just thinking about the other healers. We all share this secret and—"

She felt something press against her lips, feather-light. "I get it," said Kale.

As his heat left her face, she realized he'd kissed her. Kale. Her mate. Had kissed her.

"I'm pretty sure Peri would have zapped you for that little stunt," she said.

His throaty chuckle made her insides squirm. She felt like a schoolgirl with her first crush.

"What Peri doesn't know won't hurt her," Kale said, sounding smug and amused at the same time.

"To answer the other part of your question, I'm feeling quite good. I'm totally digging this whole supernatural-world thing. And suddenly having a man who thinks I'm the best thing since we put a man on the moon is its own bag of feels."

"You're not apprehensive about the whole true-mate thing?" Kale questioned.

Heather shook her head. "I've lived my whole life in the dark. For the first time ever, I finally feel like I'm seeing the light. Not physically, obviously, but it's as though a veil that has stood between me and the rest of the world has been suddenly ripped away. Finally, I'm living. I have relationships, with actual humans instead of just with the dogs I train. I have people I care about, and they care about me. How could I be apprehensive about that?"

She felt his arm come around her shoulders as he pulled her into his side. Heather tensed.

"Relax, mate," Kale rumbled. "I just need to hold you. You're remarkable and you're mine. What on earth did I do to deserve a gift such as you?"

"You might not be saying that in fifty years," she teased.

"I imagine in fifty years I will find you even more remarkable than I do now."

Heather hoped that was true. She hoped whatever it was the Great Luna had said they'd need to sacrifice wouldn't cause Kale to be angry or bitter at her.

"Do you think we can defeat Volcan?" asked Heather after another couple minutes.

"There is no other choice. I won't even entertain the idea that we won't defeat him."

"But what if we don't? What if…" Heather swallowed down the one fear that could take her breath away at just the thought. "What if you die? I mean, I understand Peri's reason for wanting us to hold off on the Blood Rites, but how am I supposed to go back into the dark if I lose you before I've really even gotten a chance to be with you? How am I supposed to just go on living?"

Kale pulled her tighter and began to run his hand up and down her arm. "Shh," he said gently. "You're howling at the wrong wolf, love. I've been waiting for you for centuries. The idea of something happening to you and me being left in this world without you makes me crazy. What Peri is asking of me, and of the other males, goes against everything we are destined to do. My wolf is a mess because he knows we need to mark you. We need to complete the bond in order to keep you safe. We must."

Heather felt Kale's arm tighten around her like a steel band. She felt wetness drop on her hands which were clasped tightly in her lap. She was crying and she hadn't even realized it. Her heart pounded harder and her lungs felt tight. Taking a breath was nearly impossible. She didn't understand why she was reacting so strongly. Yes, she hated the idea of losing Kale, but it hadn't been something she'd allowed herself to fall apart over. That's just not the way Heather was wired. She didn't act like a wilting flower and fall over in the face of a storm. She was an oak tree, strong, with deep roots, and she met the lightning, thunder, and rain with her branches fisting in the air, daring the storm to give her more.

"This is ridiculous." Kale suddenly growled. "Perizada of the Fae is not a *Canis lupus,* and she isn't an Alpha. Why then are we letting her order us to go against our very nature?" His breathing increased and Heather felt something sharp on her arms.

She reached her hand over, ran it down his hand, and felt sharp nails. No, not nails, claws.

"Kale?"

"I can't lose you, lass." He breathed out and then rubbed his rough cheek against hers, nuzzling her. Heather felt a rumble in his chest. "I won't," he added.

"What can we do?" she asked. "Peri said—"

Kale interrupted. "I am not subject to Peri. We can do whatever the hell we bloody want to."

Heather's thoughts clouded. Kale's words were true, of course. But something about his tone felt very wrong. She couldn't exactly put into words what she detected. She simply knew it wasn't the *real* Kale speaking, the one who was always so gentle with her. But as soon as that thought appeared, it evaporated.

They *were* true mates. Weren't they supposed to complete the bond? Isn't that the reason the Great Luna put the desire in the males so strongly, to bond the mates together so they would always be one? Did Peri really have a right to ask them not to do exactly what the Great Luna intended for them?

"I won't lose you, Heather," Kale said, pulling her from her messy thoughts. "Tell me you don't want this, and I won't do it."

"Do what?"

"Do the Blood Rites," he answered, a low growl filling his voice.

Heather sucked in a deep breath. *Did* she want that? Hell to the yes. But should they do it? They couldn't. *Could they?*

Kale's lips were on her neck, and she was tilting her head on instinct. He kissed her flesh several times and licked her as well, making her shudder. "Tell me no and I won't."

His teeth scraped across her skin, and she had to bite her lip to keep from moaning.

She wanted to scream at him, "Yes," but somehow, she held back. Heather gasped as he kissed her again. "We can't. I want this so bad but we can't."

Kale pulled her into his lap. He was panting. "Okay," he said, "you're right. I'm just so damn—"

"Ouch!" His words were cut off as Heather hissed and covered her eyes with her hands.

10

"Loose ends are never a good thing. It doesn't matter if the loose ends are someone else's or your own. They always unravel and leave some poor idiot naked ... or staring at some other idiot who's naked. In case you're having trouble following along, it's a metaphor people. Quit trying to read ahead to see if someone ends up naked. Geeze." ~Nick

When Nick could no longer hear the other two couples speaking, he knew they'd walked far enough away to have a private conversation. He'd been wondering when Kara would finally bring up her frustration over her age and how protective Peri was, and rightfully so. She was seventeen, a minor. Well, a minor in some countries. In others, she would be considered an adult. But that was beside the point.

Nick found a cluster of trees where there was some shade. He pulled his mate into the shelter and started to tug her down to the ground where they could sit, but Kara pulled against him.

"I want to stand. I can't be properly outraged if I'm sitting," she told him.

He tried not to smile, but she was sort of adorable when she was pissed.

"Alright then," he said. "We'll stand."

"I'm not a child," she began.

"No one is saying that you are," he countered. "But you *are* significantly younger than me. I'm a grown man, Kara. If you had parents, they'd be ready to kill me for pursuing you."

"I'm pretty sure if I had parents, they'd be more concerned about the whole 'sprouts fur and runs on four paws' thing."

"There is that," he conceded. "But the point is, you're in a vulnerable situation. Your life has been upended, and everything you've known turned on its head. I don't ever want to take advantage of you being in such a vulnerable state."

"Because I'm young," she asked.

The question sounded innocent enough, but Nick felt as if he was navigating a minefield and if he placed his foot in the wrong spot, it might get blown off.

"You don't have to be young to be vulnerable, but in this instance, you're both."

"Do I look vulnerable to you?" Kara bit out through clenched teeth. "Do I look like I can't make decisions for myself? Do I look like a girl who would let herself be taken advantage of by anyone, even a gorgeous, supernatural being who claims they belong together?"

Nick looked at the woman who had been given to him, who carried the other half of his soul and was the light to his darkness. What he saw stole his breath. No, she didn't look vulnerable. She looked magnificent in her anger. The wind had picked up as if in response to her temper, and her hair blew back behind her. The high cheeks on her face were flushed, and her eyes held a feral quality that called to the beast living inside of him.

"You look amazing," he practically whispered. "You look strong, determined, and fierce. You..." He paused as his wolf pushed forward, desperate to communicate with their mate, hating that the mental bond had yet to snap into place. "You look like mine. My female. My mate." He knew his eyes were glowing. He could feel how close he was to phasing.

"Then what is the problem?" Kara nearly growled.

"The man thinks like a man," Nick's wolf said as he pushed the human back even farther and took control. "He does not understand the wolf bond."

"Is there a difference? I mean, you say wolf bond like it's something separate from the mate bond."

Nick's wolf stepped closer to their mate. He took a deep breath and let her scent wash over him. The man had kept him on a tight leash since they'd found her, and though they usually were in agreement about things, on this, they were at odds. The wolf knew she was no longer a child, despite the human laws concerning adulthood. The animal within knew the bond would have never made itself known if she were still a child.

"I wouldn't have known you were my mate if you were too young. Wolves do not prey on the young as humans do. We are not attracted to a mate who is not mature physically and emotionally," the wolf explained.

"So, you're saying we wouldn't have felt anything for one another if I wasn't ready to be your true mate?"

"Exactly," he answered. "But you are ready. I am yours and you, my lovely healer, are mine." Nick took another step closer until he could lean his head down and touch it to hers. Being in the human form didn't change his need to rub up against her and cover her in his scent. His tongue darted out and licked her forehead, and he growled at her delicious taste.

"Did you just, uh, lick me?"

"I like the way you taste," Nick's wolf rumbled. He wrapped his arms around her and pulled her tightly to his body. She felt warm and ... *right* pressed against him. The wolf buried his face in her neck and nipped gently at the flesh there. He wanted to bite, needed to bite, to leave his mark and to have her blood flowing in his veins. He was angry over the fact that the high fae, Perizada, thought she had the right to tell him he couldn't claim his mate. That he couldn't offer her his full protection by marking her and finishing the bond between them that would ensure they would never be separated, not even in death.

"Nick?"

Kara's voice was breathless, and when he took another deep breath, he could smell her desire for him. His female wanted him as a woman wants a man.

"She has no right to keep us apart. It should be between mates, when the bond is completed and no one else." He pulled back and took her face in his hands. Her eyes were glazed over with passion as he pressed his lips to hers. It was one of the things the wolf appreciated about being in the human skin, the ability to kiss his mate.

She pressed closer to him as his tongue swept out across her lips, and her mouth parted with a gasp. Nick's wolf purred his approval. He tugged on her bottom lip with his teeth and then delved deeply into her mouth, their tongues tangling in a timeless rhythm. It wasn't enough though. The wolf wanted more. He wanted the bond complete.

. . .

Kara wanted to sing with joy as Nick kissed her. His hands ran up and down her back, pulling and pushing and tugging as if he didn't know what he wanted to do next—throw her on the ground or pull her on top of him. She wouldn't have objected to either. Hearing Nick's wolf tell her that he didn't agree with how Nick and Peri were treating her with kid gloves was a relief because she knew in her soul Nick was hers. They were meant to be together now, not later. They needed to complete the bond so there would be no separating them.

Kara felt the urgency growing in her as Nick did something fancy with his feet and hers, and suddenly, she was on the ground, and he was covering her with his body. She clung tightly to him, terrified he would suddenly come to his senses and stop. She needed him. Needed his touch, his taste, his love. She didn't realize she'd spoken out loud until he answered.

"You have it. You have all of me, babe," Nick said, and his voice was once again his own. When Kara opened her eyes, she saw that his were no longer glowing. "My wolf is right. We wouldn't have had even the hint of the bond if you weren't ready. And to be honest, I'm done having a fae tell me how to handle my own bloody mate bond."

He gently tilted her head back and ran his nose down her neck. "My mark is going right here." He kissed the skin between her shoulder and her neck. "And then every male will know that you are mine."

Kara started to tilt her head further back, giving him even better access. She wanted him to bite her, wanted to bear his mark, to belong, to be loved, and adored. She wanted forever with him. To be safe and treasured.

"No more waiting." Nick panted. "We can figure out something else for the sacrifice."

His words were a bucket of cold ice water flushed through her scorching bloodstream. Kara could practically feel the steam coming off of her skin. Yes, she wanted the bond complete, and no, she didn't like being told how to handle her relationship with her true mate, but, she did understand the reason behind it. Peri cared deeply for those she considered under her protection. She wasn't trying to keep them apart. She was trying to keep them all alive so they could one day have a completed bond.

"Nick, we can't," she said as she tried to push him back.

"Yes, mate, we can and we will. I'm done being kept from you. I promise you will enjoy this," he said, a hint of humor and something more sensual in his voice.

Kara wanted to say, "Of that, I have no doubt," but she was beginning to realize that something wasn't right. The Nick she knew would stop the minute she questioned him.

"I'm serious, Nick. We can't do the Blood Rites. I want to"—she reassured him when she felt him tense—"but we have to consider the consequences and how our actions will affect everyone around us."

He was licking and kissing her neck again, which was completely unfair because he'd figured out that it was definitely an erogenous zone for her. Kara tried turning her head to hopefully pull further away from him. As she tucked her chin down, she glanced up and froze as she stared at a small man. No, not a small man, a pixie, she realized. A male pixie was staring back at her from about twenty feet away. He gave her a sinister grin and a wink.

"Nick, Nick," she said urgently as she pushed at him. "Someone's watching us. Look! You big ass hairball!" She growled as she pinched and then twisted his nipple. It worked. He snarled at her and pulled back.

"Damn, female. You fight dirty," he huffed as he rubbed at his chest. Then he paused and shook his head as if to clear it. "What the hell just happened?"

"I'm trying to tell you. There was a pixie, over there." Kara pointed to where she'd seen the little creepy dude. "He winked at me."

"He what?" Nick rumbled.

"He winked at me. It was creepy." She noticed Nick rubbing his head as he stared where the pixie had been. "Are you alright?"

"My head hurts and it feels, uhh, fuzzy. Did I attack you?"

Kara chuckled. "If by attack you mean assaulted my senses with all of your male hotness, then yes, and don't worry. I liked it."

"But I didn't stop," he said, sounding very upset about that fact. "You said to stop and I kept pushing."

"You weren't hurting me and you have. You were just a little distracted, running on instinct I think. Your wolf did come out to play, so maybe he was driving you a bit?" She didn't have a clue if what she was saying could actually happen, but she hated the self-loathing look on her mate's face. "I'm fine, Nick. We're fine."

"Maybe," he said. "But whatever just happened wasn't normal. I shouldn't have lost control like that. No matter how badly my wolf and I want to complete the Blood Rites, we would never force it, not when you were telling us to stop. I couldn't think clearly. All I could think was that I was pissed Peri was trying to tell me that I couldn't claim you and that we needed to do it now. I felt desperate to complete the bond."

She nodded. "I began to feel that way too. But then something happened. You said something that made me realize we couldn't, and that's when my head cleared and then I saw the pixie."

Nick stood, pulling her up with him. He gently brushed her off, being careful where his hands touched. "I have a feeling that pixie had something to do with us both feeling so out of control, and if he was messing with us, then he's no doubt going to mess with the others. We need to warn them."

Kara agreed, but she worried that there was a certain couple with a blind chick with no self-control and that they'd be too late.

～

Ciro led Stella back to Peri's home. Since the others had wandered off into the forest there was no reason they couldn't go back to the empty house. He took a seat on the couch and motioned for her to join him. She didn't hesitate, and he noticed how pleased that made his wolf. The wolf hated that she feared them, even a little. There was no one safer in the world from him than his mate.

"I know that in my heart," Stella said, obviously having picked up on Ciro's thoughts. "It's just my head that has a hard time."

Ciro took her hand in his and caressed the top with his thumb. He hadn't realized how much he needed to touch her. "Does this bother you?" He motioned to their hands.

She shook her head slowly. "I'm sort of surprised it doesn't bother me. It's been a long time since I've wanted to be touched."

"So you want to be touched?"

She looked away shyly. "Only by you. I mean, it doesn't bother me for the other healers to touch me, but I wouldn't be able to stand it if another guy touched me."

Ciro tried to bite back the low growl. "That is a good thing, *amor*, because I wouldn't be able to stand it either." He'd never considered his possessiveness as a weakness until now.

"Don't try to change your nature for me, Ciro," Stella said. "I'm not scared of you."

"The males of my race are intense, and when it comes to our mates, well, there isn't an accurate description to explain what we become. The need to protect, possess, and provide becomes all-consuming. I am old. I am more controlled than almost all others, but having you, well, it's definitely harder than I anticipated," he admitted.

"What are you worried about?"

Ciro met her gaze and forced his hand to stay in hers instead of running his fingers across her cheek and down her neck. His wolf wanted him to bury his face in her neck so they could breathe her scent in deep. He was worried he would give in to his wolf and do something that would push her away.

"All you have to do is ask," Stella said, once again responding to his thoughts. "The worst that can happen is I might say no."

Ciro considered her for a moment before asking the question that had been burning inside him since meeting her. "This might be something you say no to, but I'm going to ask on the off chance you will say yes. Will you tell me what happened to cause you to distrust men so badly?"

Stella knew the question had been coming. How could it

not? They were soul mates. Ciro was going to be stuck with her for the rest of their lives; he had a right to know why his mate couldn't stand to be touched. It didn't mean she hadn't hoped it had been the one question she could have put off answering for as long as possible.

"You can say no, Stella, my love," Ciro said gently.

"You have a right to know."

"But you have a right to tell me when you're ready. If that time isn't now, that's okay."

She shook her head. "I think I should treat it like a bandage and just rip it off." And so she did. She told Ciro about the abuse she had endured at the hands of the one man who should have protected her—her father. Stella was shaking by the time she finished, and she wondered if she would ever get herself under control.

"I would like to hold you," said Ciro, his voice so quiet she almost didn't hear him. "In fact, if I'm being honest, I need to hold you at this moment, as much as I need air to breathe."

Stella looked at him and realized he was not as composed as she'd originally thought. His hand had released hers at some point and both of his were now clenched into fists. Ciro's shoulders were tense and his eyes were glowing.

"Please," he breathed out sounding more desperate than she'd ever heard any man before.

"Okay," she said before considering how she felt about it. All she knew was that Ciro was hurting and she wanted to offer him comfort.

Between one breath and the next, she was in his lap. He buried his face in her neck, and he took slow, deep breaths. Ciro's arms wrapped snugly around her, but instead of feeling restrained, Stella felt safe. She waited for the panic to come, but after several minutes, there still wasn't any. After another few minutes of only the need to comfort her mate, Stella wrapped her arms around him and leaned her head against his as he continued to breathe, slow and deep.

"Are you alright?" asked Stella.

"In all my time on this earth, never have I wanted to kill someone as violently and slowly as I do right now." He pulled back and looked in her eyes. "I would do absolutely anything to be able to go back and fix this, to take away the horror of what you endured and give you only beauty and good. There is nothing I wouldn't do for you, Stella. There is no depth I wouldn't swim, no height I wouldn't climb, no evil I wouldn't destroy to make sure you are safe, healthy, and happy."

Stella's breath froze in her chest as she looked into his eyes. It was at that moment that she could actually see a future with the man holding her. Not just an implied future, but one that was real and tangible. She could see herself letting him perform the Blood Rites, sinking his teeth into her neck and leaving his mark on her. In fact, she wanted it. She wanted to belong to this man who had so openly declared his intentions toward her, and not just with his words. Ciro had opened the bond so she could feel the *intention* behind his words. She could feel everything he was feeling for her, and it robbed her of all rational thought.

"How?" she finally asked. "How can you feel this way?"

"Because I was created to love you, my beautiful soulmate."

Stella released the hold she had around his neck and ran her fingertips along his strong jaw. He closed his eyes and leaned into her touch as if it was the best thing he'd ever felt.

"Ciro?"

"Yes, my love," he answered, though his eyes were still closed and he was rubbing his face against her hand much like an animal would do and it made her smile.

"Will you kiss me?"

Ciro's eyes snapped open and roamed over her face, seeming to search for something. "Is that what you really want?"

She nodded.

He leaned in closer and ran his thumb slowly across her bottom lip. "Breathe, Stella. You're in control, always."

Because her voice was apparently incapable of forming sounds, Stella simply nodded again.

Ciro's lips turned up slightly, and then he wrapped his large hand around the back of her neck and pulled her toward him at the same time he leaned in. When their lips finally met, Stella felt as if the world had stopped turning. Time had simply frozen, and the only thing important was that moment. It was the first time she'd wanted to be kissed by a man. It was the first time her desire overrode her fear.

"Shall I stop?" Ciro's voice filled her mind.

"No."

"Part your lips for me, beloved."

Stella obeyed and melted into him further when his tongue swept into her mouth. He didn't stay long, just a couple of intimate touches and then his lips were moving to her chin, jaw, and down her neck. She felt the light scrape of his teeth, and her head fell back of its own accord.

Stella barely had time to register that she wasn't freaking out about his teeth on her neck. In fact, she was enjoying the physical intimacy happening when she heard a deep bellow, followed by a shrieking banshee, or at least that's what it sounded like.

"STELLA, NOOOOOOOOOO!"

Kara's voice broke through the intense moment, and, in the blink of an eye, Stella was seated on the couch with Ciro crouched in front of her, snarling at Kara and Nick.

"Kara, what in Hades is going on, and why is your biker wolf growling like a rabid dog?" asked Stella, her eyes bouncing back and forth between Nick and Ciro.

"Nick, I think you can pump the breaks," Kara said, ignoring Stella all together. "I don't see any bite marks on her neck."

Stella's hand flew up to her neck. Bite marks? WTH? Did they think Ciro had been about to bite her? Seriously?

"Step back, pup," Ciro growled. "You are much too close to my mate and far too out of control."

"I am not out of control," Nick snapped back. "But you might be and not even realize it."

Stella nudged Ciro aside so she could stand up. When she tried to step past him, he wrapped an arm around her waist and pulled her back against him. She patted his hand, hoping her touch would calm his obviously ruffled fur.

"What are you talking about?" asked Stella.

"I very nearly performed the Blood Rites on Kara," Nick admitted. The look on his face said he was disgusted with himself. "I didn't realize something else was influencing me until Kara caught on."

Kara took over the narrative and explained what happened. Then her eyes met Stella's, and they spoke at the same time. "Heather."

"You think this pixie was influencing your emotions somehow?" Ciro asked.

Nick nodded. "It wasn't rational. I wasn't thinking like a true mate who adores his female. I was thinking like a Neanderthal who couldn't control himself."

"We need to warn Heather and Kale," Kara said.

As they headed for the door, Stella thought of something. "Did you recognize the pixie, Kara?"

The other girl paused. "Now that you ask, I think I did. I think it was the pixie king's brother."

"Penis nose?"

Kara nodded. "But minus the penis this time."

"I really do not want to know why you are mentioning another man's penis, female," Nick growled. "And my emotions are still all over the place, so could you not?"

Kara grinned and patted his back. "Cage your beast, Canada. I got no interest in another man's junk, especially when it's on his face."

Nick groaned as they left Peri's home in search of the other couple.

Stella grabbed Kara's hand as they followed the two males. "I have a feeling we're going to be too late."

"Well, I'm not going to lie. If we find lettuce wrapped around his blind healer in the throes of passion, I am totally going to be jealous," Kara bit out through gritted teeth, making Stella laugh.

"Sexually frustrated?"

Kara rolled her eyes. "You have no idea."

Bet I do. Stella didn't say it, but it was on the tip of her tongue.

"As I said before, Beloved, you are in control. I'm happy to take care of your frustration if you decide that is what you need from me." Ciro's voice sounded a tad smug. He knew how he'd made her feel, and he was a little proud of himself. Truth be told, he probably should be.

"Duly noted."

SOMETHING ... *bright* filled Heather's mind and it hurt. She forced her palms against her eyes, but it didn't seem to help. She'd detected brightness behind her eyelids before, but she'd never seen it. It had simply been a warmth on her face. Now, for a brief moment, it exploded into her field of vision. She didn't know how to describe the sensation; it was simply the opposite of the dark that she'd lived in her whole life. She pushed her palms to her eyes harder as a pounding headache began to form. "Kale," her voice was shaking as she spoke. "What's happening?"

"I think you just saw through my eyes."

"What? How?"

"I'm not sure," he replied. "Typically, after the Blood Rites, have been performed, mates can send each other images of what they're seeing. So, theoretically, you could *see* through my eyes. But it doesn't work with unmated pairs. Perhaps the mate bond within us is pulling us together so strongly, you simply got a glimpse of what it will be like."

Heather's breath came in huge gasps. "I don't know if I can handle that."

Kale couldn't help but chuckle. "You're telling me you've never seen anything your entire life, and now that you have the opportunity, you don't want it?"

"No," she replied quickly. "I do. I want it more than anything. It's just going to take some getting used to. It's all a bit overwhelming."

"I'm here for you. We'll take it slow."

"Can you do it again?" she asked, trying to keep her voice from shaking.

"I don't think I *did* anything, lass. It just happened."

"Please try."

"Okay, you concentrate on opening your bond as wide as possible, and I'll try to show you what I'm seeing. If you see a beautiful blonde pop up in your field of vision, you know it worked."

Heather scrunched up her face, reaching out for her mate. She opened her mind as wide as possible, knowing that everything within her was laid bare. If Kale wanted to, he could waltz right in and see every memory she had. She almost shuddered at the thought.

"Are you doing it?" she asked.

Kale grunted. "I'm trying."

"I can feel you in my mind, but I'm not getting anything," she said. "No vision."

"I'm so sorry, Heather. I wish so badly I could do it. I want to meet your every need, even this one."

"Dammit!" said Heather, jumping to her feet. She took a few steps in front of her, heedless of whether she would run into anything or fall into a lake.

"Do you really think I could see if we completed the Blood Rites?" she asked.

Kale rose and went to her, wrapping his arms around her from behind. "I'm certain of it."

A breath of wind washed over the couple, but she ignored it.

"Then do it," she said quickly. "Bite me, scratch me, make me your chew toy if that's what it takes. I want to see, Kale. I want to see you."

Heather felt Kale tense as he practically snarled and lunged at her, but she could tell he kept himself in check. Instead, he sat back down and pulled her into his lap. She heard him draw in a huge breath. Then she felt his lips on her neck.

"Wait!" she said hurriedly.

"Changed your mind?" he asked, his voice rough with his wolf. "We don't have to do this, love. If you're not really ready. If it's just about seeing, it will always be there waiting for you."

"That's exactly what I don't want you to think. I'm not just doing this so I can see. I don't care about that. I mean, I do, but I'm not ... I'm doing this because I want you, Kale. Because I love you. Because you are mine and I'm yours. I want that to be permanent. Even if I wouldn't be able to see, I'd still want this. You understand that, don't you?"

"Mine," he replied, and she was sure it was the wolf talking, not the man. Heather gasped as she felt a sharp sting in her neck and then nothing but euphoria. As he pulled her blood into his mouth, Heather tried not to act like a cat in heat, and she was pretty sure she failed. One of his hands ran up her back and then gripped her neck while the other held her waist, securing her body against his. Heather hadn't been prepared for it to feel so good. Her body tingled from the tip of her scalp all the way down to her toes.

When he started to pull away, she grabbed the back of his head and attempted to hold him in place as she muttered under her breath, "No, don't stop. Don't stop." She wasn't ashamed. Not. At. All.

He chuckled and then licked the spot he'd just bitten. *"It's your turn, love,"* Kale's voice filled her mind, and she was gratified in how breathless he sounded. *"You taste delicious."*

"I don't mind waiting my turn if you want to take another nip."

"Bloody hell, woman. You're going to be the death of me. I promise there will be many more times in our life that I will mark you with my teeth. But right now, I need your mark on me. I need the bond complete. Bite me, lass. Bind our souls."

Heather felt as if she were in a haze of pleasure as Kale directed her head to his neck. Her lips pressed against him, and she opened her mouth. *"I just bite? What if my teeth aren't sharp enough?"*

"We are destined for each other, mate. Don't worry about the details. Just bite me." That last part was growled out so low and with such determination that she shivered.

Heather had to admit she'd never thought she'd hear those words come out of a man, let alone a werewolf, but there it was. She bit down, and her teeth somehow sunk deep into his flesh. His blood rushed into her mouth and amazingly it didn't taste like copper. Kale groaned and pulled her more tightly against him. She could hear his breaths coming in shallow pants and could feel the rapid breathing as his chest rose and fell. He whispered something to her in another language, the lilting sound another form of assault on her senses. The warm blood continued to flow into her mouth as she sucked on the wound. The intensity of his reaction made Heather want to latch on like a leach. Sooner than she wanted, he was gently pushing her back. "It is enough, mate."

"I'm going to have to disagree because I'm definitely not sated," Heather said as her eyes fluttered open. Before she could say anything else, she gasped.

Heather felt something inside her snap into place, as though a tether that had been floating between them was now securely wrapped around them both, connecting them tightly.

"That's the mate bond," Kale said as he brushed his lips against hers. His voice was full of awe. "And it unmans me to think that I'm leaving my mate unsatisfied."

Heather was about to speak, but then she screamed as the brightness from earlier returned with a vengeance. "Kale," her voice shook as she spoke. "It's happening."

She *felt* him in her mind, so much stronger than before.

"You're seeing through my eyes," he said. "Our bond is stronger now and will be even stronger when we consummate it."

Heather couldn't even think about what that might cause. She was, to put it mildly, freaking the hell out. Slowly, the brightness began to dim and a large shape came into focus. Trembling, she reached out a hand toward the shape so she could see it. This was the way she *saw* things ... she felt them. Now, she'd actually *see* the thing she was feeling. She started when the shape began to reach back toward her. She stopped. It stopped.

"What the hell?"

She heard Kale chuckle in her mind. "You're seeing through my eyes, babe. That's you."

11

"My years in the dark forest come back to me sometimes as nightmares. The monsters I killed—the things I had to do—cause me to awaken in a cold sweat, screaming at the top of my lungs. And, yes, it was hilarious the first time Peri was jolted awake at two a.m. by my night terrors. I wish, for her sake, I would not have had to fight those monsters so she wouldn't now have to deal with my leftover mental scars. But there was one particular monster with whom I never crossed paths, that I never got the chance to battle. And, Great Luna, I wish I would have. Would he or I have come out victorious? I don't know. But I would have done everything in my power to kill Volcan before he could have escaped the dark forest and made life miserable for all of us." ~Lucian

Peri's heart sank. *The In-Between.* She could have lived her entire life without hearing those three words again and been just fine. The fae balled her fists at her sides to keep from going into a full-blown tantrum. It wouldn't do for the rest of the group to see their leader on the ground, kicking and screaming.

Peri never thought she could hate another fae as much as she had her sister Lorelle, but Volcan was testing that conviction. How in the world was he so clever? Not only had he figured out how to create an entirely new species of supernatural beings beholden to his will, but he'd also been smart enough to close the veil to the draheim realm in such a way that his enemies could only open it by submitting themselves to horrendous torture, thereby weakening themselves in the process. Apparently, Volcan had had plenty of time to plot his revenge while he was trapped for hundreds of years in the Dark Forest. Sometimes, you just had to sit back and commend the other side on their effort. Even if it did make you want to scratch an evil fae's eyes out. Oh, well. Volcan's cleverness just meant the feeling of victory would be all that sweeter when Peri was standing over his cold, disemboweled body. Bloodthirsty much? Absolutely. This situation completely warranted as much bloodthirstiness as she could muster.

"No," Elle screamed at Thadrick. The fae stood nose to nose with the djinn, or she would have been had his nose not been at least a good sixteen inches higher than hers. As it was, she was probably staring straight up into his nostrils. Still, her fury was unabated. Elle's eyes blazed and her face reddened as she continued. "There has to be another way, Thadrick. Figure something else out!"

"I wish it were different, Elle of the fae."

"If you think I'm letting my mate go through that again, you've got another thing coming. You have no idea what it's like," Elle shrieked.

"Neither do you," he replied.

"No, but I've seen its effects. The place almost killed Sorin. He won't survive another trip."

"Your mate can decide for himself," said the djinn.

Adam smirked. "You really don't understand us, do you, buddy? We don't exactly do anything without our mates' blessing. I mean, we do, but it always comes back to bite us in the ass."

Sorin, for his part, didn't appear as if he could decide anything for himself. He had sunk to the ground and sat there with his head in his hands. Peri couldn't help but feel for the wolf. She'd only been in the In-Between once for two hours. She and Elle had gone in to fetch him and the rest of the wolves. It had been the longest two hours of her life, and it still gave her nightmares.

"Maybe he won't have to," said Peri. "Thad, what's it going to take? The veil to the In-Between is far from here. Give me logistics."

"Very well. It appears that the spell requires five wolves, each chosen from a different pack, to enter the veil and travel all the way through it. If they survive, they will exit here, the spell will be broken, and the draheim veil will open."

"Five wolves for five healers. Gotta hand it to, Volcan. He certainly has a penchant for poetic justice," said Crina.

"That's one way of looking at it," said Peri.

"Sounds simple," offered Aimo. "We go in, we go through, we come out. Easy enough."

Adira laughed but there was mirth in it. "Simple, but brutally effective. You have no idea, wolf."

"Well, explain it to me then," said Aimo.

"To all of us," said Antonio. "I've heard of the place, of course, but I've never been there."

"People don't *go* there," said Peri. "They are *sent* there. Generally, they don't come back."

"Maybe the only one here who's ever been to the In-Between should explain it," said Thadrick.

Sorin looked up from his hands and realized everyone was staring at him. Elle squatted next to him and placed her arms around him. *"It's okay, Sorin."* She spoke through their bond. Sorin could feel the comfort she was pushing through to him. He couldn't receive it. All he could think about was that place and the horrors he experienced there, most of which involved her. In the visions, if Elle wasn't being tortured or killed, then she was always in the arms of another man, enjoying it. Sorin couldn't take that again. He didn't even want to think about it, much less describe it to the others.

"I know it sucks, Sorin, but these wolves need to know what they're up against," said Peri.

Sorin shook his head.

"Surely, it can't be that bad," said Bannan.

"It's worse," croaked Sorin.

"How?" asked Antonio.

"Imagine you have a mate, Antonio."

"Okay."

"Now, imagine if I have my way with her right here in front of everyone."

Antonio snarled and lunged. Elle held up a hand, knocking him back down on his rump with an invisible force.

"Enough," said Peri.

Sorin rose to his feet. He looked at Aimo, Bannan, and Antonio. "And imagine your mate enjoys it. Imagine her begging for more from another man. You want to experience that, Aimo?" The wolf didn't respond. "What about you, Bannan?"

"But it's all in your mind, isn't it?" Bannan asked.

Sorin shook his head. "Nope. It's as real as you and me. You will see it. You'll close your eyes and try to shut it out, but still, the visions will be there. You'll cover your ears, but you'll still hear the sounds. You'll hold your nose, but you'll still smell the scents.

"And after that, worse visions come. Maybe your mate is raped and murdered. Maybe your loved ones are all killed before your very eyes. You won't know you're hallucinating. You'll believe in your hearts it's real. You'll suffer pain and loss. And then it will repeat all over again. You'll beg for it to stop but it won't. *That* is what the In-Between is like.

"Sounds like a great place to build a summer home," said Adira. No one laughed. "Tough crowd," she said after a few minutes.

"I won't go back there," said Sorin.

"Damn right, you won't," said Elle, taking his hand. She spread her feet apart and stared at the others, daring anyone to defy her.

Peri sighed. "No need to make a decision right now. Let us all return to my house and regroup. We will gather everyone and then make a determination as to what must be done. Elle and Adam, if you will flash with these wolves, I need to take Thad with me. We will meet you there shortly."

"Where are you going?" asked Adam.

Peri smiled. "The Little Shop of Horrors. Thad is about to take a stroll down memory lane."

~

HEATHER STARED AT HERSELF. She held up her hand. The vision she saw through Kale's eyes held up a hand. She furrowed her brow. The figure in front of her furrowed its brow. Heather had never gazed into a mirror before, but if she had, she would've known this was similar, though not exactly the same as Kale's point of view was a little higher because he was taller than her. She tilted her head and began staring at herself, watching as she leaned closer and closer to Kale. He leaned forward and placed a kiss to her lips. Heather yelped and leaned back.

"Stop that!"

"What?" he asked.

"That was weird. It was like I was kissing myself. Hold still." She reached out and grabbed his face on either side with both of her hands, pulling him close again. She turned her head left and right, examining herself. She narrowed her eyes, then opened them wide, then narrowed them again. She pouted her lips. She stuck out her tongue. She opened her mouth, looked inside, and said, "Aaaaahhhh." Heather closed her mouth again then released Kale. She stood up and he followed. Slowly, she turned in a circle, examining herself. Heather saw long blonde locks flowing down her back. She saw big brown eyes and a girl who was very, very short. She'd known she was short, of course, because she constantly found herself reaching up to feel the faces of other people, but looking at herself from Kale's perspective, she now realized just exactly how short she was.

"So, that's what I look like, huh? Should I be impressed?"

Kale shook his head, which was disconcerting to Heather as her newly acquired field of vision shifted without warning. "What do you mean?" he asked.

"I mean ... am I ... ya know ... pretty?"

Kale chuckled. "You are the prettiest lass on earth."

"Have you *seen* all the women on earth?"

"No, but I've seen a lot of them, and I can't imagine one better looking than you."

"What do you mean you've seen *a lot* of them?" She narrowed her eyes on him, though she couldn't see out of them.

"I don't mean *a lot*, a lot. I just mean ... you know ... you walk around, you see people, that's all. Women make up half the population. It's hard to avoid them."

"Well, since I'm the *only* woman I've ever seen, I guess I'll have to take your word for it. This is so cool," she squealed. "Can you, like, look in a mirror or something?"

Kale patted his pockets. "Sorry, I don't usually carry around a mirror with me."

Heather growled. "I want to look at you."

"I can do that, sorta."

"What do you mean, sort of?"

"I can send ya an image of meeself, lass, but it won't be exact."

"Why not?"

"Well, a person doesn't exactly know what they look like, do they? I mean, ya look at yerself in tha mirror, but it's kinda hard to remember every detail, ya know?"

"I do not," she said, deadpan.

He chuckled. "I guess you wouldn't. I'll do me best."

All of a sudden, a picture of pure masculine perfection filled her mind—or at least what she'd imagined as pure masculine perfection when such things were described to her. She saw a man with dark hair, green eyes, and a red goatee set upon a broad chin. "Wow," she breathed.

"Is that a good wow?" he asked.

"That's an un-freaking-believable wow. You're hot."

"I appreciate that you find me attractive. I was a bit concerned that when you were able to see through my eyes you might not find me attractive."

"You knew this was going to happen?"

"No, but like I said, I knew it'd be possible. And I figured I'd at least be able to send you images of what I see. I wanted to surprise you. But I didn't perform the blood rites with you so that you can see. I did it because I love you, Heather, and I want to be with you more than anything. You're my mate. One of these days when this is all over, we'll go back to Ireland and have a house full of pups. I can't wait to show you my home country. It's so beautiful. Everything is lush and green. You're going to love it."

"I can't wait to go there with you," said Heather. "And you needn't have worried about me being attracted to other men."

"That's probably because you've never seen a man before. Unfortunately, now I'm going to have to keep you separated from every other man on Earth just in case you find one that you think is better looking than me."

"As long as you're there, I don't care. Lock me in a castle if that's what you want. My father did like to call me Rapunzel when I was little."

"Rapunzel's got nothin' on you, lass."

"Kale, can you show me some things? I want to see everything."

"As you wish," he replied. He turned from her and began walking forward, pivoting his head slowly so his mate might take in as much visual input as possible. She stepped up beside him and they marched in lockstep, Heather using his eyesight as her guide as she deftly, though slowly, got used to walking by sight instead of by feel.

"Okay, stop," she ordered. He did and she also stopped a beat later. "Look up." Kale complied. "I assume this humongous thing in front of me is a tree."

"You assume correctly."

Heather said nothing for several moments. The tree was the most beautiful thing she'd ever seen. Okay, so it was one of the only things she'd ever seen. Still, the sight of it caused tears to form in her eyes. Colors. There were colors everywhere. She never imagined there were so many colors. The tree itself held so many shades of green—a color she'd only heard of but never seen—she couldn't believe it.

Heather stepped toward the tree and extended her hands, almost tripping and bumping into it because she was guiding herself with Kale's eyes. She ran her hand along the rough bark, something she'd done so many times in the past. This was an oak. She knew exactly how the bark felt on many different kinds of trees because she'd felt them all on her own property. But now, she knew what an oak tree *looked* like.

"You don't understand how many times I've seen a tree like this by feeling it with my hands and now I can actually *see* what I've been feeling all these years. It's just so..."

"Overwhelming?" he offered.

"Yes, overwhelming."

Each leaf of the tree seemed itself to be a smorgasbord of greens colliding and overlapping each other. She reached up and wiped the wetness off her cheeks. The action was surreal. She didn't see her hands as they approached her eyes. She only saw herself through Kale's eyes reaching toward her own face. The process took a bit of getting used to, and she accidentally poked herself in the eye once, but she was beginning to figure it out.

Heather began to laugh.

"What's so funny?" asked Kale.

"I'm laughing because I've always wanted to see, and now, I'm seeing myself *seeing*. It's just a strange sensation. I don't know how to explain it."

"Got it. You know what's even stranger to me?" he asked. "When I look through your eyes, I see darkness. Absolute pitch black. I get to experience what you've experienced your whole life. It makes me feel closer to you."

She wrapped her arms around him. "Thank you so much for this, Kale."

"This wasn't my doing, mot. This was the Great Luna."

"And I'm forever grateful. I need to see more. Look down."

He did and she breathed, "The ground." The healer looked long at the dirt beneath her feet. She bent down and scooped up a handful. The earth had such a familiar feeling. She'd scooped up so much of it in her lifetime, feeling it, *seeing* it. She knew exactly how all the different soil types around her farm back in Texas felt. To most people, dirt was dirt. Not to Heather. Everywhere she went, the dirt felt different in its own subtle way. The dirt of the fae realms was soft and loamy. She imagined a person could grow almost anything in it if they were so inclined. She stepped close to Kale and held the handful of dirt up in front of his eyes, staring. He chuckled but she just gazed at it, gaping.

"It's just dirt, my love."

"It's amazing," she replied. "What kind of brown is this?"

"What do you mean?"

"Exactly what I said. What kind of brown? Light, dark, sandy, beige, hazel, chestnut, chocolate, khaki, desert, red-brown, coffee, caramel? WHAT SHADE OF BROWN IS THIS?" She brandished the handful of dirt at him, almost hitting him in the nose with it.

"Uh, I'd call that ... *light* brown, I guess. I'm not the best with culurs."

"What do you mean you're not the best with colors? Can't you see them?"

"Yes, I can," he replied. "But culurs are kind of a ... chick thing. I mean, to a bloke, brown is just brown. The nuances are lost on most of my gender."

"I want to know them all. Let's look at something else," she said, dropping the dirt and wiping her hands on her coveralls. She took a step to her left, off the path into some tall grass. Dutifully, Kale followed. Heather reached down and plucked a blade of the grass.

"More green," she said.

"Once again, mot, you are correct. I have to confess, Heather, this isn't exactly how I imagined spending the first few moments after performing the Blood Rites with my mate."

"And how did you imagine it?"

"With you and me wrapped in a tangle of sweaty sheets."

"Oh ... OH! No ... that's just ... eww."

"Eww?? What do you mean eww?" he asked.

"When we do ... that, I'm going to be looking at myself ... doing that. I don't think I want to see that."

Kale burst out laughing. "That would be weird. I don't think I'd want to see myself doing that either. I'll close my eyes."

"We'll talk about it later," she said. "I'm sure some type of ... arrangement could be made. For now, I'm still looking at things."

"I have an idea," he said and grabbed her hand. "Follow me."

"No," she replied. "I've been led around my whole life. I want to walk without someone guiding me for once. I'll walk beside you. But kind of keep an eye on the ground in front of me. If you look off at bird flying by, then I'll have to look at it, too. You know what? Scratch that. I *do* want to see a bird and everything else possible. If you do see a bird, look at it so I can see it."

"We'll take it slow, lass, and look at everything we come ta'. How's tat?"

"Great," she replied. They began strolling arm in arm down the wooded path, which soon opened into a clearing. Wildflowers of every color swayed in a strong breeze on either side of the trail. Heather gasped when she saw them. She fell on her knees in front of them, picking them one by one and holding them up to Kale's face so she could examine them. "What color is this?" she asked.

"That one is yellow."

"And this?"

"Purple."

"It's so pretty. What about this one?" She held up a wild daisy.

"That's white," said Kale.

"White?" Her brow furrowed. She held the flower up to her arm. "I thought I was white."

"What do you mean?" he asked. "You are white."

"I don't look like this," she said examining the bright petals laid against her pale skin.

Kale laughed. "No, your skin isn't exactly white, it's more of a ... peach color."

"So, I'm not white? I've always been told I was white."

Kale laughed more. "No, no, no. You *are* white. But that doesn't mean your skin is necessarily *white*. White is just a term used to describe the race of people. We're also called Caucasians, of course."

Heather held her arm up to his. "Our skin tones are very similar," she said. "Are all white people this color?"

Kale laughed again. "Not even close."

"Did I just hear you say I was a peach color?"

"Yes, I would say that's a good description."

"So, I'm the same color as a peach? That's strange."

"Uh, actually, no. Peaches aren't really peach colored usually. They're more of a reddish and yellow mixture."

"I had no idea colors were so confusing," said Heather.

"Neither did I until I started trying to explain them."

Heather looked at clothes through Kale's eyes. "And these overalls are blue?"

"They are."

"What color is your shirt?"

He looked down. "This is black."

"Okay, before I make any assumptions and look like a huge idiot in front of my friend later, tell me this. Stella is black, is she not?"

"She is," said Kale.

"But I bet you're going to tell me she isn't the same color as your shirt."

"She is not." He smirked.

"Then what color *is* she?"

Kale scrunched up his face. "I'm sure you'll see for yourself, but I would say she is kind of a ... chocolate color."

"Chocolate! Again, with the food. Well, I have no idea what color chocolate is, only that it tastes delicious."

"We'll get you some later, love."

"Oh, I wish I could see your face."

"If you would quit asking me questions and come along, then you might."

"Okay, okay." She grabbed him and held him by the arm.

"You're not leading me. I'm just holding your arm because that's what mates do. They walk arm in arm."

"Right," he agreed.

They walked for a few minutes, slowly and surely. All the while, Heather fought the urge to stop and gaze at every rock and stump along the path. Soon, they came to a fork. Kale turned his nose up and sniffed.

"This way," he said and pulled her along the right-hand lane. "There's water close by."

Soon, they came to a large steel-gray lake. Sunlight glinted off the surface and Heather had to stop.

"It's magnificent."

They walked up to the bank. "Be careful near the edge," he told her.

"Water. So, that's what water looks like? Unbelievable."

"This is what I wanted to show you. I don't have a mirror, but I have this. And this way, you don't just see yourself through my eyes or see a picture of me in your head that I conjured up. You can see us as we're meant to be—together. Kale put his arm around her shoulder. They leaned out over the water's edge and he looked down. The bright sun shining from behind him placed their reflections in stark relief on the water's surface. A ripple or two caused by the wind occasionally distorted the image, but all in all, it was a reasonable facsimile.

Heather gasped. After a few moments, she said. "I can't even... I don't know what to say." She grabbed his face and turned it toward her so she could look into his eyes, but then she saw herself again. "Dammit." She turned him back toward the water so she could continue to take in the picture of them together. She stared for some time, studying every detail. "I never want this moment to end, Kale."

As she continued to look at the reflection of them

through his eyes, she felt his hands on hers as he guided them up and then her fingertips were brushing across his skin. She stared at the reflection of him with her mind while she allowed her fingers to roam over his physical face. His jaw was strong and had a rough hint of stubble on it. His eyes were intense as they looked straight at her. His lips were thin, but his mouth had a sexy smirk on it that made her feel like he knew something that no one else knew and he found it incredibly amusing.

"You're perfect, Kale," she admitted. "Well, your face is perfect," she teased.

"What's that supposed to mean, mate?" he asked.

"I have it on someone else's authority that the rest of your physique is quite exceptional but I've only seen your face, so I have to qualify my perfect statement."

"Aye," he purred. "So in order to get your full approval, you'd need to see a bit more?"

She shrugged as if it wasn't a big deal, as if she wasn't bouncing up and down on the inside while gesturing greedily with her hands and screaming 'gimme gimme gimme.' There was something seriously wrong with her.

"Pay attention, my female." Kale's voice was against her ear and his breath warm on her neck. "I wouldn't want you to miss anything."

Kale's face was in her mind again, but this time she was seeing the rest of him. He was standing a couple of feet away, without a single stitch of clothing on.

Heather's hands flew to her mouth as she witnessed her mate through their bond. "You're picturing yourself fully naked for me?" She asked, her mouth tripping over the words as she stared at the beautiful male specimen. Once again she allowed her hands to rove over his physical body as she stared at the image in her mind. His muscles were firm against her hands, his skin was ... it was a color she didn't know how to describe. Just that it was lovely. She didn't allow her gaze to wander down because she was sure she would do something stupid like giggle or completely lose her mind and jump on him both mentally and physically.

"We can go over the body parts when we have a little more time," he said, humor lacing his voice. "This is just the beginning, mot. I want you to see everything you've missed, Heather. Every sunrise, every sunset, every cloud in the sky, every tree, every mountain, every city on earth. I'll take you there, and I want you to see it all through my eyes."

Their images became distorted as her tears began to fall freely, splashing the surface of the water and sending ripples across the reflection. "I can't wait," she breathed. "I can't wait."

"Are we too late?" Kara's panting breath came from behind her and suddenly naked Kale was gone and the bond was closed down tight. Kale swept her close to his body, and he was shaking as he growled at the intrusion.

"Are ye' too late for what?" he barked.

"Watch it, Kale," Nick's voice joined in. "There's no need to bite my mate's head off."

"Why are you all here?" Kale asked. "This time was supposed to be private, not a damn orgy."

"Orgy?" Stella's voice was next. "What were you two about to do that you think we wanted to join in?" Her voice rose several pitches as she became more indignant at Kale's suggestion.

"There was nothing happening," Heather said, trying to defuse the situation.

"So, that isn't blood that I smell?" Ciro asked.

"Great," Heather muttered. "The gangs all here."

"That's none of your concern, wolf," Kale snarled.

"Heather, honey," Kara spoke again. "Your mate is looking decidedly wolfy and seems a tad edgy and extra protective. Could you explain why this might be?"

She could. The question was, should she? Her friends were going to bitch-slap her when they found out that she and Kale had performed the Blood Rites. She didn't want to admit that they'd totally failed in their no-biting mission. But she did want to tell them that she could see, well, sort of see. She wanted to scream it from the rooftops. She hadn't had time to let her heart really absorb the fact that Kale had just given her such an amazing gift. She'd seen her face for the first time, a tree, her mate, her *naked* mate. Had she known that morning when she'd woken up that she'd get a glimpse of Kale and all his incredible fleshly glory, she'd have been in a much better mood.

"Why does she have the euphoric look on her face?" Stella asked. "It's creeping me out. I've seen that look on the faces of men who'd come into the bar and watch women dance. It's the naked-dance face."

"The naked-dance face?" Kara asked at the same time Heather giggled. Yep, she was about to lose it. The composure she'd maintained was about to come crashing down.

"Yes. You know, the face men get when they see a naked chick jiggling about."

"Nick, do you have a naked-dance face?" Kara asked her mate, sounding much too intrigued.

Heather snorted when Nick sighed. "How about you let me know the first time you dance naked for me. Then you call your girls and let them know, too, since the question has just been tossed out there in front of nature, the Great Luna, and everyone."

"I'm still trying to figure out why in the bloody hell you all are here." Kale nearly bellowed.

"Kale, sweetie, I think you need to take a breather. Calm down."

"They interrupted something private," he countered. "Something precious between us. We just performed the Blood Rites, Heather. That's extremely intimate, and we should be spending this time alone. Not explaining ourselves."

"I hear you, but I don't think you're hearing them. They are concerned about something. I could hear it in their voices. They're our friends, Kale. They aren't here to rip us apart."

"Honestly, we were worried we were going to show up and find that we needed to rip you two apart and separate you for a while," Kara said, interrupting their dialogue through the bond and saying the complete opposite of what Heather needed her friend to say.

"Dammit," Heather muttered under her breath when Kale roared, sounding more like a lion than a wolf.

"NO ONE IS TAKING MY MATE!"

"Kara, Stella, step back," Ciro said calmly.

"We're too late," Nick said quickly. "I can see his mark on her neck."

Heather sighed. "Well, it's out there now." Then she clapped and squealed like a damn child in a candy store. She managed to surprise Kale and was able to free herself from his grip. Running forward in the direction she thought Kara and Stella's voices had come from she yelled, "I can see!" One second the ground was beneath her feet and the next she was falling forward to meet it with her face.

"But apparently not that hole in the ground. In front of you. Right. There," Kara said dryly.

"Shut your trap, Orphan Annie," Heather snapped as Kale's large hands helped her up. "I seriously can see. In fact, I saw Kale naked."

"Okay, that's it. We're out," Nick said. "We will be at Peri's. We will fill you in on what might have helped cause you two to completely disregard Peri's warnings and do the Blood Rites anyways. Take your time as I'm pretty sure there's no rush at this point. Damage is done."

"Wait, she just said she saw her mate naked. That is *not* the moment when you exit a conversation, Canada," Kara balked.

"You are not going to listen to another woman talk about seeing her mate naked. I don't give a damn if it was the first time she's ever seen anything in her entire life. March, woman. If you're that desperate to talk about seeing a naked man, you and Stella can get a Ken doll, unclothe him, and then discuss it to your little heart's content."

"What crawled up your butt and died?" Kara all but snapped back at her mate. Heather had to admit, things were getting interesting despite having been interrupted.

"Nothing. Everything. I'm just frustrated and you aren't helping!"

"ME? What did I do?"

"Nothing! That's the bloody problem. You did nothing, I did nothing, and they have done everything! And it pisses me off."

"Whoa, hold on there, Sons of Anarchy," Heather said to the biker wolf. "We did not *do everything*."

"You're bonded. I can smell it all over both of you. His blood is pouring through your veins as we speak, while my mate stands next to me without my bite, without my blood, and without having her own stupid grin over seeing her mate naked! Forgive me if I don't give a damn about the technicalities of what *everything* extends to."

"You have a death wish if you continue to speak to my mate that way," Kale said, his voice so low and deadly that Heather was worried anything living might have simply dropped dead from hearing it.

"Guys, something isn't right," Stella said slowly. "Nick's not acting right and neither is Kale. Ciro, babe, you okay?"

Ciro didn't answer right away. Heather could feel the tension around them and wanted Kale to open the bond so she could see what was happening, but she knew she'd be too distracted with getting a first look at her friends to worry about whatever danger had wandered into their midst.

"Ciro?" Stella tried again.

Finally, Ciro answered. "We must get back to Perizada's home. Now."

From one breath to the next Heather was whipped up into Kale's arms, wind blowing across her face. Her wolf was running full speed as if the hounds of hell were on his heels, and for all she knew, perhaps they were.

12

"Occasionally, I get bored and complacent and entire years pass by without my notice. If the supernatural races do nothing of note, then I'm not required to record and remember their actions. How do I decide what is and is not 'of note'? That's a good question. It's solely up to me to decide. If I feel their actions will affect the course of events in some significant way, then I record it. Rarely do I bother with the affairs of humans. I only record their events if they directly affect the lives of supernatural beings, and that doesn't happen often, though it's been happening more and more lately. But most of the time, I try to ignore the actions of humans, especially if what they do is personally embarrassing to me." ~Thadrick

"Why are we here, Peri?" asked Thad as he stared at the storefront of the Little Shop of Horrors. The discomfort on his face was glaring.

"Do you recognize it?"

"Of course, I recognize it. Have you forgotten it's my job to record the happenings of the supernatural world? How can I record those happenings if I don't know the locations of all the supernaturals?"

Peri tilted her head. A thought suddenly popped into it. Shouldn't Thad know exactly where Volcan is at this very moment? "Are you saying you know the location of all the supernaturals in the world?"

"No," he replied. "Some go to great lengths to conceal themselves and are successful."

"Like Volcan?"

"Yes, like Volcan."

"And what about the owner of this shop?"

"Yes, she, too, tried to conceal herself from me."

"Why has she concealed herself from you? Is there anything you need to tell me, Thadrick?" Peri tried to keep the grin off her face but failed.

Thad turned his impassive gaze upon the fae. He looked down at her, and Peri saw the exact moment he realized she knew his secret. His gaze turned from impassive to ... slightly passive.

"She told you."

"She did," said Peri. "I don't suppose there's any way that you're *not* still angry at her? And we can all just let bygones be bygones?"

"Why would I be angry? It wasn't a serious relationship. It's not as if we were mates."

Peri thought about calling BS. But djinn were hard to read, and Thad's expression had returned to its normal statuesque state. "Um, yeah, I kind of feel like you're not being totally honest with me."

"We have a job to do. Let us get on with it."

"Okay then," said Peri. "Professionalism, exactly what I

like to see in my djinn. Very good. Let's go." She started toward the shop. It took a few steps before Peri realized Thad wasn't following. "What's wrong?" she asked, turning back to him.

"All of a sudden, I find myself ... hesitant about speaking with the witch."

Peri narrowed her eyes. If it had been anyone else, she'd have thought he was being insulting. But this was a djinn. She didn't know if he had the understanding of social norms to insult someone. And Jezebel *was* a witch, after all.

"Why not?"

"I'm unsure. I feel ... apprehensive. As if seeing the witch might reawaken old feelings."

"And here I was thinking djinn didn't actually have feelings."

"Of course, we have feelings. We are flesh and blood, after all."

"Could have fooled me. Doesn't matter. You're going to have to speak to her. We must perform the creation spell you, Jezebel, and I performed long ago. You concealed the missing pages of the spell book and gave them to Jezebel. I will need you both to cast the spell."

"I wonder ... how she looks."

If Peri had been drinking something, she'd have spit all over the djinn. "Are you kidding me right now? Are you telling me you still have feelings for her? My goodness, man, it's been over a hundred years. And not to make you feel like I don't care—I don't, by the way—but we don't have time to deal with any revelations you might suddenly have in regard to past relationships. We have something small to do, and it's called saving the world. Maybe you've heard. It's kind of our thing."

"The world isn't going anywhere. What is a hundred

years to you and I, Perizada? Her betrayal isn't so easily forgotten."

Peri shrugged. "A hundred years for me is like a decade. But I guess for you it's like an afternoon."

"Perhaps, Perizada of the fae, rather than speaking with the witch, I shall burn this shop to the ground. Perhaps, I'll burn this whole city block to the ground. Maybe the entire city itself."

"You won't," she said. "I don't know what kind of cosmic being or beings control you, but I've known you long enough to know you have rules. You're an observer, not a participant. You're not allowed to go around burning down cities."

"The rules for the supernatural world are changing. Wolves, fae, humans, and warlocks, all able to be true mates now. Maybe the rules are changing for me, as well."

"I doubt they've changed that much."

"Regardless, I'm not going in." He crossed his arms over his chest. If he had boobs and a monthly cycle, he would have been the epitome of a teenage girl.

Peri put her hands over her eyes. *I so don't need this right now.* "Thad, you have to help us. We cannot do this without you."

"Then don't do it."

"If we *don't* do it, innocent people will die. Volcan will become too powerful."

"And how does that affect me?"

She wanted to rage at the djinn's stupidity, but she knew it wouldn't do any good. Even if Volcan became so powerful he enslaved the entire human race, it would make no difference to the djinn. Volcan would never be powerful enough, nor would he ever even have any desire, to challenge the djinn. Thad was, after all, just an observer. Peri took a deep breath before she spoke.

"Okay, I understand what Jezebel did wasn't exactly ... nice, but let us look at this from a different perspective. You only agreed to help me to begin with because you were bored, correct?"

"Correct."

"And has helping me been boring?"

"Not at all, Peri. I've had more distraction these past few weeks than I've had in decades."

"Okay, perfect! And were you bored when you were with Jezebel?"

The djinn didn't say anything, so Peri continued. "Look, Thad, you could refuse to help me. You could go back to the djinn realm, rot in your dilapidated mansion *or* you could continue to help us and experience whatever exciting adventures await you. You're not going to let a silly little breakup that happened over a hundred years ago keep you from that, are you?"

Seconds stretched into minutes and Thad said nothing. Peri could tell he was weighing his options. She was just about to try a bit more coaxing when he spoke.

"I will not speak to her."

Peri threw up her hands. "Thad, c'mon, we need you. No one else—"

"I didn't say I wouldn't help," he interrupted. "I said I would not speak to her."

"I don't understand," said Peri thickly. "You have to speak with her."

"No, you will speak to her on my behalf. If I must relay information to the witch, I will tell you. You may relay that information to her if you so choose."

"What are you in third grade?"

"Those are my terms. If that arrangement is not satisfactory, I will happily return to my own realm."

Peri shook her head. "I doubt you do anything happily." She stared at him, but he didn't move. His expression remained as blank as ever. "I cannot believe I'm doing this," she said under her breath. "Fine, if that's what it's going to take, I will speak to Jezebel on your behalf. Now, c'mon on!" She grabbed Thad's arm and dragged him into the shop.

∽

JEZEBEL TOOK A STEADYING breath before walking to the front of the shop. When she heard the bell over the door ring, she knew exactly who it was—someone she thought she'd never have to face again.

The wolves and fae had flashed away just a few minutes ago. Jezebel would like to say she hadn't run straight to the bathroom afterward and emptied her stomach because she was so nervous about seeing Thad again. She would also like to say she hadn't spent the remaining minutes afterward applying makeup and trying to tame her dark, unruly locks into something that looked semi-decent.

Maybe he's forgotten about it. A girl can hope, can't she?

Jezebel walked out from behind the counter and saw Thad and Peri standing there, facing her. Peri had a hold of Thad's arm. She released it and stepped forward. Thad didn't move. Nor did he look at her. The djinn was staring straight past her at the far wall as if the most interesting painting in the world was hung there, when in reality, all that was there was a sign that read All Sales Final.

Nope, he hasn't forgotten.

"Okay," said Peri, "best to just rip this bandage right off as quickly as possible. We all know you two had a relationship. We all know it ended badly." Jezebel didn't miss the pointed look the fae gave her. "But that has nothing to do with me or my healers. We are facing a very bad dude who wants nothing more than world domination. The only way that stops is if you two can put your past behind you. I think it would be best if we dealt with this right here in private. My place is crawling with people right now—wolves, fae, and healers alike. I don't see any reason to air your dirty laundry in front of them."

Jezebel didn't say anything. She couldn't make her mouth form words and she couldn't take her eyes off the djinn, who still refused to look in her direction. He looked exactly as she remembered him. His hair was still that stunning, white blonde that contrasted with his dark eyebrows. He still had eyelashes much too long for a man to be deserving of and the dark eyes only made him even more striking. His nose was straight, his jaw strong and his lips thin. She had to tilt her head back a bit to look at him because of his height. All in all, he was a magnificent specimen of a male. Exactly as she'd imagined him so many times since that fateful day when she'd knowingly and very purposefully ruined whatever relationship might have been left.

"You may tell the witch that I stand ready to do what is required of me. I have promised you my help, and I have promised the wolf, Dalton, my aid in exchange for..." Now, Thad finally looked at Jezebel, but she couldn't read his face. "Certain efforts on his behalf."

Peri spun to the djinn. "What efforts?"

"That is between me and the wolf."

Peri rolled her eyes. "I know exactly what you are talking about, Thad, and I really don't think this is the time."

"What *is* he talking about?" asked Jezebel.

Peri's brow lowered. "It'd probably be best if I didn't discuss it. Forget about it. Let's just get on with this."

Jezebel couldn't help herself. "I want to know. This whole situation concerns my daughter, and I'm not doing anything until I find out what is going on."

Thad stuck his chin in the air and looked away. Peri shrugged. "Well, you heard her. What do you have to say to that?"

Thad looked down at Peri. "I did not hear her. I have lost the ability to hear witches. It is a strange phenomenon. It happens sometimes."

Peri growled. "This is ridiculous. She said she wants to know what's going on with you before she agrees to work with you."

"Tell the witch my affairs have long ceased being any concern of hers. Ask the witch if she is willing to play her part in helping the healers. Tell the witch the sooner this business is done, the sooner I can get on to … more important things. Things that have nothing to do with her or her daughter or any of the healers, for that matter. I came here because I was bored. I am quickly becoming annoyed."

"Seriously, Jezebel," said Peri. "Don't worry about it. It's just more of Thad's nonsense. It has nothing to do with Anna. Let's just get this business over with."

Jezebel gaped. She couldn't believe what she was hearing. She had no idea how this meeting was going to go, though she'd rehearsed it a million times in her head over the long years since the incident. None of those fantasies involved the presence of a high fae and Thadrick acting like a spoiled toddler. Though, now that she thought about it, they probably should have. The djinn was acting exactly the same as he always did. Like a complete ass.

She knew she'd have to be the bigger person. That had

always been the case with Thad. That's okay, she would do it for her daughter. "Thad, I'm sorry," said Jezebel when she'd finally found her voice again. Thad didn't acknowledge her.

Peri huffed. "Thad, she said she's sorry."

"Tell the witch she has nothing to be sorry for," Thad replied.

"Really, Thadrick," said Jezebel, "you're just going to pretend nothing happened?"

Again, the djinn did not respond. Peri repeated, her voice rising, "She said, 'You're just going to pretend nothing happened?'"

"Tell the witch I don't know what she's talking about, and I have no desire to know. Tell her I simply want to complete my tasks and go on my way."

"Stop calling me *the witch,*" Jezebel yelled. *So much for being the bigger person.* "You know my name."

Thad didn't acknowledge her. "Okay, that's it," snapped Peri. "I agreed to speak to her on your behalf, not listen on your behalf. That wasn't part of the deal. Quit making me repeat what she says."

Thadrick pursued his lips. "You have caught me on a technicality. What you say is true. Our bargain did not include relaying the witch's words to me. Tell the witch of course I know her name. I know the name of all supernatural beings."

Jezebel ground her teeth. "Then why don't you use it?" she spat.

"Tell the witch it's nothing personal. It's simply a matter of convenience for me. Sometimes, it's easier for me to do my job when I classify supernaturals according to their race or supernatural ability instead of actually naming them."

An avalanche of emotions warred within Jezebel. She wanted to scream at Thadrick. She wanted to slap him across his face. She wanted to cry, but she wouldn't give Thad the satisfaction. "Fine," she said through gritted teeth. She turned to Peri. "You, tell *the djinn* that I will not discuss the spell book until he acknowledges my apology."

"Jezebel." Peri's voice was pleading but the witch ignored it.

"Those are my terms," she snapped. Jezebel stood as straight as possible and crossed her arms, thrusting her own chin the air.

Peri looked up at the sky. "I need a moment," she said quietly and walked away from them to the back of the store. In a few moments, Jezebel heard the fae scream at the top of her lungs, "DAMMIT! DAMMIT! DAMMIT!" Perizada reappeared a few seconds later with a smile plastered on her face. "Okay," she said sweetly. "Let's continue. Jezebel, you appear to have some unfinished business with Thadrick, is that correct?"

"Yes."

Peri turned to the djinn. "And, Thad, it sounds like you don't want to revisit your collective pasts, is that correct?"

"Yes."

"Very good," said Peri, putting her hands together. "I think we can find some common ground here."

"Thadrick, I understand what Jezebel did to you was—"

"The witch did nothing to me."

"Thad, I'm not asking you to forgive Jezebel."

"Neither am I," added Jezebel quickly. She knew he could never forgive her for what she'd done. She'd had her reasons. She'd been so very hurt, and she just wanted him to hurt as badly as she had. Two wrongs did not make a right. No matter what century it was. But she didn't want him to hate her, either. And it wasn't just because he was the most powerful thing walking on two legs. They had some good times together ... before.

"Good, because that would never happen," said Thad quickly.

Peri smiled. "Wait, I thought you said Jezebel did nothing to you. If that's the case, then why would you *never* forgive her?"

"Do not try to trick me, Perizada of the fae. I'm older and wiser than you."

"You're definitely older," said Peri. "We can talk about who's wiser later. If you admit Jezebel did something terrible to you, then you'd have to admit her actions hurt you, wouldn't you, Thad?"

Jezebel leaned forward, desperate for Thad's response. The djinn said nothing for several moments.

"You are not incorrect, Perizada."

Jezebel's mouth fell open.

"And if you admit her actions hurt you, then you'd also have to admit that you cared about her, that your relationship wasn't just a casual fling."

Again, Thad hesitated. Jezebel was practically on her tiptoes. She couldn't contain herself any longer. "Thad, I'm so sorry. Please..."

"Do not speak to me," he roared. Jezebel flinched and shrank back.

Peri appeared unfazed. "Thadrick, that's not polite."

"Polite? Polite! You want to lecture me about what's polite. She brought another man into MY bed! I am a djinn. My family is powerful, old, and respected. She made me into a laughingstock! I should have destroyed her the way she destroyed me. I should have done it then and I should do it now!"

Jezebel took a trembling step backward. Her heart raced.

"But you didn't," said Peri quietly. "Why?"

Again, Thad went silent. Seconds stretched into minutes. Try as she might, Jezebel couldn't keep the tears from her eyes. It was all she could do to keep herself together. She was just about to tell Peri they should leave when Thad finally spoke.

"Because I cared about her."

Peri held her fingers in the shape of a gun. "Bingo!" she said in a tone Jezebel thought was entirely too cheery for the situation. "And you still do."

"Maybe I do." He turned his eyes on Jezebel. "But that doesn't matter, I will never forgive her."

"Like I said before," said Peri, "no one is asking you to. I just need you to work with her for a short time. Can you do that?"

"I can."

"Is that okay with you?" Peri asked Jezebel.

The witch's voice was anything but steady when she replied. "Yes," she whispered, wiping the tears from her eyes. There was so much more she wanted to say. Seeing him now after so many years, she realized what a mistake she'd made. It wasn't just that what she'd done was despicable. It was that she'd done it to someone she cared about. Though she knew it was impossible, she *did* want Thad to forgive her, despite what she'd told him. She wanted to go back and change what had happened, to open her mouth and communicate instead of simply reacting out of anger and hurt. "It'll have to be. I'll do it for Anna."

Peri mimed brushing her hands together. "There now. Done and done. When I took this job, I had no idea I'd have to be a relationship counselor as well as an ambassador. But such is the cross I bear."

"Don't push it, fae," said Thad.

"Now that that's settled, I'll take off my therapist hat and put on my hard hat. I've still got to clean up this mess those kids made here earlier," she said, indicating the back of Jezebel's shop. "A couple of quick spells and I'll have it back as good as new ... or, at least as good as it was before Dalton, the healers, and I destroyed it. Then, we're out of here, people. While I'm at it, Jezebel, do you want me to change the wallpaper in here? It's hideous."

13

> "I was young during the Great Werewolf Wars. Though I begged them, my parents wouldn't let me fight. They said I was too young and I wasn't ready for the horrors of war. I've fought in many battles since that day, seen many tragedies, and now I know how right they were. Those horrors were but an appetizer compared to the buffet of terror I now face." ~Crina

Peri's sitting room was getting crowded. While he waited for his mate to return with Thadrick and Jezebel, Lucian surveyed the occupants, analyzing them each in turn, judging strengths, weaknesses, and how each might aid them in the quest to defeat Volcan. He noted who was doing well under the stress of their current situation and who needed encouragement. He constantly released a little of his Alpha power in waves, ensuring that everyone present knew who was boss and that he would suffer no divisiveness at this critical juncture of their mission. He also put a calming influence into the magic, hoping to keep everyone peaceful and focused.

Mostly, Lucian kept an eye on Anna and Jewel. He'd been terrified when the two healers had attacked Peri. He'd felt every physical blow his mate had taken, as well as felt her fear that she might not actually be able to defeat Jewel. Though his mate was the most powerful thing walking—or had been up until recently—he still worried about her when he wasn't around to protect her. As with all dominant wolves, it was in his nature to protect his mate. Yet his mate rarely needed protecting and, even when she did, Peri still had trouble accepting it. Sometimes, it was maddening to Lucian.

After Jewel and Anna returned, he and the healers had explained to everyone else what had happened in the fight with Peri. Lucian had felt it important that he inform the others what Jewel and Anna had done, not so that anyone would mistrust the healers, but to ensure everyone knew how serious the situation actually was. After a period of stunned silence, the room erupted in questions, but he silenced them, insisting that they wait for Peri to return and explain everything.

Now, Dalton and Gustavo clung to their mates like white on rice. Whatever they were doing seemed to be working. The healers hadn't tried to kill anyone since they'd been back at Peri's house. Lucian hoped the two girls would continue to have the strength to keep Volcan at bay.

The three unmated wolves, Aimo, Antonio, and Bannan, Betas of the Italian and Spanish packs, and Third of the Irish pack, respectively, stood whispering together quietly. Adam could be seen stroking Crina's hair. Sorin clung to Elle as if he could somehow shake off the memories of the In-Between just by holding her closely enough.

Peri finally arrived back with Thadrick and Jezebel in tow. Though he knew it was necessary, Lucian hated every second his mate wasn't in his arms. He went to Peri and wrapped his arms around her. He knew she wouldn't appreciate it, especially with so many people watching. There were few things she hated more than public displays of affection. The wolf didn't care. It could feel Peri's tension through the bond. He knew it seemed to Peri as if each step she took brought them closer and closer to ruin, and Lucian could sense her growing frustration. Lucian knew she was doing her best and that without them, the healers would probably already be dead or worse. But it didn't matter to Peri, and she felt their situation spiraling out of control. So many times, they'd face down darkness in the past. She'd been able to trust her own strength. Lucian could tell she didn't know if her strength was enough.

"You and I need some alone time together," he whispered to her through their bond.

"I know, but we have something more important to deal with right now."

"What's more important than our relationship?"

"That's not a fair question," she replied.

"Probably not. Though you know the entire world could crumble around us and, as long as I had you, I would be okay."

"Maybe so. And that's terribly sweet, my love. But how about we put off the world crumbling as a last resort if we can, okay?"

"If it helps me be alone with you sooner, I'll tear the world apart myself."

She didn't respond, but Lucian felt her relax and soak up the feelings of peace and comfort he was sending her through their bond. The reprieve was only short-lived.

"Okay, everybody, listen up," Peri said to the room. Lucian smirked. His mate had put on her camp counselor voice. It was the tone that said 'I love each and every one of you, but I'm about to give you some bad news, and you're going to have to eat it by the spoonful and like it. If you don't, I'll show you just how much I love you by knocking the crap out of you a couple of times.'

Her brow furrowed. "Where the hell are the other healers and their fur rugs?" Her head whipped around as if they might jump out at any moment and yell "Surprise!"

A few seconds later, the door to her home burst open, and six new bodies barreled in. Out of instinct, Lucian pushed his mate behind him, his teeth bared, as he prepared to attack. The scent of the males' rage mixed with the females' fear hit him hard, and his wolf snarled.

"I feel pixie magic," Peri said through their bond. "Royal pixie magic, to be exact," she added out loud.

"I smell a new bond," Lucian said as his eyes landed on Heather's neck and the bite that now marked the previously unblemished skin.

"What?" Peri barked. "Who?"

"Don't react before hearing them out," he warned. "We need to be united. Pointing fingers and assigning blame will simply divide us. That is the strategy behind any worthy opponent—create dissension in the opposing side."

"You're being the voice of reason again. It's pissing me off."

"I live to please you, beloved."

"Can you ward this house?" Kale asked as he set Heather down on her feet but didn't release her.

"It's already warded," Peri answered.

"Not just the ability to enter it. I'm talking about making it invisible to someone's senses," the Ireland beta clarified.

"We've been toyed with, and I don't want our enemy listening in."

Peri's lips moved and Lucian could barely hear the ancient language she spoke. "The ward is done," she said after a couple of minutes. "Now, tell me about the pixie."

"How do you know it's a pixie?" Kara asked.

"I sense the magic that has been used around you. What happened and who bonded?"

Heather's chin rose in the air, and Lucian recognized the defiant move as one his own mate had perfected.

"Heather and Kale completed the Blood Rites," Ciro answered. "But it wasn't entirely their fault. Magic has been used to mess with our emotions, and whoever it was knew how strongly we males are driven by our instincts. I felt the magic, as did Nick, and it made me want to immediately give in to my wolf's need to mark our mate."

"Did anyone get a look at this pixie?" Asked Peri.

Kara raised her hand. "I'm pretty sure it was the pixie king's brother."

Peri cursed under her breath. "Ciesel. There's no way Ansel would be behind this. Ciesel has to be working for Volcan."

"And the hits just keep coming." Anna sighed.

Peri sighed as she stepped away from him and rested her hands on her slender hips. "There's nothing that can be done about it now. Ciesel is no doubt long gone. He probably fled the moment he picked up on my return to Farie. We will just have to figure out the sacrifice thing for Kale and Heather."

"Peri," Heather stepped toward the high fae. "Do you trust us?"

"You're asking me that as I stand here staring at the wolf bite on your neck? A bite I specifically said to avoid."

"Neither of us planned this." Heather pointed to her neck. "But it happened. Now, do you trust the healers in this room? If not me, then at least the others?"

Peri sighed. "Yes, I trust you all." Lucian knew his mate had purposefully worded her answer so that Heather would know she hadn't lost Peri's trust.

"Then quit worrying about the sacrifices. We've got that covered."

The other healers were nodding in agreement as Peri glanced around the room.

"The Great Luna help me if so much as one of you sacrifices your life. I will kill each of your mates in the most painful and humiliating way possible."

"Considering it's the Great Luna who revealed to us these sacrifices we must make, you might not be so eager to invoke her help," Heather pointed out.

"Bloody hell," Peri spit out.

"Slow your roll, angry fae woman." Stella spoke up. "Not one of us wants to die. You don't have to worry that any of us are about to thrust daggers into our hearts."

"Fine. I'll leave the sacrifices to you five. I don't like it, but I don't like anything that takes control away from my hands."

"That's not entirely true," Lucian teased. He was trying to ease the worry he could feel building inside of her.

"You are the exception to my every rule," she replied.

"So, moving on," she began out loud. "At this point, I'm not sure what everyone does or doesn't know about our current situation. Other than the present information we've all just been privy to." She took in each of them in turn. No one said a word. "So, I'm just going to give you a quick rundown and tell you how we're going to defeat that son of a bitch, Volcan, despite my not knowing exactly how the sacrifices will happen. The bastard has currently locked himself in the draheim realm. And he has put a spell on the entrance so that it will not open unless five wolves from five different packs cross the In-Between." Lucian could see the wolves in the group shifting. Peri held up a hand. "Let me finish. I'm not looking for volunteers just yet.

"If we are somehow able to open the veil to the draheim realm, then I think I have a plan that can take him down. It's going to take said sacrifice from our new healers." Peri nodded to the girls and gave them a long look.

"We've still got some details to work out on the plan, but I think it's going to work. There's a spell that must be deciphered, and that's where this guy comes in." She indicated the giant djinn next to her. "I think you've all met Thadrick, the djinn, by now. I can see some of you wolves still have the scars from training with him. He and Jewel, along with my friend, Jezebel"—she pointed to the woman on Thad's other side—"are going to study the spell and attempt to find the information we need."

She took a deep breath. "Now, we've come to the time for volunteers. While the ladies and Thad work on the spellbook, some of you, if you're willing, shall cross the In-Between. We should probably decide now who that's going to be. It's my guess that those who cross the In-Between are going to be in no position to help us fight Volcan once the veil is finally opened. I trust everyone here knows the risks associated with entering the In-Between, much less crossing its entirety."

"I'll go," said Bannan immediately.

"And me," added Aimo.

"Are you sure?" asked Peri.

"Aye," said Bannan.

"Absolutely," said Aimo.

"Me too," said Antonio. "We three are not mated. We have the least to lose. If we do not make it back, no one else dies. Plus, without knowing our mates, the evil in the In-Between has less to use against us."

"It will find something, believe me," said Sorin, speaking up for the first time since they'd returned from the draheim veil.

"Nevertheless, we will do this for our packs," said Bannan.

"I appreciate your bravery, wolves," said Peri. "For all the faults of the *Canis lupus*, loyalty and bravery are not among them." She drew in a breath. "That's three taken care of."

"Four," said Crina as she stepped forward. "I will represent the Romanian pack."

"The hell you will," Adam yelled.

She turned to face him. "I am sorry, my mate, but this has to be done."

"Well, it can be done by someone else," he replied. "

"Anyone from the Romanian pack can do it. Call Decebel, call Fane. Hell, call Vasile himself, I don't care. Anyone but you. I'm not letting you go through that. I saw the effect it had on Sorin."

"Which is why he, for sure, is not going back in there," she replied. "And we don't have time to summon someone from another pack."

"Not to mention, I would not ask it of them," said Peri. "They have their own issues to deal with battling the Order of the Burning Claw. I do not think Vasile can spare a single wolf right now."

"Then I'll go in her place," said Adam.

Thadrick shook his head. "It must be a wolf. I am sure of that."

"We can talk about this later in private if you want, but

you are not going to talk me out of it." Adam and Crina stared at each other for a long moment. Lucian could tell they were conversing through their bond. He didn't know what was said between them, but Crina must have won out because a defeated look passed over Adam's face.

"You do Vasile and his wolves honor, Crina," said Peri. Lucian could feel Peri's despair coming through their bond. She and Adam had been friends for a long time. Peri hated sending his mate to the In-Between.

No one in the crowded room said anything for a long time.

"You know what comes next?" said Lucian through the bond.

"I don't think I can do it."

"You must."

Peri exhaled deeply. If anyone besides Lucian saw the tremble in the action, no one acknowledged it. From the looks on their faces, everyone else felt the heaviness in the air as strongly as he did.

Peri's fear and pain assaulted the bond. Lucian stood like a rock against the oncoming tide of her emotions. In contrast to his stoicism, Lucian could tell his mate felt as if her feet were resting on a sandbar and the currents and waves were about to sweep it out from under her.

"How can I choose between the healers I am sworn to protect and my own mate? It's an impossible choice."

"The choice is not yours to make, my love. It's mine. I am here to protect you. To support you no matter what happens. That is why this task falls to me, and I undertake it willingly."

"You can't. Let us discuss other options."

"There's nothing to be discussed. I may never have been to the In-Between, but I have been in the dark forest and I survived. I can survive this. As long as I know I have you to come back to, I will make it through."

Finally, someone broke the silence. "And who is the fifth wolf?" asked Jezebel.

"I will be the fifth," answered Lucian.

"But you're not part of a pack," said Bannan. "Thad said we must have five wolves from five different packs. No offense, Lucian, but you have no pack."

"That's where you're wrong, Bannan," said Ciro. "Lucian is the Alpha of this pack. Everyone here knows it. Since we've been here, we have operated as an impromptu pack with Lucian as the Alpha because he is clearly the most powerful. How else would he have been able to use pack magic to bind us from speaking to our mates?"

"Do you think it will work to open the veil?" Aimo asked Thadrick.

Before he could respond, Lucian said. "Everyone here who has come at the behest of my mate is under my protection. I have led you these many weeks, and I would willingly lay down my life for each and every one of you. We may not have a name or a territory, but we are a pack and I am a part of it."

"Here, here!" said Gustavo.

Ciro spoke up again. "It's my belief that if these wolves are to have any chance of making it across the In-Between, Lucian must lead them. He is, besides myself, the oldest and wisest among us. They will need his strength."

"I agree," said Sorin.

They all looked to Thadrick, who nodded. "I am confident these five wolves will be sufficient to break the spell."

"I agree with Ciro and Sorin," Peri said to the room, though she looked only at Lucian. "These wolves won't survive the In-Between without your help." She paused and stared at him for a long time. Finally, she looked away to everyone else watching and waiting. "Well, then that's settled. Aimo, Bannan, Antonio, Crina, and Lucian will cross the In-Between for us and open the draheim veil. May the Great Luna have mercy on their souls."

There was a collective symbolic exhale from the room, and the tension dissipated as if everyone had been holding their breath at the same time, waiting for a violent tornado that finally passed them by. All except one. The tornado hit Peri full in the face and, though her outward appearance remained as impassive as a statute, inside her emotions were a tempest threating to tear her apart.

"On a happier note," Heather said suddenly, her bright smile in complete contrast to the heavy topic, "I can see!"

"And yet she trips over stuff more than when she couldn't see," Kara added.

"But, I can see," Heather pointed out again, undeterred.

"Does that mean we don't have to keep pretending your clothes don't look ridiculous?" Peri asked dryly.

Heather's brow dropped low. "My clothes look ridiculous?"

"Your clothes look delectable, lass. Don't listen to the grouchy fae," Kale said gently.

"Oh yes, because you're a completely unbiased voice of reason who would definitely tell her the truth if she asked you if her butt looked big in a pair of jeans," the high fae said, rolling her eyes.

"The mate bond has allowed you to see?" Lucian asked.

"Yes," said the enthusiastic healer.

The others smiled at her joy, and for a moment, all the ugly they were facing was set aside as Heather began using her mates' sight to meet everyone as if for the first time. It was a much-needed moment of peace.

"I can't begrudge her this," Peri said through the bond as they watched Heather touch Stella's face, telling her friend how lovely her brown skin was.

"Volcan meant for the pixie magic to be used for evil, to cause turmoil for us, but instead he inadvertently brought joy to our pack. He gave us a gift without knowing he would do so. That, to me, is the sweetest kind of victory."

She laughed and looked over at him. "It's wonderful when evil's plan backfires. Perhaps the result of Heather and Kale's bond will be the moment's peace that will give us the energy to get through what we will soon have to face."

14

"Kill. Eat. Kill some more." ~Grus

"Eat. Kill. Eat some more." ~Volaman

Jewel felt the pull inside of her, the dreaded call from Volcan to the dark magic inside of her. She looked over at Anna and their eyes met. The pain on the other girl's face, no doubt, mirrored her own.

"What's wrong?" Dalton asked as he tugged her to a quiet corner in the room. "You're pale."

Jewel raised her brow at him. "I'm a redhead."

"Okay, paler than usual."

She rubbed her chest. "Volcan's calling." She watched as his jaw tensed. She hated this. She hated hurting him. Hated feeling like she was betraying him.

"It's not your fault, Little Dove," he said as he pressed a hand to her face. "I'm not angry with you. I'm just angry at the situation. I'm angry that I am so helpless to help you."

"But you are helping me," she assured him. "You're here, taking care of me, checking on me. Being strong for me and loving me. Those things are priceless to me. I couldn't do this without you."

"You're stronger than you know, Jewel Black."

Jewel's eyes widened at the use of his last name attached to her first one. "Did we get married while I was sleeping?"

"We performed the Blood Rites quite a while ago, Little Dove. In my world, that's the same as a wedding. You're my mate. Every part of you is mine, just as every part of me is yours. If that isn't reason enough to join our names, I don't know what is."

Jewel flinched at his mention of every part of her being his. She wondered if he'd still feel that strongly if he knew that Volcan's name was permanently cut into her abdomen. And of course, her mate was so attuned to her that he picked up on the tiny movement.

"Do you not feel the same?"

Jewel took his hand, but before she pulled him from the room she looked back at Anna. "Fifteen minutes. Then we will have to go." Anna nodded and leaned back into Gustavo, who had wrapped his arms around her, his lips pulled into a grim line.

Jewel led Dalton up the stairs to the bedroom she shared with the other girls. She closed the door behind her and took a deep breath. It was a moment she'd been avoiding. She felt violated and ashamed despite the fact it wasn't her fault. That was the worst part about being a victim. She'd learned, no matter how it happened, you still felt somehow responsible.

"Talk to me, Jewel."

Here goes nothing. "When Volcan was holding Anna and

me in his dungeon, he had a vampire torture us. And he marked us."

When she looked up into his face, she could see how tense his jaw was but his voice was calm as he spoke. "Marked you how?"

Jewel slowly lifted her shirt, her eyes never leaving his face. When he saw the letters on her stomach, he frowned and stepped closer. "It says Tainted and that's the letter—"

"V," he finished for her. "I recognize the lettering." Dalton's eyes were glowing with his wolf. "You think this means you aren't mine? Or that I wouldn't want you?" he asked.

"How can you know my thoughts and feelings when there's no bond between us?" she asked.

"There's a bond, Little Dove, make no mistake. There is definitely a bond, and you wear your every emotion on your pretty face. Jewel, this"—he pointed to her stomach—"doesn't make you less mine nor does it make me want you less." He stepped closer to her and got on his knees. Dalton placed his hands on her hips and pulled her forward until he could press his lips to her marred flesh. Over and over, he kissed the skin that had been so cruelly carved. "You are precious to me. Every scar you bear is my own. Every hurt you've endured, I wish I could have endured for you. I am so sorry this makes you feel less. It is a reminder to me of how incredibly strong you are."

Tears ran down her cheeks as she ran her fingers through his hair and gripped as she pulled, letting him know without words that she wanted him to stand back up. Dalton got to his feet and took her face in his hands. His lips met her own, but Jewel couldn't let it last. They couldn't forget that Volcan had a curse at work that could cause the darkness in Dalton to spread quickly, driving his wolf to become feral. She may have wanted her mate like she wanted her next breath but it wasn't to be. She wouldn't be the cause of any more pain in their relationship.

Jewel felt the pull again, only it was more insistent. She pulled back and caught her breath. "I'm sorry. I have to go. I need to get Anna. It will be worse if we don't show up quickly."

Dalton gave her a single nod and linked his fingers with hers, leading her back downstairs. Anna and Gustavo were waiting at the bottom, but they only had eyes for each other. Jewel hated to interrupt, but it had to be done.

"Anna, we need to go."

Anna nodded and closed her eyes as Gustavo pressed his lips to her forehead. When she stepped back, Jewel released Dalton and took Anna's hand. She flashed them without another word because it would just make it harder if they drew out the goodbye. The quicker they got to Volcan and dealt with his insanity, the quicker they could get back to their mates.

ANNA STARED at the veil to the draheim realm as they waited for Volcan to retrieve them. "How'd we end up here?" she asked Jewel.

"Volcan's power," answered Jewel. "He's obviously being extra careful since the others were trying to get through the veil."

"Come through." Volcan's voice filled Anna's head.

"Did you hear that?"

Jewel nodded and then reached for Anna's hand. Together, they crossed into the other side. But instead of entering a forest, they stepped directly into Volcan's study.

"The veil opens into your lair?" Jewel asked, her brow drawn down in a deep frown.

"My power is increasing," he informed them. He stood from where he'd been sitting at his large desk, piled high with books. "I would be even stronger if you two had succeeded in the task I commanded you. Have you figured out how to make the witches?"

Jewel nodded. "We have."

"Tell me," snapped Volcan.

Anna wanted to *tell him* to get some freaking manners but figured that wouldn't go over too well with the crazy fae freak, CFF for short. It was a fitting title, she decided.

Jewel began explaining what they'd learned, and Anna tuned her out the minute she heard Gustavo's voice in her mind.

"Are you alright, my female?"

"I'm not chained to a table with a vampire carving me up like a Christmas ham, if that's what you mean."

"You are not putting my wolf at ease, Anastasia," he growled.

"I didn't realize it was my job to take care of your wolf," she snapped. "I sort of thought you were a grown man and capable of taking care of yourself." Anna couldn't believe those words had filled her mind let alone that she'd sent them to her mate. Gustavo had been nothing but kind to her, so why on earth did she feel like clawing his eyes out?

"We are two halves of the same whole, mi amor. We were meant to take care of one another," said Gustavo, his voice still calm and patient.

Anna wanted to scream at him that she didn't need anyone to take care of her. She'd been taking care of herself long before he came along, and she'd still be doing it long after he was gone.

"This is his magic speaking. The darkness of Volcan's power is growing in you, and being there in his place of power is making the darkness spread faster in you. Please fight it, Anna. If not for me, then fight it for yourself. Don't be a slave to Volcan's power."

"I am a slave to no one," Anna bit out. "You would do well to remember that."

She heard a sigh that sounded full of exhaustion and weariness, and Anna wanted to say she took the words back. She wanted to beg him not to leave her, but something was keeping her from saying those things.

"Come back to me, mi amor. I realize that right now you probably don't feel like yourself, but please come back to me."

Anna realized Jewel was shaking her arm and pulled her mind from Gustavo's. She looked at the other healer and then at Volcan, who was smiling. It wasn't a happy smile. It was one of those creepy ones that made you want to spit in the person's eye just to wipe the smile off their face.

"We've been given our orders," said Jewel. "We are to do the spell tomorrow, when the moon is at its highest."

Anna nodded. They took hands again and flashed from the CFF's castle. As soon as they were standing back in the forest on the other side of the draheim veil, Anna released Jewel's hand and stepped quickly away. She leaned over as her stomach heaved, and she vomited up the contents of her stomach.

She heard Jewel's own retching sounds and realized the other healer was just as sick as she was.

"What the crap is wrong with us?" Anna asked "And why is my puke black as if I'd eaten a couple pounds of licorice?"

"It's Volcan's magic," Jewel said in between retching. "Our healer magic is trying to fight it."

"I think mine is losing. I just treated my mate like dirt," admitted Anna, and it twisted her stomach, causing her to vomit again.

"I think we should take a few minutes to compose ourselves before we flash back to Peri's," Jewel suggested. "I'm not in control of myself. I feel so angry, and I don't really know what about. I just want to ... to..."

"Kill something or someone?" Anna offered.

Jewel flinched at the cruel words but nodded. "Exactly."

"I can feel Gustavo trying to get through the block I've got in my mind. I don't want to say anything more that could hurt him."

"It's not like he would hold it against you. Those damn males are so forgiving. It's like we can do no wrong in their eyes. It kind of makes me want to push the boundaries of Dalton's patience and see how far I could go before he'd finally say he doesn't want me or can't forgive me. I've lived all these years without him anyways. It's not like I couldn't live without him again. Especially once we have changed the others. We won't need anyone else. We will have our family in our coven."

Anna found herself nodding even though there was a small voice in her mind screaming that what Jewel was saying was so wrong. "You don't really mean that," she finally said, though she felt like she was going to choke on the words.

"I know, but it feels like I do."

"Maybe if we go back, it will help. Being farther from Volcan and being back in Peri's home, with our mates."

Jewel took several deep breaths. Anna imagined she was attempting to figure out a way to keep her mouth from spewing awful things to people they cared about because she was doing that as she took deep breaths. "Did you know that the average dog can learn about 165 words?" Jewel asked. "And in the 1600's cannibalism was a common practice among some Europeans? And during the Cold War the military trained dolphins to find explosives and bring equipment to divers, among other things?"

"Is this you trying not to want to kill someone?" Anna asked, recognizing Jewel's penchant for reciting facts when she was stressed.

"Pretty much."

"Is it working?"

Jewel shrugged. "Maybe it would be better if we just didn't talk once we got there."

"Good idea."

"Better yet," said Jewel, "maybe we should have Peri bind us so we can't move or speak. That way we can't hurt anyone with our words or actions."

Anna considered it, and when she thought about the things she'd said to Gustavo through their bond, she finally nodded. "I think you're right."

Jewel nodded. "Alright. That's settled. Let's go."

They flashed from the draheim veil and were in Peri's living room a few seconds later.

JEWEL'S FEET landed on Peri's living room floor and the rage she'd been feeling while at Volcan's only intensified. She knew it wasn't her own emotions. It was Volcan's magic but it felt so real. She had no idea if she'd be able to control herself.

Her hands were raised before she even realized it, and she said a word that she didn't even recognize. Light flew from her hands at the high fae. Peri flicked her hand as if she were batting away a fly, and the bolt of power Jewel had shot at her was redirected toward the wall beside Peri.

Before Jewel could speak another word she didn't know she yelled, "Bind us!" A second later, Jewel couldn't move or speak. If she could have sighed in relief she would have.

Dalton and Gustavo came barreling into the house, and their eyes jumped from Peri to her and Anna. Both males looked enraged.

"Release my mate, Peri," Dalton snarled.

Jewel wanted to shout her agreement at the same time she wanted to scream for Peri to do no such thing.

"Even if I did take orders from you, my answer would be no. But since I don't take orders from you, my answer is go jump off a cliff, wolf," Peri said calmly.

"Why have you done this?" Gustavo asked.

"Because Jewel demanded it."

Dalton looked at Jewel, and his eyes were full of worry. He stepped toward her and ran a finger gently down her cheek. "Why, Little Dove?"

Gustavo was the one who answered, which was a good thing, considering Jewel couldn't speak and didn't have a magical bond to communicate with her mate.

"Anna says that Volcan's magic has a stronger hold on them. They can't be trusted not to try to hurt us."

"Well, considering Red just tried to fling a spell at me, I'm going to have to agree with your female," said Peri.

"So we're just going to leave them like that?" Dalton asked.

Gustavo spoke again. "Anna says they think they will be better once they've been here awhile. That being around us"—he motioned between him and Dalton—"will help as well."

Dalton walked over to Jewel and wrapped an arm

around her waist and a around her mouth. "Can you unbind her long enough to let me sit her on the couch with me? I want to hold her, and she doesn't need to be standing for a long period. It can't be comfortable."

Gustavo nodded and headed for Anna. Jewel couldn't see him but assumed he was probably holding Anna in the same manner.

Peri rolled her eyes but nodded. "Fine." For a heartbeat, Jewel was able to move, but Dalton had her in his lap and restrained and then she was bound again by Peri's magic. Dalton had been right. It was much more comfortable being frozen and sitting instead of standing. She'd have to thank him later for being so considerate, if she ever got past the darkness that wanted to harm him. It made her sick to her stomach to feel any sort of anger toward him, especially when she knew it wasn't her own but simply a product of the magic Volcan had infused into her blood.

Dalton nuzzled her neck, and she felt his warm lips on her skin. "Don't let him win, Little Dove," he whispered in her ear. "Come back to me."

Jewel wanted to do just that. She didn't want to be controlled by a mad man. But her head was a jumbled mess of her own desperation to be free of Volcan and Volcan's voice commanding her to harm those she loved. She just had to last until tomorrow night. Then they would do the spell, and the darkness would no longer have a foothold. *Five more minutes, Jewel. Be brave for five more minutes.* She would continue to tell herself that until those five minutes ended with the full moon tomorrow night.

15

"Sometimes love is beautiful and wondrous. But sometimes love is the darkest kind of dark—all-consuming and without any care for who it destroys."
~Jezebel

"Thad, what is this word?" asked Jewel. She'd spent all morning poring over the pages of Jezebel's spell book, cross-referencing the spell to the ancient texts Wadim, the Romanian pack historian, had brought. It would've been nice if the man had stayed and helped. Jewel could tell right away he knew his business when it came to supernatural history. But, apparently, he had a new mate back in Romania and, according to Peri, he was needed to help the wolves there fight a threat even more sinister than Volcan. Jewel shuddered at the thought. She didn't see how anyone or anything could be eviler than Volcan. "Sengoisegnom. It looks to be some derivative of

Latin, a combination of signum, symbol, and sanguis blood."

"Very astute, young healer," replied the djinn. "Sengoisegnom is an ancient word from the fatimil."

"Fatimil?"

"Yes, it's a long-dead language. Generally spoken only by supernaturals even when it was in common usage."

"Can you please read the text following the words of the spell to me again?"

Thad pulled the crumbling tome back across the desk to him.

"Easy!" said Jewel. "That book is about to fall apart. We can't exactly run down to the local pharmacy and grab a paperback copy if it disintegrates."

"My apologies," said Thadrick. "I, of course, have the pages committed to memory. As such, its preservation isn't my top priority."

"Wait a second. You have it memorized? Then why bother reading it to begin with?"

"You asked me to. Had you asked me to recite the text following the spell, I would have done so."

Jewel rolled her eyes. Then a realization hit her. "Thadrick." She said and bit her lip to keep from chuckling. "Have you always known what was on the missing pages of the book?"

Thad tilted his head. "That's a strange question, healer. I thought you were a genius, at least according to human standards."

"I am," she said.

"Then why would you ask something that hinges on an impossible premise. I can't have *always* known what was in the book because, at some point, the book didn't exist.

Before it was written, I couldn't have possibly known of its existence."

"That's not what I meant."

"And even after it was written," he continued without acknowledging her statement, "before I was shown the book, it existed outside my awareness."

"I *mean* did you know what it said before you visited Jezebel at her shop?"

"You must be able to deduce, given the information available to you, the answer to your question."

"I have. I just want to confirm my suspicions."

"You should trust your own considerable intellect, healer. You needn't rely on the confirmation of others."

"Humor me."

Thad shrugged. "Very well. Of course, I've known since I read the spell when Perizada, the witch Jezebel, and I cast it a hundred years ago."

Jewel nodded. "That's what I thought. And, unless I'm wrong—and I'm very rarely wrong—at any point, while we were discussing our predicament, you could have said, 'Hey guys, guess what? I already know a spell that will create good witches, and I can tell it to you. There's no need to involve Jezebel whatsoever. I don't need to remove the spell from the pages because I keep a record of everything in my giant djinn-computer brain, and I can simply recite the pages to you.' Isn't that right, Thad?"

"Your statement has no fallacies I can detect."

"Hmm." Jewel tapped her bottom lip with her finger. "That is strange behavior, even for a djinn."

"I don't know what you mean."

"You're a strange cat, there's no doubt about that. But even as obtuse as you are, I don't think you would have withheld this information without a good reason."

"I withheld the information because no one asked me directly if I knew the language of the spell."

"Tut, tut, tut." Jewel narrowed her eyes. "I thought you might say that ... but I don't think that is entirely factual, Thadrick, my good man."

Thad began to turn red, and Jewel knew she was on the right track. "Are you accusing me of lying, healer?"

"Of course not. No one asked you what the spell said so you weren't obligated to tell us. That's certainly true. BUUUTTT ... that's not the reason you willingly withheld the information."

"And why would I do such a thing?"

"Simple. You knew there was one other person who knew about the spell, and you knew Peri would get her involved eventually. Had you intervened earlier, Jezebel's help wouldn't have been necessary. We could have done this entire thing without her."

"That's a considerable logical leap."

"Nope, that's the only logical conclusion. But it does raise one very interesting question. Why, djinn, would you put us through all that just to force a confrontation with Jezebel?"

Thad blanched. "Force a confrontation? I've done no such thing."

"You could have easily visited Jezebel countless times, couldn't you, Thad?"

"I'm a djinn. I go where I will when I will."

"Exactly. But you haven't. Instead, you fabricate a scenario where you're forced to come into contact with her after a hundred years."

"I haven't fabricated anything!"

"What's going on between you and Jezebel?"

"Nothing!"

"I've seen the way you two look at each other when you think no one is watching. You two have a history."

Anna's voice came from the doorway. "They don't call her a genius for nothing." Thad and Jewel looked up to see Anna and Jezebel watching them.

"You might as well tell her," said Jezebel. "I've already told Anna everything. I'm done keeping secrets. They do nothing but hurt the ones we love. I'm tired of hurting the people I love, including you, Thadrick."

"Perhaps you should have considered that a century ago," Thad said, his voice as cool as a winter night in Maine. "You could have saved us all from your secrets."

Jezebel didn't respond. She simply stared at the man she'd been telling herself she was over for the better part of a hundred years. The lie was getting old.

"Jewel, can you come have a chat with me?" Anna asked.

"No can do, voodoo woman," Jewel said, completely oblivious to the fact that Anna was trying to give Jezebel and Thad some privacy.

"Heaven save us all from oblivious geniuses," Anna muttered as she walked over and tugged on Jewel's strawberry blonde locks. "Come on, wheeler. Let's give the adults some space."

Jewel's eyes widened as she glanced between Jezebel and the djinn. Realization dawned and she hurried to her feet. "Right, um, we'll just go, we've got to, uh, wash our hair," she said, tripping over her words. "But separately. Not together. That would be weird. Two grown women washing their hair together. I mean, who does that?"

"Jewel?" Anna asked.

"Yes?"

"Shut up."

"Thank you." Jewel sighed as if Anna's words had somehow been the dam she'd needed to stop the word flood.

When the girls were gone, Jezebel stood there, unable to take her eyes off Thad. He was as handsome as the day she'd first seen him. He held the same intensity and cold aloofness that had drawn her to him in the first place. It was also the same thing that had pushed her away and into another's arms.

"You may exit with the healers," he said, staring down at a book he had likely memorized.

"I think we should talk."

"I have nothing to say."

"Then will you at least listen?"

"There is nothing you could say that I could possibly need or want to hear."

Ouch. Thadrick never was one to beat around the bush. It was time she took a page out of his book. "You left. One minute you were there and then you were just gone," she said, the pain from that time welling up inside of her. "I waited for you. I worried about you. I was terrified something had happened to you."

"I told you I had to take care of something very important," he argued. It seemed his obvious exasperation at her words was finally getting the better of him. "It wasn't like I fled in the cover of night without a word."

"No, but you failed to mention that you would be gone for five damn years!" She hadn't meant to yell, in fact, she'd specifically told herself that she would remain calm. Apparently, her other self was telling her rational self to go jump off a cliff.

"I *said* it was important."

"Is that code for 'I'll be gone, without a word or reassurance, for half a decade?" Jezebel snapped. "I took care of your home. Watered your plants and tended your garden. I fed that demon of an animal you called a horse so you wouldn't come back to find him dead, because I knew what he meant to you. What I hadn't realized was how little *I* had meant to you."

"Those are your words," he barked.

"No! Those are your actions! People who care about someone don't stay gone for that long with no word of reassurance or even a 'Go to hell. It's over.'"

"And what of your actions, Jezzy? What did your actions say about how you felt for me?"

The pet name cracked something inside her, and she bit her lip to keep the tears at bay. One slipped down despite her effort, and she hastily wiped it away. "I was angry. I hadn't realized until you'd been gone for half a year just how much I cared for you. The longer you were gone and the more the pain ate a hole inside of me, the angrier and more bitter I became. I didn't know how ugly I was inside until I stooped to the low of taking another man to your bed." Jezebel wiped away more tears. Even though she desperately wanted to keep her emotions in check, they continued to flow.

A low rumble rolled out of Thad as he stood up and towered over her. "I didn't expect you to wait on me," the djinn said. "I also didn't expect you to be angry at me for being gone."

"Did you even miss me?" She whimpered. "Did you feel anything for me at all?"

"Of course!" he roared. "I am not a heartless monster. If I hadn't felt anything, I wouldn't have cared that you were with another man, regardless of where you slept."

"But you just said you hadn't expected me to wait on you."

"I also hadn't expected it to bother me if you were touched by another. It wasn't until I knew for sure that you indeed had moved on that I realized just how much it enraged me. Still enrages me. I don't even want to consider the number of lovers you've had in the past century while you've lived in the human world."

"Only one," admitted Jezebel. "And the one time I was with that man, Anna happened. I cannot regret that night because it gave me her."

Thad's eyes narrowed as his gaze fell on her. "There has only been one man, one time, in a hundred years?"

She shrugged. "I didn't want the pain that came with caring for another and if I couldn't have who I wanted, there was really no point in being with someone else. What about you? How many hearts have you broken?"

Thad scoffed. "You cured me of any need I might have once felt for female companionship." He frowned and then muttered, "At least until recently."

"What do you mean by that? Have you found someone? A mate?" Why was she asking? Because she liked to have her heart split open, stomped on, and then spit on for good measure? Apparently so because she was hanging with bated breath to hear his answer.

"I thought I wanted a mate," answered Thad. "After being around the wolves and their true mates, I thought that maybe it would be a cure for the melancholy that I'd found myself feeling. But"—he shook his head—"seeing you, feeling these emotions that I thought I'd long ago released, I find that once again I have no desire to endure such torment again."

"We could try again. Start over. Start new."

The bitter laugh he let out had her flinching away from him.

"I've lived a very long time, Jezzy. There is too much pain between us to ever be able to try again."

"I looked for you," Jezebel said quickly as he started for the door. She couldn't let him leave, not until he knew everything. "I was so worried that something had happened to you. Four years after you'd gone, I went searching. I went to the veil of every supernatural realm and asked any being I came across." This was something she hadn't told anyone. She hadn't been able to because it had taken every ounce of strength she had not to shatter when it had happened the first time. She hadn't wanted to relive it by telling someone else about it, not until now. "Finally, one kind soul pointed me in the direction of your family. I was shocked, of course. No one visits the djinn realm because no one knows where it is. But I went."

"What?" he growled.

"I went because I needed to know you were alive and well. I thought that would be enough for me to be able to move on. When I entered the veil, one of your sisters, at least that's how she introduced herself, greeted me. When I told her I was looking for you and that I hadn't heard from you in so long she assured me you were fine. I told her I wouldn't believe her until I saw you with my own two eyes. So, she presented me with a scrying glass. When she called forth your image, I saw you, whole, unharmed, and wrapped in the arms of another woman."

"You lie. Even now you're willing to continue your deceit!"

"NO," she yelled back. "I have no reason to lie. I lost everything when I did what I did. Why the hell should I lie now? Your sister smiled coyly and practically told me to be on my way and that you were no longer in need of a pet. She said you'd been betrothed to another djinn since your childhood, and the female had finally come of age."

Thad's face looked murderous. His fists clenched at his sides, and his eyes turned solid black, the whites completely engulfed. "So, you were a woman scorned and decided to get back at me? Is that it?"

"I was a woman in love with a man who didn't want me and didn't have the decency to tell me. Or at least that's what I thought."

"In *love*?" he spat out. "You never once hinted you felt so strongly for me, and you expect me to believe you?"

"DAMMIT! I don't care what you believe. I don't give a rat's ass if you even care. I *need* you to know the full story. I've never told anyone, not even Peri, what your sister told me."

"Why didn't you confront me about her information? Didn't you think that hearing it straight from the source would have been a more accurate way to know the truth?"

"I wasn't exactly rational, Thadrick. A year later I was still taking care of your place and horse because it made me feel close to you. I was pathetic, pining away for scraps of you in your things and home. I just wanted to be over you. I wanted to be free of the grasp you held on me."

"Well, you certainly got what you wanted. You're free. I release you. Is that what you need? I have no claim on you, and I wish you the best for your future."

His words were flat, and the only emotion Jezebel could see in his face was complete and utter rage. If anything, she was even more caged now than she'd ever been.

"My house is practically shaking with the amount of power being poured into it. Holy hell, Thadrick of the djinn, get yourself under control!" Peri's voice broke into their little emotional bubble. Thad didn't pay her any attention.

"What was the name of the sister you spoke with?" he asked Jezebel.

"Myanin," she answered.

The power grew even stronger. "I don't have a sister named Myanin."

"I'm not lying!"

"Thad, you need to rein it in. If you cause my house to implode, I am going to be most put out," warned Peri.

"I must go," the djinn said suddenly.

"What?" Another voice joined them. "You can't leave. We have to prepare the spell," Jewel said. "Anna and I are on the verge of going dark, and we need to get this show on the road."

"It is of little consequence to me, child, if you go dark, as you put it. You aren't the first pure person to give in to their darker side, and you won't be the last. Volcan will not be the cause of the end of the world."

Jezebel's mouth dropped open at the cold tone in Thad's voice. He sounded as if he couldn't care less if they all were crushed beneath Volcan's heel.

"You have to stay," Peri added. "You gave your word."

"You see my eyes, Perizada of the Fae?"

She nodded. "I do."

"And you know what it means?"

She nodded again.

"Then you also know if I use my magic right now, I might just destroy the world, instead of save it. I. Must. Leave. There are things I must attend to."

"Please, Thad," Jezebel tried. "I've caused enough harm by my actions. Don't let me be the reason you don't help these girls. They need you."

He shook his head. "No. The intelligent healer can figure it out." He turned to Peri. "It was a mistake for me to leave my home. It was a mistake for me to come here." Without another word, he was gone, out the door, out of Peri's home, and out of Jezebel's life, again.

"Shit fire!" Peri bellowed.

More was said, but Jezebel couldn't hear any of it. Her heart was shattered. Her daughter was in danger of becoming evil, and the man she loved had basically said it was a mistake he'd ever seen her again.

Thad was breathing hard as he moved through the fae forest toward the veil. It wasn't exertion that had him out of breath. It was how tightly he was trying to keep from releasing the anger that was causing his blood to boil. If he released his power now, he would destroy all of Farie. He shouldn't be leaving them. He'd indeed given his word, but neither could he stay. Thad was roiling over Jezebel's revelations. He hadn't known that she'd cared enough for him to be worried about him, let alone actually search for him. He also hadn't known that she'd been deceived by his own people, that he'd been betrayed by a childhood friend.

He'd known that Myanin had had feelings for him, but he'd made it clear numerous times that there would never be more than friendship between them. He hadn't thought her capable of something so lascivious. A woman whom he'd grown to care deeply for and cared for like a sister had purposefully hurt another—the woman Thad hadn't even realized he loved, not until after he'd caught her in his bed with another. Jezebel's actions still burned him to the core, but he at least understood the motivation behind them. She'd been in love and thought he'd left her to be with someone he'd been betrothed to. She thought he'd lied to her and never admitted that he was to be married.

How would he have responded if the tables had been turned and he'd been the one to find out such information about her? That was easy, he shrugged to himself. He'd have killed them both. Did that make him slightly unhinged? Probably, but then any being that had lived thousands of years was bound to be at least a little twisted.

He moved at inhuman speed as he headed for the veil of his people. There were multiple locations all over the world that would allow him entry, though few people, supernatural or otherwise, knew that. It had been a few decades, maybe five, since he'd been to the djinn realm. He didn't miss it. He found that his own people tended toward callousness as they aged, and he was callous enough. He didn't need their pissy moods adding to his own. Needless to say, he was looking even less forward to his return than usual.

When he finally reached the veil, he didn't hesitate to cross and knew exactly who he'd find on the other side. She was, after all, assigned as the veil guard for the current thousand-year rotation.

"Thadrick?"

Myanin's voice, one he was usually happy to hear, felt like blades running across his skin. She stood ten feet away and started to take a step toward him but stopped when she noticed his eyes, which were, no doubt, solid black.

"Is everything alright?" she asked. "Has something happened in one of the other realms?"

He took a deep breath before he spoke, hoping to keep from strangling her. "Why have you never taken a mate?"

It wasn't what she been expecting him to say, judging by

the shocked look on her face. Myanin composed herself quickly and then responded. "You know why."

"And I've told you several times it will never happen. I will never desire you that way."

"You don't know that. We live very long lives. Our emotions change, feelings grow."

Thad shook his head. "You have always and will always be like a sister to me. I could never see any of my sisters, including you, in a romantic light, no matter how long I walk this world."

As she often did when he said something she didn't like, Myanin changed the subject. "Why are you here?"

"I've come to address a grievance I have with a clan member. It has been brought to my attention that I have been betrayed by one of my own, and I am petitioning the ruling elders to discipline the one who knowingly and purposefully acted in a way that brought harm to me and one I cared about."

Myanin visibly paled. "Who would dare such a thing?"

Betrayal among the members of the clan was akin to murdering one of your own. After all, how could there be any kind of healthy society if they were willing to harm one another? "Who indeed?" he asked, glaring daggers at her. "Are you really going to play this game?"

Her chin tilted up and she pulled her shoulders back. "Thadrick, what are you implying?" She had the gall to look offended.

"A century ago, you told a woman who came looking for me that I was betrothed. You told her that she'd been nothing more than a pet to me and to be on her way. You lied. You hurt her. And you hurt me. If you had any idea of the pain your selfish actions have caused, you'd turn yourself into the elders."

"She was a witch," Myanin spit out. "She didn't even deserve to breathe the same air as you, let alone share your bed."

"That was not your decision to make!"

"It would have been a disgrace. You would shame our clan with such a union! Who do you think the elders would side with?"

Thad was older than Myanin and knew the elders far better than she. "I don't know where you're getting your information, but our people don't think themselves better than any other race."

"We don't mate with others," she said.

"Only because we rarely socialize outside of our realm, not because we have some superiority complex. We are the keepers of the supernatural history. I have seen the amazing things each race is capable of, and we would be blessed if any of those would choose one of us as a mate. They are out there fighting the evil in the world while we sit back in the safety of our realm and do nothing but observe and record."

"It is not our place to interfere."

He growled at her and took pleasure when she took a step back. "It is that kind of thinking that creates bullies and victims. If it is not our place than whose is it? If everyone stood back with their hands held up saying 'Not I', then WHO?"

"You will bring ruin to the djinn's if you join the battles of the other races. You will break the order of things." Myanin touched the stone hanging around her neck. It was a direct link to the elders.

"Did you ever think that maybe things are already broken and that is why there is so much turmoil in the world? Did you ever think that maybe we were given so much power for such a time as this?"

"Myanin, you summoned us?" The voice of elder Clarion joined them just before five djinns stepped from the surrounding forest.

Thad bowed his head and pressed his hand over his heart. "Elders," he said, offering them the respect they were due.

"Thadrick," Lyra, one of the two female elders said. "Do you have news that we need? You usually don't come unless that is the case."

She wasn't wrong. Whoever the current historian was, they rarely were around the clan. It was easier to see the other supernaturals if they were living in the human realm instead of one of the supernatural realms.

"I have a grievance I wish to bring before the council. It is something that has just been brought to my attention," explained Thad. "And it involves Myanin."

All five heads turned to look at the female. She stood tall and defiant as she stared at Thad, her eyes narrowed and filled with anger. To his surprise, he didn't see any pain. It was then that he realized her obsession with him was just that: an obsession. There was no love in her for him. It was simply that she couldn't have something that she wanted. How he'd never seen it before, he didn't know.

"Let us convene in the hall of justice," Clarion said and motioned for them to follow.

Thad glanced back at the veil and felt himself being pulled in two directions. The words he'd spoken to Myanin were truer than he realized. They needed to be helping their fellow supernaturals and the humans. They needed to be offering the aid of the power they held. And yet, for the sake of his honor and Jezebel's pain, he needed to see justice done. He would just have to make sure it was served quickly so he could get back to help defeat Volcan, and then after, he had a certain witch he needed to apologize to. They'd both endured pain but maybe she was right. Maybe they could start over. They'd both learned things about themselves that would make them better prepared for a relationship. He just hoped he hadn't ruined any chance with her when he'd left her standing there needing his help. He would make things right. He had to. After seeing the woman he loved again, he was sure he didn't want to spend the rest of eternity without her by his side.

16

"I would rather face a thousand of my foe in battle than be betrayed by one person I care about." ~ Thadrick

Once they had entered the hall of justice, the five elders took their places at the front of the room. They each had a chair with an emblem on them that represented what their role was as an elder.

"Will you allow me to see the proof I need, Thadrick?" asked Synica, the only one of their elders who could see the true memories of a person. She could discern the truth, no matter how badly one might want to hide it. Synica's chair had the emblem of an eye with no eyelid. The implication was clear. Nothing could be hidden from her.

"I will," Thad agreed. He stepped forward and she met him halfway. Thad bowed his head as the elder placed her hand on his forehead. He relaxed and left his mind open. He had nothing to hide, and even if he did, it would be pointless to try.

After several minutes, Synica stepped back and dropped her hand. Her face looked grave as she met his eyes and then turned to Myanin. "Why would you do such a thing? Why would you hurt someone you claim to care so desperately for?"

Myanin's eyes narrowed on the elder. "I was trying to protect his honor. Even humans are not worthy of us, let alone a witch. They are evil, vile creatures. They have no care of the others in this world. They are leeches who destroy everything they touch. Why should one of them have one of our strongest males? She is nothing, she—"

"ENOUGH," Clarion bellowed, his voice echoing off of the high ceilings of the hall. He took a step toward her. The elder's eyes were practically glowing with rage. "The djinn have always kept to themselves, but we have never preached such disgusting beliefs such as those you just spewed. For thousands of years we have kept the history of all the other races, and we know that each race has spoiled offspring. Each race has its faults. There is none of such purity or innocence that they don't bring darkness to the universe in some way. We also know the history of Desdemona and her sister. Jezebel is not a typical witch, if she can even be called that anymore. What has made you believe such nonsense?"

Myanin was practically shaking with anger as Clarion cut her down to size. Her mouth opened and closed several times, but no words came out. Finally she turned to look at Thad. "Why am I not good enough? What more did you need?"

For a brief moment, Thad actually felt sorry for her. Obsession could make a person do irrational things. But then he remembered the pain in Jezebel's eyes, and his sympathy was gone. "Those are your words, Myanin. I never said those things. I said that I cared for you as a sister and friend. You chose for that not to be enough. This isn't about me. It's about you and what you wanted. You didn't care who you hurt to obtain it." Thad stared at the woman he'd considered a dear friend. How he'd never seen the contempt that obviously lived within her, he didn't know. But it was clear to him now she was wicked through and through.

"Synica," Clarion said. "Could you please relay to the rest of us what you have discovered?"

Synica turned to the other elders and explained all that she'd seen in Thad's memories. He flinched when she got to the argument he'd had with Jezebel only a short time ago, hearing Synica's description of the pain she'd seen on woman's face. When she was finished, the eyes of all the elders were on Myanin.

Myron, one of the eldest of their clan, spoke first. "This is a serious offense. We do not take it lightly. To lie to one of your own clan members, even by omission, is not tolerated. To lie to someone he was in a relationship with, someone he cared for, is equally offensive. It shows that you have no regard for your clan members."

"But..." Rouse spoke up. "This is not something that often happens, and therefore, we need to consider what the punishment will be. We will discuss this matter privately. Myanin, you will be detained in a null room. Thadrick, you will wait here."

Myanin's face paled. "Why the null room? I won't attempt to flee."

A null room was a room that neutralized a supernatural's powers. It was like losing a piece of yourself, and the dread it caused was painful to the one enduring it. Their power was an extension of themselves, like an arm or leg. Having it removed, even temporarily, was like cutting off and appendage.

"You have lost our trust," said Synica. "You will be taken to a null room. Do not fight us on this. It will only make your punishment worse." A guard entered the hall and took Myanin by the arm. Thad didn't watch her leave. His mind was too focused on a certain witch he needed to get back to.

Once alone, he walked over to one of the seats that lined the wall. During a public hearing they would have been full of clan members ready to defend or condemn the one on trial.

Thad leaned forward, resting his arms on his knees. He was tired, which surprised him. He tried to remember the last time he'd felt tired and frowned when he realized it had been when he'd found Jezebel and the male in his bed. He'd been angry for so long and then he'd just been numb, refusing to even acknowledge that she'd existed. But since seeing her, it had stirred up all sorts of memories, and he honestly hadn't been expecting it. He felt as though he'd been blindsided by a wolf paw to the temple, and he couldn't regain his footing.

As he sat there he reflected on his time with Jezebel. He couldn't pinpoint when, during their romantic entanglement, he'd fallen for her, but it had shocked him. The possessive feelings he'd had when he saw her with the other male had truly taken him by surprise. He wondered if that was how the wolves felt all of the time toward their females and then puzzled at how it didn't exhaust them to be continually bombarded with such strong emotions.

After half an hour, Thad leaned back in the chair and closed his eyes. He let himself drift into a light slumber. Within seconds he was pulled into a dream that he quickly realized was actually a memory.

"You prepared a meal for me?" Thad asked as he entered the small cottage where Jezebel lived.

"Why are you shocked?" she asked, wiping her hands on the apron she wore. "We both eat. I just thought it would be nice to share a meal together instead of just jumping into bed."

A smile spread across his lips. "I like jumping into bed with you."

She laughed and her eyes lit up with amusement. "I would hope so, considering it's becoming a bit of a regular thing."

Thad stepped closer to her until he was able to wrap a hand around her small waist and pull her to him. He could smell her lavender scent just beneath the aroma of the food, and it was her that had his mouth watering. "I have to admit, it is nice to have someone else feed me, instead of having to do it myself."

"You might want to reserve judgment until you've tried it. It might taste like ash in your mouth, and then I bet you'd have wished you'd prepared your own meal," she teased.

"I highly doubt it will taste like ash, and if it does, I will simply replace it with the taste of you."

He loved the beautiful shade of red on her cheeks as she blushed at his blunt words. Jezebel wasn't some innocent, young flower, but she was easily embarrassed and it was an endearing quality. He'd seen her completely naked, and yet he could still shock her with words, and he did it as often as he could get away with it.

"Come," she said as she took his hand and led him to the small table. "Let me feed you and then we can enjoy dessert."

"I'm really hoping by dessert you mean se—"

Jezebel shoved a roll in his mouth to keep him from finishing his sentence, and the act was so surprising that he couldn't help throwing his head back and laughing. He pulled the roll from his mouth and continued to chuckle as she fixed him a plate.

"You're an impulsive wench, Jezebel," he prodded.

"And you're an insufferable ass."

"We're quite the pair."

"That we are, Thadrick. That we are."

The dream shifted and they were in Jezebel's bed. Candles had been lit all around the room, and darkness had fallen. Jezebel was sprawled across his bare chest, and he was running his fingers through her hair. They both looked thoroughly satiated. Of course, leave it to his luck for his dream to skip the best part.

"Does it bother you?" Jezebel asked, her voice soft and tentative.

"You're going to have to be more specific than that, Jezzy," he said.

She sighed. "The fact that I have witch magic in me. Does it bother you?"

"If it did, I would not be in your bed. You are no danger, my sweet. You're too kind to ever be evil. It's why the spell the fae and I did on you worked."

"I wish she'd never done this to me."

"Your sister is a selfish creature. There is no point in wishing for something to change that cannot be changed. You simply must accept it and make the best of it. That's what life is. Taking the worst situations and making the best of them."

"And what about when things aren't bad?" she asked.

"Then you must soak it up like a dry sponge because that's what gets you through the hard times."

"Thadrick?"

"Yes, my sweet?"

"Would you consider us something you're soaking up?"

"If you're wondering if my time with you will be something that will get me through dark times, you would be right. This time I have with you will be something I always treasure, even long after we're through."

Thad's eyes snapped open as the dream faded away. He rubbed at his chest where pain suddenly throbbed. He hadn't wanted to admit it to himself that night in her bed, because he'd been afraid, but he was in love with Jezebel. He'd watched so many relationships over the centuries and how they destroyed people. Some of them people of great power, and the damage those relationships had done had led to great destruction. What would that kind of pain do to someone like him with such power? Apparently, it simply made him a moody recluse.

The doors at the front of the hall, behind the chairs of the elders, opened. Thad stood and straightened out his clothing. He had no idea how long he'd been asleep and hoped that, for the sake of Jezebel and the healers, it hadn't been too long.

"Thadrick," Clarion said as he and the rest of the elders filed in.

"Yes."

"We apologize that it took so long."

"How long has it been?" he asked.

"Twelve hours."

Thad's jaw clenched, and he forced himself to remember that these were people who were very well respected in their clan. "Why did it take so long when you had the proof you needed?"

"Myanin's sire showed up when he realized she wasn't at her post. He was worried she'd crossed into the human realm. Once we explained the situation to him, well, let's just say he was less than happy that his offspring was being detained."

Thad forced himself not to roll his eyes. Myanin's father was a pompous ass. It was no wonder it had been twelve hours, and he was actually surprised it hadn't taken longer than that with him involved.

"Have you made a decision?" Thadrick asked the elders.

"We have," Synica answered.

"Myanin will be removed from her post as guard of the veil," Lyra said. "Her willingness to deceive one of her own clan members has made her untrustworthy. She will be demoted to a servant of the elders. She will receive a small pay, obviously, as we don't condone slavery. But it will be much less than what she was making. She will be watched closely. And she will receive counseling from one of our empaths. It is obvious she has emotional issues that need to be dealt with."

"We are sorry that you and the female you cared for suffered for Myanin's indiscretion," Clarion said solemnly.

"I am as well," he agreed. "I am also sorry that Myanin was hurt by my rejection. I never realized how strongly her emotions were. She obviously hid much of her feelings from me."

"Just because you have certain powers does not make you all knowing, Thadrick," said Rouse. "We aren't gods. We are flawed just like every other species in existence."

Thad bowed his head. "Thank you. I appreciate your wisdom and for hearing my grievance. I must be on my way. There are serious matters at hand."

"We have been informed of the situation with the high fae, Volcan," said Myron. "We cannot interfere. Our power could be more of a hindrance than a help. But we wish you well in this battle and pray that evil will fall."

"I understand and thank you." Thad turned from the elders and left the hall without a backward glance. He needed to get back to Peri's and finish helping the healers with the spell, and he needed to make things right between him and Jezebel. He just prayed she still wanted him.

~

Volcan stood atop a small hill in the draheim realm. Next to him was a stone altar. He was flanked by Evanora, Morfran, and two scaly beasts. Volcan and Evanora had just returned from the human realm, and they hadn't come back empty-handed. Ten women knelt before him. Some whimpered. Some smiled beatifically. Others just stared around wide-eyed.

"Impressive," said the vampire.

"Did you expect anything less,?" Volcan asked, daring the vampire to question him.

"You know that these won't be as strong as your gypsy witches."

"Oh, how I know, Morfran. Nothing can stand against the gypsies. But I'm not one to put all my eggs in one basket. The more witches, the merrier, I've always said. And my gypsy commanders will need an army to command. These will be the first. I would have loved it if the gypsies would have been able to create more witches before we took on Perizada, as they would have been even more powerful, but I think these will be sufficient to bring the bitch low."

"Ladies," said Volcan, "arise. The time is nigh. I'm about to make your wildest dreams come true." He nodded to the first one in the line, and Evanora and Morfran took the girl by each arm. This was one of the whimpering ones.

"I'll go," said another of the women, raising her hand.

"Love the enthusiasm," said Volcan. "In due time, my love. We all have to take turns."

The woman held by Evanora and Mofran began to protest, but Evanora waved her hand in front of her face. The woman went mute and wide-eyed. The girl tried to yank free, but Morfran clamped down hard on her bicep and hissed. "Be still, fool."

"Do not try to run, my pretties," said Volcan. "If you get too far, I have to let loose the dragons." He indicated Grus and Volaman. "They so seldom get to eat humans and they do love it. But I'd much rather you join my forces. You're much more valuable to me as witches than as dragon meat."

The dragons let out matching snarls making it perfectly clear that they agreed with Volcan on the whole don't get to eat humans nearly often enough.

Mofran lifted the first convert like she was a throw pillow and sat the girl upon the altar. Evanora cast a spell to stop the woman from squirming.

"There now," said Volcan. "Much better." He lifted the girl's shirt so her stomach was exposed. He slit his own hand and let the blood drip down upon her stomach. "Let us begin," he said and placed the knife upon the woman's exposed flesh where his blood was pooling and drew a long red line there. "Bloody work this witch creation," he said to no one in particular as he began chanting the spell to transfer a portion of his power to his latest convert.

∽

THE FIVE HEALERS sat in a circle around a small campfire staring at one another. It was midnight and the forest was still. Their mates watched from a distance. Though it had been difficult, the girls had finally convinced the wolves to allow them this time together. The air was thick with tension. All the waiting, all the preparation, was about to come to fruition one way or another. They could all feel it.

Occasionally, one of the girls would pat the leg or the arm of another. They spoke in hushed voices, afraid speaking loudly might make the reality of the situation become a little too clear.

"Are you sure the sacrifices will work, Jewel?" asked Kara.

"I'm not sure about anything anymore," she replied.

"I guess we're about to find out," said Stella.

"I've never called up a goddess before," said Heather. "Any suggestions?"

"Neither have I," said Jewel, "but I *do* think she will answer us."

"I feel that way, too," said Kara.

Stella turned and looked at Heather. "Are you sure about this, Heather? Yours is the greatest sacrifice."

Heather was looking at the ground. Had she wanted to, she could have opened the bond to Kale and seen that he was currently talking to Gustavo. But she kept it shut tightly, which meant she could see nothing at this moment. Heather shook her head. "Mine is not the greatest sacrifice. What good will it be to see the world if it is burning down around me and I'm one of the ones helping start the fire? No, I think Anna's sacrifice is the greatest. I can't imagine not knowing who my father was."

"It's not great," said Kara.

"See there," said Anna, "at least I have had one parent. And since I've never known my father, I really won't be giving up anything. I don't know what I'm missing. It's practically no sacrifice at all. Kara will bear the greatest brunt. I cannot fathom knowing I could never have children."

Tears glistened in Kara's eyes, and the other girls saw them fall. She sniffed and wiped them away. "This world is no place to bring up children anyway. It's better this way." The words sounded hollow to Heather, much like her own had been. But she said nothing. Kara continued. "Besides, it's like Anna said. I don't really know what I'm missing. Stella has the greatest sacrifice. She and her brother are close. Giving him up is unimaginable." She turned to Stella. "I know you love each other. It will be like losing your best friend."

"Nobody ever said this would be easy," Stella replied. "In fact, I believe the Great Luna specifically told us this would be difficult. But it will be for the best. He doesn't need to know about this world anyway. I've already realized the people who are awoken to the supernatural world don't live very comfortable lives. I can spare him from knowing about all the hidden dangers out there. For that, I'm grateful."

Now they all turned to Jewel, but she said nothing. "Are you certain you cannot share with us your own sacrifice?" asked Anna.

Jewel shook her head and pursed her lips. "No. When the Great Luna visited me, I told her what I would give. She approved and counseled me to tell no one. I trust her. I will remain silent."

"Okay, then. What's done is done," said Heather. "We won't press you any further about it."

Stella reached out a hand to Kara on her left and Anna on her right. "I think we should all hold hands," she said. They took Stella's hands and offered their own to Jewel and Heather.

"Agreed," said Heather. "Like in church."

"Everyone ready?" asked Jewel.

"Yep," said Stella.

"Aye," said Heather.

Kara giggled, then said, "Full throttle."

"Go for it," said Anna.

"Great Luna," said Jewel, "we beseech you. Please accept these sacrifices from your servants. We make them on behalf of everyone we love, our mates, our friends, and our families. We make them on behalf of those people we don't even know. We pray we make them with pure hearts, and we ask you to accept them in the spirit with which they are intended."

All of a sudden, the area surrounding them shimmered, and the Great Luna stepped into the firelight. The pale glow from the fire was dwarfed in comparison to the goddess, who shimmered like a thousand lighted candles contained in a glass jar.

"I heed your call, healers." The Great Luna turned first to Stella. "Stella James, I accept the sacrifice you have offered, the relationship with your brother. Henceforth, it will be as if he had never met you, as if he'd never known you, as if he'd never had a sister. He will live a long and happy life, and I will watch over him. I will bless the spell because of the sacrifice you have made."

The Great Luna turned to Kara. "Kara Jones, I accept the sacrifice you have offered, the chance to ever bear children. Though you would have been the finest of mothers, lavishing the love upon your child that was so often denied to you during your life, and Nick would have made the finest of fathers, guiding his pups into adulthood with love and patience, you shall, all your life, remain barren." Kara began to sob, but stifled them and focused on the goddess. "I will bless the spell because of the sacrifice you have made."

Next, the goddess turned to Anna. "You are strong, Anastasia French, I accept the sacrifice you have offered, a relationship with your father. It would never have been my will for your father to have abandoned you. He is a broken man because of what he did. But his reconciliation with you would have given him a new life. And the relationship, even after so much has been missed, would have been rich and full of love and benefited you both. I will make it so that he forgets he ever had a daughter, and he will be happy the rest of his days. I will bless the spell because of the sacrifice you have made."

Next, the Great Luna faced Heather. "You, Heather Banks, know above all how precious is the gift of sight. Having lived so long without it, and now having experienced it for such a short period of time, you appreciate it more than anyone. You also *see* so much more than anyone else. You see through the façade, right to the core person. That has always been the case and will never change regardless of whether you can see the physical features of a person. I will bless the spell because of the sacrifice you have made."

Finally, the goddess turned to Jewel. "And you, Jewel Stone..." The Great Luna hesitated. "As every pack has an Alpha, you are the leader of these healers, that cannot be denied. They look to you for guidance, for strength. Are you confident of your decision?"

Jewel did not hesitate. "I am," she said.

"Very well," said the Great Luna. "When all is said and done, these great women will perform deeds that will be whispered about for generations. All of that is made possible because of what you have done. I will bless the spell because of the sacrifice you have made.

"Farewell, brave and noble healers. You shall perform the spell at sunrise tomorrow. Though you may not see me, I will be in your midst. I would counsel you to spend the remaining moments of this night in the arms of your mates. This time of peace is fleeting.

"And for those of you who have yet to perform the ceremony binding you to your mates, I would ask only this. What are you waiting for?" There was a flash, and the Great Luna was gone.

17

"The darkness that comes from within is more absolute than any darkness that might dwell on the outside, because the darkness that lives inside of us doesn't just cover us. It has the power to consume us if we let it."
~Crina

"I understand why you're doing this, but I don't like it," Adam said as he pressed his forehead to Crina's.

"Your complaint has been noted," she teased, hoping to ease some of the tension in him.

"As much as I want to allow us each the luxury of a long goodbye, we don't have time," Peri said as she stood in the center of her living room. "All of you going to the In-Between, place a hand on my arms. Let's get this over with."

Adam pressed his lips to Crina's in a firm but quick kiss. "Don't believe anything you see in there."

She nodded and then reached out to place a hand on Peri's arm. The other wolves had done the same. Within seconds, they were standing in the forest. A troll stood on a small bridge, and he seemed to be guarding it.

"Perizada, this is becoming a habit of yours," the troll said. "I'm beginning to think you want my job."

"I would never attempt to take your job as you so obviously are overjoyed with the task," Peri said dryly. "I am simply dropping off five wolves who wish to take a tour of the In-Between."

"A tour?" the troll asked, his eyes going wide. "Do they realize that the chances of the tour ever ending are slim?"

Peri clucked her tongue at him. "Don't insult me or them. These aren't the first wolves to enter."

"True. But things have changed since then," he said.

"What things?" Peri asked as she took a step closer to the troll.

"The In-Between has always been an entity with its own magic. But another has come along and joined his magic with it. I honestly couldn't tell you what effect that will have on it."

"Volcan," Peri spat out. "Did you see him when he joined his magic with the In-Between?"

It was obvious to Crina that the troll hadn't expected Peri to just call him out like that. He stumbled around his words a bit before finally speaking a clear sentence. "Do you have a toll to pass?" It appeared as though he was simply going to ignore the high fae's comment altogether.

Peri reached into the pocket of her robe and pulled out several gold coins. There was no telling how old they were. She flicked them at the troll, and one second they were flying through the air, and the next they were gone. The troll stepped aside and motioned for them to cross.

They were silent as they walked. None of them acknowledged the troll as they passed him. When they were standing in front of a large cave-like entrance, Peri turned to face them.

Crina glanced at the four other wolves. Aimo and Antonio seemed anxious as they shifted their weight from foot to foot. Bannan was cool and calm. His arms were folded across his chest, and he watched Peri expectantly. Lucian didn't appear worried, either. He almost looked bored. Crina tried to mimic Lucian's face, but inside, she was already feeling sick. She'd heard the stories of what the In-Between had been like for the males of her pack, and she was dreading it. Who wanted to live through their most horrific fears? Apparently, she did because she'd volunteered to waltz right into hell.

"Volcan's magic has grown stronger," Peri began. "Joining it with the In-Between's magic will probably make it unstable inside." She motioned to the entrance. "I'm going to be honest. I'm not sure how you will defeat this. But somehow you must overcome the spell that the In-Between casts over you. When you're able to do that, you will be able to exit and end up at the veil to the draheim realm. He wanted whoever was able to enter the realm to be weak. Forcing someone who wanted in to the draheim realm to go in the In-Between would ensure that if they made it, they wouldn't have any fight left in them. But you five need not worry because you will have the rest of us."

The five nodded in unison.

"When you exit the In-Between, call me immediately, Lucian." She pointed to her temple. "I'll be here in a flash ... pun intended."

"Do not worry yourself on our behalf, Peri," he replied, his voice strong and confident. "Prepare the others for battle. We will make it through."

"Good. Now, time is of the essence. This isn't a vacation. Get in there and kick some In-Between ass."

"Jen would be proud," Lucian said, making Peri and Crina smile.

Peri's smile melded into a smirk. "Well, since I live for her approval, I'm so glad."

Crina and the other males turned away as Peri and Lucian said their goodbyes. She glanced at the males again. "You three ready?"

They shrugged. "It's not like we have a choice," Antonio said.

"Just remember it isn't real," Crina told them. "If you can do nothing else, repeat, out loud, over and over, it isn't real."

Peri moved out of the way and, as one, all five of them stepped into the darkness.

Crina made it several steps before she felt the chill creeping into her bloodstream. It was as though ice water was being poured straight into her veins. She continued forward as her breathing became labored despite the fact she was walking slowly. She couldn't see anything, and she didn't want to call out to the others in case she broke their concentration.

Crina felt something nudging her in her mind and knew it had to be Adam attempting to reach her through their bond. She'd locked it down tight. She wasn't about to let him experience this with her. She knew it would make him angry, but she'd deal with that once she'd gotten out.

She took another ten steps before anything happened. But then, suddenly, standing before her was Adam. He looked as real as her mate, as if he were truly standing mere feet from her. She could even smell his scent. For a moment she wondered if he'd flashed himself there and entered without her knowledge, but then a cruel smile twisted his lush lips and she knew it wasn't really her mate. Her Adam would never look at her that way.

"Knock, knock," the In-Between's version of Adam said.

Crina glared at the false image. "I'm not here to play games."

The false Adam chuckled, low and dark. "You're a wolf. Wolves love games. I could get a ball if they're more your speed."

"I think I'm good, just not playing. Thanks for caring." She smiled politely at him and began walking again. She wondered for a minute if she would physically run into him, but he just seemed to move farther back as she moved. He wasn't walking. He would just reappear a few feet in front of her. Crina couldn't see anything around her, except for Adam.

"Crina, my dear mate," the false Adam began, "I think it's time we had a talk about reality. We've been living together as though we were equal, as if we belong together, and we both know that isn't true. We need to accept that our kind were never supposed to join. You're a wolf, for goodness' sakes. I'm a fae. My kind is far superior to your kind. I thought that perhaps I would give this whole true mate thing a try. I mean, I've been bored as hell since the werewolf wars, and you aren't exactly hard on the eyes, but I'm just not feeling it anymore."

Crina was trying to tune out the harsh words, but it was difficult because what he was saying was exactly what she feared. Regardless of the fact that the Great Luna had made them true mates, Crina wondered if she was good enough for Adam. She wondered if she measured up to lovers he'd taken in the past. She feared that there would come a day when he would get bored of having a mate and being committed to one woman.

Peri flashed back to her home, and into her and Lucian's bedroom. His sent filled her and her stomach twisted at the thought of him in that awful place. She wished she could hear Lucian's voice in her head. It was strange how accustomed she'd become to hearing it when it been so startling in the beginning. Now, she was like a city-dweller who'd been transplanted to the country and missed the constant drone of automobile engines, sirens, and people. The silence in her mind was deafening. Though she knew it was futile, Peri reached for his mind. Nothing. The In-Between was too far, too impenetrable. She took a small measure of comfort in knowing that wolves had survived the In-Between before. And Lucian was one of the strongest wolves of all. If anyone could do it, he could. She only hoped he was the same wolf when he emerged on the other side.

The high fae fidgeted. It wasn't long now. She could feel the storm brewing. Volcan had been silent for entirely too long. Peri felt she needed to make a move against him as quickly as possible. The longer they hesitated, the stronger his dark presence became in Anna and Jewel. Not only that, Peri wasn't fool enough to believe Volcan would place all his eggs in one basket. He'd have something else up his sleeve besides the healers. He was sitting behind that draheim veil plotting, working, increasing his strength. She just wished she knew exactly what he was up to so she could be ready for it.

The room became bathed in white light. Peri knelt. "Great Luna."

"Haven't I told you I will always come when you need me most?"

"And you've never failed me," replied Peri, as she bowed

her head and closed her eyes. She could feel the power and glory of the goddess but that wasn't what held her on the ground. It was the all-consuming peace that the creator of the wolves filled the space around them with. Peri could feel her shoulders relaxing despite all of the weight that was practically breaking her back.

"The hour is almost upon you, Perizada of the fae," said the Great Luna. "You shall cast the spell at sunrise. I have spoken directly with your healers. Each has chosen a fitting sacrifice. The lives of their mates are no longer necessary."

"But I..." Peri began but her words faltered. She had no right to question the Great Luna and yet she desperately wanted to know why her role had changed.

"You what, Perizada? You wanted to sacrifice yourself? Of course you did. But that won't happen."

"They've suffered enough." Peri's voice was pleading and she nearly raised her head but forced herself to maintain the respectful pose.

"And you haven't?" The Great Luna asked.

"I have more to give," Peri sighed and despite her words, she could hear her own weariness. She was tired, immensely so, but she knew that she didn't have time to be exhausted. Evil didn't rest and that meant none of them could rest either.

The goddess laughed, and the sound was like an accompaniment of harps playing in perfect harmony. "Perizada of the fae cannot control everything, no matter how hard she tries. It's time to trust in those who have trusted in you, Peri. I have asked each of the healers to spend the remaining hours of this night with their mates. The two that remain unbonded will not be so by morning. They will need the strength of their mates."

"And Dalton?"

"I shall speak to him before the night is out. Concern yourself with only performing the spell adequately. I would, however, ask this one thing of you. For the spell to succeed, the circle must not be broken until the entire ritual is complete. To ensure that happens, you are to bind the others until the spell is complete. Do not let them break the circle or all is lost."

"I will do as you say, Great Luna."

"We shall see," replied the goddess.

"What's that supposed to..." The fae's words fell flat as the Great Luna faded from view. "Really? That's all I get," yelled Peri at the ceiling. "Thanks a ton, Great Luna. I feel so much better now." Peri shook her head. "Sometimes, she's worse than the damn wolves."

18

"I thought it was difficult not knowing my true mate and having to wait for her, but I'm beginning to think that knowing her and having to wait might even prove to be more difficult. Guess it's a good thing that I like challenges." ~Nick

Jezebel was trying her hardest to remain optimistic, despite the fact that Thad had left them high and dry with an incomplete spell. He said he'd be back, and regardless of the anger he'd obviously felt toward her, she had to trust that the fate of the healers and all those involved was more important to him than their relationship issues.

It was late afternoon when she heard his deep voice.

"Where is your mother?"

"She's in that first bedroom down the hall," Anna answered. "If you hurt her, I'll figure out a way to destroy you," her daughter answered, bringing a smile to Jezebel's lips.

"I would expect nothing less, but rest assured, that is not my intention."

"We all know where intentions lead us," Heather jumped in. "The good ones and the bad ones."

There was a soft knock and then the door opened. He'd never been a patient man, and it appeared that he still was not if he couldn't even wait for her to invite him in. She turned to face him and was struck, not for the first or fifty-first time, by how handsome he was. He'd always taken her breath away and that hadn't changed.

"Thank you for coming back," she said after several heartbeats of simply staring at one another.

"I said I would."

She nodded. "Yes, you did."

"I need to ask you something before I explain where I've been." He looked a tad unsure of himself, which was something she was not used to seeing on him. "Is there still a chance for us? I mean, would you be willing to try again with me?"

Jezebel felt as though she'd been punched in the gut. Breathing suddenly became difficult and she swayed slightly. She'd longed to get a do-over with Thadrick but was sure it would never come, not after what she'd done to him.

"I'm so sorry, Thad," said Jezebel. "I know what I did hurt you and I was so angry, but it was wrong, and I am truly, so very sorry."

"I accept your apology," he offered. "It happened a long time ago, and new things have come to light, which we will discuss. First, I just want to know if you still have feelings for me."

"I'm in love with you. I've never stopped being in love

with you. I never imagined you would give me another chance, but I'm willing to take it if you're offering."

He took a step toward her and held out his hand. She took it without hesitation. "I didn't realize how strongly I'd felt about you when we were seeing each other," he admitted. "And honestly, I've been in denial about it all these years. I want to be with you. I want to see where this can go between us."

Jezebel nodded her head because at that moment words simply failed her. She'd never thought she'd hear those words from Thadrick, not after what she'd done. She wasn't about to let the opportunity pass her by.

"I need to tell you some things." He pulled her toward the bed and sat, motioning her to sit next to him. "The woman you saw when you went to the djinn realm a century ago was not who she claimed to be."

Jezebel listened as Thad explained everything that had happened. When he was finished, she simply sat there, stunned. Because of one selfish woman's actions, Jezebel had been separated from the man she loved for a century.

"She is being punished for her deceit," said Thad. "We do not take lying and hurting others of our clan lightly."

"Wow. I can't believe that all of that was between us, all this time."

"I understand why you were so hurt."

"It still wasn't right," Jezebel said.

"No, but it is more understandable. I can't say that I wouldn't have done the same thing in your shoes because I've never been in them. I can, however, tell you that I'd rip any man who touched you, limb from limb."

"Are you sure you're not part werewolf?" Anna's voice came from the doorway. "That possessive streak sounds just like one of them."

"Perhaps it's a supernatural thing," Thad said with a shrug.

"Are you good with this, Mom?" Anna asked.

Jezebel nodded. "I am. I'm sure there will be more for us to discuss and work through, but that will have to wait until after we save the world."

"Agreed," said Thad.

"So, are you ready to get back to work, and do you promise not to bail again?" Jewel asked as she stepped up next to Anna. "Because I do not have time for your drama."

"One, drama-free djinn, at your service," he said as he stood and then bowed gracefully.

"Fantastic. Let's go. We've got a spell to learn." Jewel motioned for them to follow.

Thad pulled Jezebel up from the bed and then quickly leaned down, surprising her when he pressed his lips to hers. "It's been far too long since I've been able to do that. Forgive me if I take liberties and do it often."

Jezebel laughed. "Considering I like it when you kiss me, you have my permission to take all the liberties you want."

"I think I just threw up in my mouth," Anna said dryly as she turned to follow Jewel.

Thad's brow drew down. "Why would someone throw up in their mouth instead of spitting it out?"

"Probably because she's a girl who just saw her mom kissing a guy, and it grossed her out," explained Jezebel.

"I'm not sure why that would gross her out. She kisses her mate."

"Because, I'm her mom. Seeing me be affectionate with a man isn't her idea of stellar entertainment. Maybe it's a human thing," she offered.

"Perhaps. I've come to the conclusion it's just easier not

to try to understand the healer females. They talk strange and laugh at things that aren't the least bit funny."

Jezebel smiled as they started for the door. "That's probably for the best. Trying to understand them might cause you mental distress."

As Thad held her hand and led her back to the room where Jewel had been working on the spell, Jezebel couldn't stop glancing at Thad. She was sure at any moment he'd disappear and she'd wake up and realize it all had been a dream.

"I can feel your worry," he told her and gave her hand a gentle squeeze. "I'm not going anywhere and if I need to, this time, I'll just take you with me."

That's one problem solved. Now just a few more to go.

∼

PERI WAS TRYING HARD NOT to worry about her mate. There was too much to be concerned about already, and he was a strong, powerful wolf. He'd survived the dark forest, and he would survive the In-Between as well.

"Could I have a moment of your time?" Z said as he stepped onto the back porch where Peri stood.

They'd all shared an early dinner together and had dispersed to go their separate ways for a short while. Peri knew the others needed time with their mates. Adam was off throwing knives at something, and Adira, who'd been strangely silent through the last few days, had taken off without a word. Peri imagined she might want to spend the night in her home, away from the constant bickering of the wolves and their mates.

"What can I do for you?" Peri asked. She was too tired for smartass remarks.

"Volcan still has my sister. I need to know you're going to do everything you can to get her out safely."

"You have my word," Peri said. "How is Sly holding up?"

"He misses her. We both do. We just keep trying not to dwell on it. It's not like Volcan is an honest man. Just because he claims he won't hurt her doesn't mean he will keep his promise."

"You are correct, but don't give up hope."

Z shook his head. "I wouldn't dare. After all, it's all we have."

~

HEATHER WAS SITTING on Kale's lap in Peri's living room listening to the chatter of conversations taking place. Jewel, Thad, and Peri had rewritten the spell and felt confident it would work. Her stomach was full of good food, and she was enjoying the sounds of her friends' voices.

"Do me a favor?" she asked softly, knowing Kale would hear her.

"Anything," he answered.

"Show me the room. I want to see everyone and what they're doing."

Heather felt the bond open up and light flooded her mind before fading and becoming something else. She knew who everyone was the moment her eyes landed on them. Stella and her beautiful brown skin was sitting in a chair with Ciro next to her. His arm was draped over the back of her chair, and his fingers trailed gently over her shoulder. Her New York friend seemed completely at ease with the touch. It made Heather smile.

Then she saw Jewel, her strawberry blonde hair glistening from the light of the lamp she sat next to. Dalton was standing beside the chair, leaning against the wall watching his mate. His eyes never left her as Jewel talked with Stella and the two laughed.

Heather's view shifted, and she realized Kale must have turned his head or moved his eyes because now she was looking at Kara. She was the youngest of them, yet her eyes held age beyond her years. But when she turned those eyes on Nick, her mate, they lit up, and she looked like the teenager she was. Heather watched as Nick brushed strands of hair from Kara's face and let his fingers linger on her cheek. It was something so simple and yet Heather was so thankful to have seen the love that was so obvious between the two.

Movement next to Kara caught her attention, and Heather watched as Anna stood from where she'd been sitting in Gustavo's lap. He stood with her and wrapped an arm around her waist. The heated look he gave her was so intimate that Heather felt bad for seeing it.

Sorin and Elle where on the floor close to where Gustavo and Anna had been and seemed to be wrapped in a deep conversation. The love in Sorin's eyes as he stared at his mate was undeniable.

Sly and Z were both leaned up against the wall closest to the front door of Peri and Lucian's home. They both seemed lost in thought, neither of them really seeing the room. She couldn't imagine how hard it had been for them both to be wondering if their mate and sister was safe, or even still alive. Through all of this, they'd both continued to do what they had to do in order to get to the battle that would hopefully help them get Evanora back safely.

"Thank you," she told Kale through their bond. *"I need a break now."* Heather had found she couldn't look through his eyes for too long or it made her a little queasy. She likened it

to motion sickness. Heather wasn't feeling queasy in that moment, but she'd seen what she wanted to see—each of her friends, girls she'd grown to love, happy and loved by their mates. Whatever happened tomorrow, they at least had all experienced the kind of love and care that many would not.

"You never have to thank me for caring for you," Kale said. "It is a pleasure and honor."

Heather snuggled back into his chest and closed her eyes as she continued to listen to the voices that surrounded her. Kale tightened his hold and brushed his lips against her ear as he spoke out loud. "Do you need anything?

Heather's lips turned up. "Only you. Just hold me like this, please."

"As my lady wishes," he murmured and pressed a kiss to her neck.

***

"WHERE ARE WE GOING?" Anna asked as she held onto Gustavo's hand. They walked outside in the early evening twilight, away from Peri's home.

"It's a surprise," he said, his beautiful Spanish accent sending chills down her spine.

The landscape of Farie was breathtaking and seemed to be ever changing. Anna had begun to wonder if Peri was capable of changing the scenery around them but she hadn't had time to ask about it.

Her thoughts were distracted as they walked between two trees that had grown across from one another and acted like an entryway into a small cove. The branches of the tall trees that encircled the area hung thickly over top, completely blocking the sky. Small lanterns had been hung from the tree branches, and there were at least thirty lighting up the interior of the cove. In the center, thick blankets were arrayed into a pallet, and a wide circle of candles surrounded them.

"Did you do this?" Anna asked Gustavo as she turned slowly, taking in every detail.

"I might have had a little help," her mate admitted.

She turned to look at him and smiled. "It's breathtaking."

"I'm glad you like it. Come." He motioned to the blankets. "Sit with me."

Anna accepted Gustavo's help as she stepped over the candles and then sat on the pallet. He knelt beside her, removed her shoes, and then took his own off. He reclined on his side, propped up on an elbow.

Anna took the same position, and they stared at one another. She took in his elegant but masculine features and strong, solid build, marveling in his physical beauty. Anna didn't consider herself ugly, but she didn't think she was in the same league as Gustavo.

"You're wrong," he said softly. "You are incomparable in your beauty, *mi amor*. You are regal and graceful. With all the class that comes with your name, Anastasia. You're perfect."

Anna scooted closer to him. Like a moth to a flame, she wanted to feel his warmth. Gustavo placed a hand on her hip and pulled her even closer until she could feel his soft breath on her face.

"I would very much like to kiss you," he told her. His voice was like a caress on her skin.

"I would very much like to be kissed by you."

Gustavo's hand ran up her hip, her arm, and her shoulder, until he cupped her neck. He leaned in as he pulled her to him and crashed his lips against hers. It wasn't slow or gentle as she'd come to expect from him. It was passionate and urgent. His tongue pushed into her mouth, and Anna moaned as his taste filled her.

He rolled and she was suddenly sprawled across him, but their lips never broke. Anna ran her hand up his chest to his neck and then up into his hair. She tugged gently and grinned as he growled. Gustavo's hands ran up and down her back and into her hair as if he couldn't touch her enough.

"I will never get enough of you," he whispered against her mouth. "For as long as I live, I will crave you."

He ran his lips across her jaw and then down her neck. Anna felt the scrape of his teeth against the sensitive skin, and she gasped at the sensation. When he bit a little harder, words slipped out that she hadn't even realized were hovering on the tip of her tongue. "Bite me. Please."

Gustavo froze. "*Que?*"

"I want to perform the Blood Rites," Anna said as she pulled back just enough to look at him without her eyes crossing. "There isn't a reason not to. The sacrifices have been decided, and it has nothing to do with the bonds. Please, I want this. I want to be yours completely."

Gustavo cupped her cheeks in his hands as he stared up at her. He seemed to be searching for any doubt but she knew he wouldn't find any.

"You're sure?"

She nodded.

"I want that too. But I will not make love to you."

Anna felt her face heat up. Okay, she wasn't going to lie, she had sort of thought the two were synonymous.

"They do usually happen together," he said, answering her thoughts. "But not always. You were raised in the human world, not ours. Marriage is important, and despite the fact that our bond is actually more permanent and sacred than marriage, I won't consummate our union until we've married in the human way."

"But you will bite me and I will bite you?" asked Anna.

He chuckled. "Yes, there will definitely be biting." His face grew serious and then he leaned up to press a kiss to the place where her neck and shoulder met. "Are you ready?" he whispered, his voice husky and sensual.

"Oh boy." Anna breathed out as she nodded.

Gustavo ran his teeth across the flesh again and then struck. His teeth sank into her neck easily, and the pain was sharp and sudden but then it was gone, replaced by intense pleasure. Anna clutched his shoulders and pulled him more tightly against her. She heard a mewling sound and realized it was her. She thought maybe she should be embarrassed but couldn't bring herself to feel anything other than sheer bliss. A moment later she felt his tongue licking her neck and heard a rumbling growl from him.

"You taste delicious," he purred and then added, "Your turn."

Gustavo guided her face to his neck and said, "Don't think, just bite."

Anna did as he instructed and sank her teeth into his neck. She thought that there would be some sort of resistance, but there was none. His blood hit her tongue, and to her surprise, it didn't taste bad. She felt his chest rumbling and gasped as he pulled her tight against him. Anna swallowed several times and then pulled back when she felt a sharp tug in her sternum. It was as if she'd been tethered to something and the string had been pulled taunt.

"That's the bond," Gustavo said as he pushed her hair from her face. "We are forever joined. Where you go, I go."

He pulled her face down to his and pressed his lips to hers. This kiss was gentle as his tongue tangled with hers. Anna's hands itched to touch him everywhere and to feel his hands all over her own body. She wanted to be closer to him, to have nothing between them.

"You tempt me, mate," Gustavo growled. "I want you, too, but we will wait."

She sighed. "I suppose I should be happy you're such a gentleman, but right now my hormones don't like you."

He chuckled. "Believe it or not, you will survive."

"Just remember that payback isn't pleasant."

"Are you planning to tease me?" His brow rose and his sensual mouth turned up slightly and his eyes began to glow with the presence of his wolf.

"Once we're married, all bets are off," she countered.

"Fair enough," he said and then rolled again until she was beneath him. "Just remember you said that, because I plan to thoroughly corrupt you once you're my wife. Now we must go or my willpower will fail, and I will allow myself to dishonor you."

She slapped her cheeks with her hands and gasped. "Oh, the shame that you would be intimate with your soul mate."

"Don't make me spank you, minx," he said and then snapped his teeth an inch from her lips.

"Now you're just being cruel with the teasing."

Gustavo practically jumped to his feet and pulled her with him. "We need to be around people now."

Anna laughed as he tugged her behind him. "Hey, Gustavo, do you want to see my markings? It's been a while since you last saw them." Okay, so now *she* was just being cruel, but she was sexually frustrated so it was a little out of her control.

Gustavo didn't respond to her taunting.

"What about the marks on my stomach? Would you like to kiss them better?"

A second later he opened the door to Peri's home and shoved her inside. He stuck his head in and growled, "I'm going on a run. Don't let her leave this house." Then he slammed the door and was gone.

Kara whistled. "What on earth did you do to rattle his cage?"

There were some sniffing noises and then Kale chuckled. "So you two gave in, too? Welcome to the Blood-bonded side. We have cookies."

Anna grinned. "Thanks."

"So is that what he's in a huff about? Did you get his motor running and then climb out of the cockpit? Pun totally intended," Heather said with a snort.

"Actually he shut me down," Anna said and shrugged. "Apparently chivalry is alive and well."

"Aw, damn, chivalry sucks when it's your soul mate telling you no." Kara cursed. "Can I get an amen?"

"Amen," the three other girls said at the same time.

"I'm going to take a cold shower," Anna said. "Then we're having a girl's night."

Nick started to object, but Kara put a hand over his mouth. "If one of us doesn't get loving, then none of us do. It's a gypsy healer rule."

"Since when?" Nick asked.

"Since you males decided to be all respectable."

"So we get punished for making sure to keep your honor intact?" Kale asked.

"Pretty much," Heather said.

The males growled, and all four of the girls laughed.

"Did you all know that men have to eja—" Jewel began,

but Dalton wrapped his hand around her mouth and pulled her back against him.

"What my mate meant to say was, Anna go take your shower and the rest of them will meet you outside. We males will set you gals up a campfire for your girls night."

Anna laughed as she winked at Jewel. "You can fill us in on what you were *really* going to say later."

19

"I'm happy my packmate has found his mate. And I'm happy others have as well. It makes all *Canis lupus* stronger. But I'd be lyin' if I said I wasn't just a wee bit jealous. I cannot help but wonder. Is my own mate out there somewhere? Is she close by? Or halfway around 'da world? Will I find her before 'da darkness overtakes me? Every day that passes without her, I travel a little further down that dark road. ~Bannan

"You don't have to play, only watch," said the In-Between vision of Adam. A bed appeared and two beautiful women lay naked within. Adam turned his back on her and joined them, doing things that made Crina want to vomit. Her blood boiled. She wanted to tear the two women apart for touching her man.

"It's not real. It's not real," she said walking past the bed. She almost made it...until she heard Adam speaking softly to the women.

"It's so good to finally be with a fae again. You don't know what it's like for me, having to be with that ... that ... beast of a woman."

"It must have been terrible," purred one of the women.

"Ew, she doesn't go all furry when you're in bed together, does she? I'd hate for her to scratch this perfect body." The woman stuck out a long pink tongue and ran it down Adam's naked torso.

Crina leapt upon the bed, intent on tearing the women limb from limb. Adam threw out a hand and blasted her backward with a bolt of power. There was a look of pure hatred on his face. "Get away from me," he said. "I never wanted to be mated to a werewolf." She fell backward on her rear end.

Crina heard her name being called. All of a sudden, a pair of strong hands held her in place. "It's not real," someone said loudly. She shook her head and her vision cleared. She was staring into Lucian's face. "Ignore whatever you're seeing," he said.

Her eyes went wide. She looked around and saw Aimo, Antonio, and Bannan staring at her openmouthed. Her eyes glanced over to where Adam had lay naked in the bed. He was gone and so were the two women. Even the bed had disappeared.

"It was real," she said.

"What was real?" asked Bannan.

"I saw..." she began. "Never mind."

"Why did you fall?" asked Aimo.

"What do you mean?" asked Crina, seeming to only just now notice she was sitting.

"You fell down for no reason. It looked as if someone shoved you," said Antonio.

"It was Adam. He knocked me down. I felt it." She

placed a hand on her chest. "I'm telling you, Lucian. This wasn't a vision. I actually felt him knock me down."

Lucian's face went grave. "I guess we know how Volcan's magic has affected the In-Between. It appears the visions are even more dangerous now if they can physically affect our bodies as well as mentally torment us. We must proceed all the more cautiously. Do not engage with your visions, whatever you do. I still believe we will make it across safely if we simply ignore what we see in our minds. Look at one another," he commanded. "Remember these faces. These are the only things real within this realm. Nothing else you see is the truth. When you see a vision, call out to the rest of us. We will help one another."

~

LUCIAN FELT as if they'd walked for miles. He had no idea how long they'd been in the In-Between, but he knew he couldn't go much farther. He'd seen Peri defiled so many times now, he knew he'd never get the memories out of his head even if he lived a thousand more years. He'd seen his beloved raped, murdered, tortured, and ... perhaps most painful of all, give herself willingly to other men. Most of them he knew personally. So many times he'd been on the verge of phasing and acting on the visions. But each time, he'd called out to the others. If no one answered, he knew they were wrestling their own nightmares. It was then he knew he was needed most. He would wait for their call. When he heard it, the sound would give him the strength to turn away from the terrible things in front of him and go help his friends. He couldn't see what they faced, but he knew it was completely real in their minds.

They walked along through the darkness, the heat of

fires below sometimes spurting up through cracks and fissures to reach them. Just when Lucian thought he couldn't take another step, just when he thought he couldn't handle another horrendous vision, the path upon which they walked widened into a large chamber. Candles lined the walls, casting shadowy light across the large cavern. A large stone door stood opposite them. "Finally," he muttered. "Stay together, everyone. Let's join hands. I wouldn't be surprised if this place had one more trick to play." He put out a hand and Crina took it. Aimo took his other. He looked over and saw Antonio grab Aimo's free hand. Bannan was just about to take Crina's hand when the wolf's head turned too quickly to one side in response to a voice only he could hear.

"Bannan," Lucian yelled. The wolf didn't respond. He took a step away from the group, seeming to stare off into nothingness. Then they all began shouting his name. Crina reached out and grabbed his arm, but he shrugged her off. He started running across the chasm. In an instant, Bannan phased and there was a huge brown wolf leaping away from them.

BANNAN HEARD HER VOICE. It was his mate. He ran to her. Soon, he saw her standing beside a flowing brook, her long blonde hair blowing in the wind. The sunrays seemed to break through the clouds, putting a spotlight on her alone. He took a step toward her, calling her name—Lavinia. He wasn't sure how he knew it. He just knew that was it. She didn't seem to hear him. The woman took a step away from him. He ran toward her but never seemed to gain any ground. Finally, he came around a large tree and saw her standing in the arms of another man. It was a wolf he knew —Kale.

"Get the hell away from her," he yelled. "She's my mate."

Kale shook his head. "I don't think so, brother."

"You have a mate," said Bannan.

"Who? That little blind chick? Nah, that's just a hobby. Lavinia is my true mate."

Bannan made a guttural sound in his throat. *Why was Kale acting like this? He loved Heather.* "Step away from her now, Kale," said Bannan past canines that were growing longer.

"Or what?"

"Or I'll kill you for touching my mate."

The girl laughed, and the sound was vicious and haughty. "You?" she asked. "You're just a Third. I could never be with someone so weak."

Bannan didn't think. He just reacted. He leaped upon Kale, phasing as he flew through the air. Kale responded in kind. The two wolves met with a thud, each going for the other's throat. They snapped and snarled, lunging at one another again and again. The fight went on for what seemed to Bannan like hours. He'd scored a few hits on Kale, but he'd taken more damage himself. He was bleeding from a dozen different bite marks and his back left paw was hanging on by nothing but a piece of sinew. It had always been this way. Kale had always been more powerful; he'd always been the Alpha's favorite. Bannan never got the spoils. Only the dregs. The thought enraged him. He gathered his strength for one final leap at his opponent. Given that he was fighting on three legs, it wasn't powerful.

Kale seemed to sense what Bannan was thinking, and he anticipated the move. As soon as Bannan jumped, Kale rolled to the side and sprang on to the other wolf's back, sinking his teeth into the back of Bannan's neck. Bannan roared and tried to shake Kale free. The wolf held fast. Bannan felt the strength leaving his body. He collapsed, the weight of Kale's body driving him to the floor. Bannan's vision swam and then went dark. He thought he heard someone calling his name ... several people ... his friends. Aimo, Antonio, Crina, and Lucian. Bannan tried to respond but he couldn't speak. The last thing he saw in his mind's eye was sweet Lavinia. She was coming to him, placing her hands on either side of his face, kissing him softly. Then Bannan knew no more.

~

"Don't phase!" yelled Lucian to Crina, Aimo, and Antonio. "It won't help Bannan. We need to be able to speak to him, convince him what he's seeing isn't real." Lucian ran after the raging wolf. Bannan was thrashing all over the cavern, slavering and biting. Lucian tried to jump on the wolf's back but was thrown back by an invisible force. He tried again with the same result.

"What's happening?" asked Crina.

"It's this accursed cavern," said Lucian. "Volcan must have cast a spell upon it. I can't touch Bannan.

"Bannan, stop," roared Lucian. The wolf either didn't hear him or didn't care that Lucian was calling and the alpha power he'd put in the command seem to have no effect. He just kept on fighting against whatever or whomever it was that only he could see.

Crina screamed. All of a sudden, a huge gash appeared on Bannan's side and blood began to pour from it.

"We've got to stop him," said Lucian. All four of them ran at Bannan but were thrown back. They stood at the invisible barrier and called to him, pleading. He gave them no heed. He only fought. Soon more cuts and gashes appeared. Seconds later, Bannan let out a sickening yelp as one his rear paws was almost ripped completely off.

"Stop him, Lucian!" yelled Crina.

Lucian just shook his head. "There's nothing we can do. He has to beat this demon on his own."

The four wolves continued to pound on the invisible barrier with no effect. Crina gasped when Bannan fell flat on his belly. He was struggling to rise, but something unseen was holding him down. Blood poured from his neck. "Bannan! Bannan," they yelled over and over again. Bannan gave one last twitch and went still. Crina and the three men stumbled forward as the invisible barrier dissipated. They ran to Bannan and knelt by his side. Crina placed her hand on his back. The wolf was completely still. Slowly, the hairy beast became a naked man lying on the floor. A large pool of blood began to form beneath him.

"He's dead," said Crina.

Lucian snatched up the body and threw it over his shoulder. "Join hands again," he said extending his free hand. Crina took it, and the four wolves formed a chain with Lucian at their lead. He ran across the chamber, careful to keep his eyes focused straight ahead on the door, and the others followed. He began to hear a voice calling out to him. It was Peri. "Lucian! Lucian! Help," it screamed.

"Ignore the voices!" Lucian yelled back at the others. He gripped Crina's hand with all his strength. She couldn't have broken free if she wanted to. They reached the door and Lucian threw himself against it. Bannan's naked body flopped around on his shoulder. The door didn't budge. Lucian swore. Peri's voice grew louder, beckoning him from across the chamber. He didn't dare look back.

He sat Bannan's body on the ground. "Push," he commanded. All four wolves strained against the door. Still, it didn't move.

"What was that?" said Antonio as he took a step away from the door, cocking his head as if listening to something only he could hear.

"No!" Lucian grabbed him and threw him against the door.

"Wait," said Crina. "Thadrick said five wolves must make it across. Touch the door." Aimo, Lucian, and Antonio all touched the door. Crina knelt down and took Bannan's hand. She pressed it against the door along with her own. Instantly, the stone door swung outward. Lucian picked Bannan up again, and they all stumbled out into the human world, landing at the entrance to the draheim veil. With a snap, the door shut behind them. Antonio rose on shaky legs and went to the shimmering veil. He stuck his hand through it.

"It worked," he said. "The veil is open."

"Come and get us," said Lucian to Peri through their bond. "And you'd better bring Kale with you."

20

I don't want to do this anymore. ~Peri

The morning dawned bright and clear. Seven wolves, five healers, a djinn, a pixie, and two fae stood in Peri's kitchen. No one talked. Everything that needed to be said had been spoken already. Peri had made sure Bannan's body was safe until they returned to lay him to rest. That had been the last thing that had need to be taken care of before they went to face their enemy. With no discernible signal, they all walked out and began marching toward a small clearing a quarter mile away from Peri's house that she had consecrated and prepared for the spell. At some point, Jezebel, Thadrick, Elle, Sorin, and Adam peeled off to find a spot to wait. Peri had given them an order to stay away. After what the Great Luna had told her, she didn't want anything to interfere with the spell. The more people involved, the more likely something would go wrong.

. . .

Dew glistened on the grass. Heather saw it through her mate's eyes. Though he kept his bond open to her, she was closed to him. She tried to commit everything she saw through his eyes to memory and tried not to mourn the loss of her sight. At least now she'd better understand the things she felt. She'd have the memories of her vision.

Kara thought only of Nick. She squeezed his hand tightly as they walked and looked forward to the day when they would complete the Blood Rites so that they would be able to speak through their bond. And despite the fact that they would never have children together, they would have one another. They would have a future together and with the pack that she would join with him. She would never be alone again. He would be there. All her life, she'd needed someone to just be there. And now she had that.

Stella and Ciro walked arm in arm.

"I want you to know that I support whatever decision you have come to," said Ciro.

"You mean the sacrifice?" She asked.

He nodded. "And I thank you now, for making the sacrifice."

"You would do the same," Stella said. "Whatever you needed to give up to protect those you love and those weaker than you, you would do it."

"I hope that I would. I hope that I would be as brave and gracious as you and the other healers have been through all of this and are continuing to be.

"Just know that I love you. I realize that we are still new to one another but I do love you and I am so very proud of you. Your brother would be as well."

A lump formed in Stella's throat as she thought of Derrick. She clamped down on the thought before it could travel to Ciro. Still, he must have felt something in her spirit.

"Be strong, my queen. No matter what happens, we will survive it."

"Your queen?" She asked with a smile.

He bowed his head and on anyone else it might have looked silly, but Ciro had an old world charm about him. "You are every bit a queen in my eyes. You rule my heart and you own my soul."

Stella was breathless as she felt the truth of his words to her marrow. She could see how much he meant the words in his eyes and feel it through their bond. "Thank you, Ciro. That means more to me than you know."

ANNA SHIVERED AS SHE WALKED. It was if two voices warred continually within her mind. One, a voice of darkness, of power, and hatred. The other, a voice of unyielding love and acceptance. Each pulled at her with an undeniable force. Since she and Gustavo had completed the Blood Rites, the link to Volcan felt a tad weaker but she could still feel it trying to woo her. She was happy they were about to perform the spell, regardless of what happened. She couldn't bear being pulled in two directions any longer. She needed Volcan out of her mind one way or the other. It was going to happen now if she had to dig her own brain out with a plastic spoon.

"I'm here, Criña," said Gustavo through the bond. "And

I'm not going anywhere, no matter what happens. I'll be with you every step of the way."

"Thank you." It was all she could say. She had no more words, no more strength. She'd been fighting Volcan's influence for so long. Without Gustavo, she'd long ago succumbed. Now, she could only say thank you.

"When this is all over, I'll take you to the Sagrada Família in Barcelona. After you, it's the most beautiful thing I've ever seen."

"I look forward to it," she replied.

Jewel said nothing as she and Dalton walked hand in hand. She didn't trust herself to speak. Dalton, always a wolf of few words, followed her lead. He just stroked her fingers with his thumb as they walked. *Thank you, Great Luna for giving me Dalton. I would be worse than dead without him. Please protect him through all of this.*

The wolves, healers, and Perizada reached the clearing. Five points were marked, evenly spaced around a circle. The mated pairs moved to their appointed spaces. The healers each separated from their mates and stepped to the side a few spaces and stopped.

Peri waived her arms and uttered a few words. Muttered cursing came from the males in the group.

"Peri, why do you bind us?" asked Ciro.

"Just a precaution, Alpha. Once we begin, the spell cannot be interrupted. We must all stay perfectly still. We only get one shot at this."

"I don't like this," said Dalton.

"None of us do," said Gustavo.

"I don't care," said Peri. "I have orders from the GL. She pulls rank on moody wolves." Peri walked around from healer to healer and held out a hand. One by one, she ran a blade across their hands so that when they joined hands their blood would mix. Once all were joined, she moved to the middle of the circle. She held her hands up and began to chant.

"I CALL upon the power given to my ancient race,
   The light that lives inside, I fully embrace.
   Fill the darkest places inside each of these,
   Cast out the shadows and bring darkness to its knees.
   Bind the evil magic that tries to own each soul,
   Give them what they need only you can make them whole.
   Goddess of the moon and wolves, we ask for your ear,
   Take notice of our battle and our petitions hear.

A LIGHT FELL from the sky. It hit Peri and exploded outward in five directions, connecting the healers like spokes in a wheel. The five fae stones appeared, each hovering in front of one of each of the girls. "Great Luna, we beseech your blessing on this spell. The sacrifices are prepared," shouted Peri. Wind began to blow about the clearing, and dark clouds formed above them. Soon, the sky opened up and rain came pouring down. Lightning crashed around them.

"Peri," yelled Gustavo. "Is this normal?"

"Everyone, hold on," she yelled. "Not much longer now."

"Stella, go," commanded Peri.

"I sacrifice the relationship with my brother," said the healer, raising her arms.

There was an answering clap of thunder that shook the surrounding trees.

"My queen, what's going on?" asked Ciro.

"Leave it, Alpha," said Peri.

"I sacrifice my ability to bear children," said Kara without being prompted.

Another answering clap of thunder.

"What the hell?" said Nick. No one responded.

"I sacrifice my relationship with my father," said Anna. Gustavo stood next to her with his mouth open. He reached for her, but she was just out of his grasp. He strained against Peri's bond but couldn't move to reach his mate.

"I sacrifice my sight," said Heather.

"NO," yelled Kale, who looked pleadingly at Heather. "No." She just shook her head and faced the ground.

Dalton screamed at Peri. "What the hell is going on Peri? Answer me, dammit!"

Peri looked sad as she answered. "This is all their doing, wolf. I couldn't stop them. The sacrifices had to be blood sacrifices but not necessarily the shedding of blood. Everything they are giving up is bound by blood in one way or another. This is between them and the Great Luna. Just be thankful no one has to die."

DALTON TURNED to Jewel and his eyes narrowed. She could feel the worry and fear coming off him in waves even without the magical bond.

"I'm sorry," she said softly, knowing he wouldn't be able to hear her above the roar of the wind and the pounding of the rain, but he would be able to read her lips. "I'm so, so sorry." And she was.

But what other option did she have? She started this

whole thing. She was the original witch/healer. It was up to her to end it. The others had done what they could. Each of them had given a sacrifice in their own way. No one had died, but there was plenty of pain associated with what the others healers had given up.

Still, Jewel knew it wouldn't be enough. All five healers needed to provide a sacrifice, and since Jewel had the most of Volcan's blood coursing through her veins, her magic was the darkest. Which meant her sacrifice would have to be the most painful.

"JEWEL!" Dalton bellowed her name as she drew the fae dagger from her boot. She'd stolen the blade from Elle—borrowed was actually the better term. Jewel wouldn't have much use for it soon. The fae would be free to take from Jewel's dead body soon enough.

Jewel had waited for the precise moment to make her move. Now that they were all arrayed in the circle and the spell had begun, none of them could move from their spots or the spell would be broken. Peri had cast a spell ensuring no one would move until the spell was complete. No one could stop Jewel now.

"It has to be done," Jewel whispered to herself. "And I'm the only one who can do it." She knew her words to be true. There was no mate bond between her and Dalton. If she died, he would continue to live. He would have another chance at love. That was all that mattered to her now.

"JEWEL STONE, DROP THAT DAGGER RIGHT NOW," Peri yelled, drawing Jewel's attention from the face of her mate. Jewel's eyes met the piercing gaze of the high fae, and the pain hidden in their crystal depths nearly drove Jewel to her knees.

"DON'T DO THIS. I'VE BEEN HERE BEFORE, AND

FRANKLY, IT PISSES ME OFF WHEN YOU DAMN HEALERS GET HEROIC."

"There is no other way," Jewel shouted back as water matted her hair to her face and dripped across her lips as she spoke. "No one else can do this, and you know it must be done."

"Someone else can do it. I've already told you I would take your place."

"This world needs you, Perizada. We'd be lost without you. I cannot do what you do, Peri. I cannot fight the darkness like you can," said Jewel.

"You're just as important as me, if not more so," Peri yelled. "I cannot heal others like you can. I cannot bring unity to the packs. Luna knows I've tried over the years."

Jewel shook her head. "The only job left for me is to end this. I started it. It's only right I stop it."

Now it was Peri's turn to shake her head. "No, Jewel, you mustn't. This is madness." Jewel could hear the fae's voice quavering as she spoke. Jewel knew she couldn't drag this out. The longer she waited, the harder it would be. Still, she couldn't leave this world without taking another look at her mate, something to carry her through to the afterlife.

The pain of Jewel's decision hit her as she turned to gaze at Dalton. Jewel hadn't even pierced herself with the dagger and yet it already felt as if the blade was slicing through her heart.

"NO!" Dalton's voice filled the night and sounded like thunder as he realized what she was saying.

He couldn't move, none of them could. Dalton stood there staring at her, anger radiating off him even as the helplessness he felt was glaring at her from the eyes that now were filling with tears. Her strong, steady mate was crying ... for her.

"Don't do this, Jewel," he cried. "There's always another way. Don't do this! If you love me, please, Little Dove, don't do this!"

Jewel gasped as the sobs she'd been holding back burst forth. "It's because I love you that I do this, my mate," Jewel shouted back. "I will not allow you to live with a woman whose darkness will eventually consume us both, nor will I allow my sisters to live in such a state. I am the only one who can do this. Please, my love, please understand." She took a deep breath, holding his gaze even as he shook his head at her. "Dalton Black..." Her voice was as firm as she could make it as she screamed into the storm. "I love you. Every single cell that makes you the man you are, every bone, muscle, and tissue, I love. I love your stubbornness, your determined will, and your faithfulness. And I am beyond thankful I've had the privilege of being loved by you even for such a short time."

"PERI! Don't you let her do this!" Heather suddenly shouted. "By the stars, I will kill you myself if you let her do what I think she is going to do!"

"PLEASE, JEWEL!" Anna joined in, her voice every bit as loud as the others. "Don't leave us!"

"BREAK THE DAMN CIRCLE, PERIZADA," Stella screamed.

Jewel couldn't look at them. She couldn't take her eyes away from Dalton. "I will be with you always," she said as she poised the sharp dagger at her chest. "Take care of my sisters, Dalton. If you love me, you will protect them with your life." It was a jackass move, but it was the only thing she knew to do to keep Dalton from taking his own life once everything was said and done. She pulled the dagger back, and after hesitating for the briefest of moments, Jewel plunged it through her chest, aiming for the space between her ribs that would leave her heart unprotected.

The blade slid in effortlessly.

She heard the gasps and cries of the others, but one voice rose above the others. It was the cry of a man who had just lost any reason to live, and it hurt Jewel worse than the blade she'd just plunged into her chest. Dalton's voice was the last thing she heard as the world went dark. It was the last thing she wanted to hear, but not like that.

DALTON COULDN'T STOP SCREAMING. His mate lay lifeless on the wet ground with a fae blade sticking out of her chest, and he couldn't move to get to her. He couldn't save her. He couldn't hold her. All he could do was stand there, frozen by fae magic, watching the woman who held every part of his soul die right before his eyes.

Suddenly, his knees hit the ground and he fell forward, his hands barely catching himself before he face-planted onto the ground. Dalton breathed in great heaves as he processed what had just happened. He could move. Without another thought, he scrambled across the forest floor, pushing aside two of the females who'd reached Jewel before him. He took Jewel's still form into his arms.

"Little Dove." He growled as he shook her, even though he knew he wouldn't get an answer. "No, no, no, no," said Dalton over and over as he buried his face in her hair and fell to the ground in a heap. Everything around him disappeared, and all he could hear was his mate's voice in his mind. All he could smell was her scent as it washed over him. All he could feel was her cooling body against his own. Dalton could feel his wolf pushing against him, begging to get closer to their mate, needing to feel her against his fur, but Dalton couldn't release Jewel from his arms, not even for his wolf.

The wolf in him snarled and then forced the man to throw his head back and release a howl that any supernatural within fifty miles would hear. It was a howl that spoke of pain, loss, terror, and grief on a level Dalton had never felt before. It was a howl he didn't even know how to stop. He feared if he did stop, he would destroy anyone near him. So, he just howled as he held his mate and hoped someone would kill him next and put him out of his misery.

"Peri! Stop!" Lucian snarled as Peri reached to take Jewel away from Dalton. She needed to do something. She had to fix this.

"Not again," Peri muttered. "Not bloody again!" Firm hands wrapped around her waist and pulled her back before she could touch the girl's body.

"You can't touch her, mate," Lucian whispered harshly in her ear. "He will kill anyone who tries to take her. You know this."

"This can't be happening, Lucian. This wasn't supposed to happen. HOW THE HELL DID THIS HAPPEN?" Her voice pierced the air as her hands fisted, and she threw her head back against her mate's shoulder. Peri wanted to hit something. She wanted to rage against everything and curse the world.

"Hit me, my beloved. Take it out on me," Lucian said softly into her mind.

But Peri shook her head. "It wasn't supposed to end like this," she said.

21

"For a genius, Jewel does some really stupid things ... like sacrificing herself when I've specifically told her not to." ~Peri

Waves of peaceful thoughts came to Peri through the bond. *"You must be strong now, my love. For Jewel."* Peri knew he was right, but how could she go on?

"You do not honor Jewel's sacrifice by mourning her now," said Lucian. "The healer will be celebrated, but only if we defeat Volcan. Otherwise, her sacrifice was in vain."

Peri nodded, drawing in a huge breath to calm her trembling body. "I'll see you again, Jewel Stone. And when I do, I'm going to slap you so hard..." she whispered.

"Take her back to my house, Dalton," said Peri. "We cannot wait or we risk the draheim veil closing again. We have to move against Volcan now. I am so sorry for your loss. We will mourn Jewel properly after."

The large man said nothing. He simply lifted Jewel's body like it was an overstuffed pillow and began running back toward Peri's home. He was met by the other wolves and fae as they approached. They tried to hail him. He simply snarled and ran past them.

"Peri, what happened?" asked Crina.

"Jewel sacrificed herself."

"Oh my god," gasped Elle.

"What do we do now?" asked Adam.

"We stick to the plan," Peri replied. "We have to attack Volcan now."

"How can you be so callous?" asked Kara through a rush of tears. "We can't go on without Jewel."

Peri looked around, steeling herself. There was shock on every face. "I hate to use a cliché at a time like this," she replied. "But it's what Jewel would have wanted us to do. She sacrificed herself so that we might defeat Volcan. We cannot hesitate." There was a murmur of agreement from the others.

"But what do we tell Volcan?" asked Stella. "He's expecting five healers, not four."

"Tell him Jewel attacked me and I killed her. The rest of you were only able to escape during the chaos. Tell him we're on our way but in no position to fight," Peri replied.

"Will he believe that?" asked Anna.

"He'll have to," said Peri. "Good luck, girls. It's all up to you, now."

The high fae watched as the four healers stepped away from the group and embraced their new mates. She could only imagine the conversations going on in their bonds. The wolves weren't happy to let their mates return to Volcan, but it had to be done. A few moments later, the girls joined hands and disappeared as one, flashing to the entrance of the draheim veil. It was no surprise to Peri that the four men immediately transformed to wolf form. They raised their snouts and released a unified howl. It wasn't a mournful sound. It was frightening, a howl to signify the start of a hunt. They came back to the group, hackles raised.

Peri turned to the others. "The rest of you, sharpen your blades and your fangs. We leave in five minutes."

She stepped up to Thad. "Noble djinn, we thank you for your help, but I think you've done all you can do."

"I agree, Perizada of the fae. I wish you luck. I hope I will soon record your greatest victory. If not, I will write that you died honorably, fighting for those you loved."

"Just make sure it says I was having a good hair day."

VOLCAN FELL to his knees and clutched his chest. He felt as if a piece of him had been ripped away. Jewel was gone. He wasn't sure what had happened, but her spirit was gone. Seconds later, he watched the four women rush through the veil, like the hounds of hell were on the heels. *Four. So his queen was* truly *gone?* They ran stumbling up the hill toward him. He rose to his feet.

"Where is Jewel?" he asked them.

"Peri killed her," said Anna. "She attacked Peri again, and the fae got the best of her. She didn't want to kill Jewel, but she couldn't defeat her otherwise. We only escaped because the others were distracted."

The dark fae screamed. "No! It can't be! My queen is twice as strong as that damn fae. Why didn't you help her?"

"We were going to," said Stella, "but there were too many. We would not throw our lives away needlessly. We thought you'd have more use for us here."

Volcan growled. "Good thinking, gypsies. I do. But I'm

going to peel Peri's skin from her body," Volcan spat out. "Let's go!"

"No need," said Kara. "They chased us. I'm sure they'll be here any second."

"Then ready yourselves for battle. Even though Jewel is gone, her power is still my power. I will show Peri just how strong I am."

"THE TIME HAS COME," said Peri. "I don't know what awaits on the other side of the veil, but I'm sure it won't be pretty. Fight for everything you hold dear. Fight for Jewel. Let her sacrifice not be in vain."

As one, Peri's army, consisting of nine wolves—four of them weary and beleaguered from the In Between—two fae, and a pixie stepped through the shimmering veil into the draheim realm.

～

AS SOON AS she stepped through the portal, Peri had about half a second before a burst of fire engulfed her and her comrades. She threw up a shield and blocked the blast of flame released by the giant draheim swooping down on them. She held it in place as another dragon, twin to the first, passed over.

"Scatter," Peri yelled, and the wolves and fae broke apart, moving in every direction.

The two minutes of warning the healers had given Volcan had been enough time to prepare his forces and take her by surprise. Peri saw the four healers standing around Volcan, who was pointing at her and shouting. She couldn't tell from this distance what the girls might be feeling. Of course, they'd seen some terrible things since they've been introduced to the supernatural world, but they'd never seen a full-blown battle before. Peri hoped their resolve would hold.

A large group of women came barreling down the hill toward Peri, shooting fireballs as they came. Apparently, Volcan had made more witches apart from her healers. Peri hated that the women had been subjected to that, but there was nothing she could do. She didn't see how she'd be able to spare any of them. The wolves met them head on, and the battle was joined. "Adam, Elle, hang back," said Peri. We'll need to deal with the draheim."

"Sly, is your mate here?"

"There," said Sly pointing to dark-haired woman wearing a red tunic and leading the enemy's charge. He ran to her, yelling her name. "Evanora!" The woman didn't seem to acknowledge she knew him. Z followed after him.

"Don't kill the one in red," Peri shouted, though she wasn't sure anyone heard her. She didn't have time to notice what happened between Sly and his mate as the draheim swung around for another attack.

They seemed to be focused on her alone. That was a good thing, as she and the other fae were the most equipped to handle them.

"Adira, you're with us, too," shouted Peri. Truth be told, she hadn't given much thought to how she'd take down the giant beasts. She'd had too many other things on her mind to plan that far ahead. Now, she knew how foolish that had been.

"There!" She pointed to a high hill opposite the one on which Volcan was standing. She, Elle, Adira, and Adam flashed to the top. The shadow of the dragons were above her, and she threw up another shield, again blocking two blasts of flames from the beasts. From the top of the hill, she could see the battle more clearly. Peri wasn't encouraged by what she saw. Some of the wolves—probably Nick, Gustavo, Ciro, and Kale, she couldn't tell with any certainty—had managed to take down a couple of witches. The others—most likely those who'd survived the In-Between—were being beaten back. She couldn't make out the warlocks amongst the chaos, but she knew they'd probably be close to Evanora.

"Adira, see if you can draw the dragons in close. But be careful. They're faster than they look."

"You got it, boss," said the pixie before she leaped into the sky.

"Elle and Adam, time to bust out your best trapeze moves. I'll toss you up. See if you can land on the backs of their necks. Adam, take the first one. Elle, the second."

They both nodded. "Easy, peasy," said Adam.

Peri watched as the pixie zoomed in front of the first draheim. Adira drew a small sword and charged right toward the beast. It opened its huge jaws, and Peri thought for a moment Adira would simply be swallowed whole. But at the last possible second, the pixie swerved upward and drove her sword directly in between the draheim's eyes, which probably felt like nothing more than a thorn to the monster. Still, the pixie had done her job. The draheim roared at Adira as she released the sword and sped away. The dragon gave chase, and Adira led it right back to where Peri and the others were standing. The second dragon followed his partner's lead.

"Here we go," said Peri.

Adira zoomed past. A second later, Peri threw out her hand and issued forth a great blast of wind. Adam and Elle jumped. The gale caught them up, and they directed their bodies toward the oncoming beasts. Adam somersaulted and landed on the back of the thing's neck. With an *oomph*, he hit with his legs splayed on either side of the monster's neck. The fae grimaced in pain but held on.

Elle wasn't quite so lucky. She hit the side of the second dragon's back and almost bounced off. She was just able to get a fingertip grip on one of the scales, hanging on for dear life as the creature slipped and spun through the air. The fae reached to her waist and drew her fae blade, recently returned to her from Jewel's lifeless body. Elle shook away the thought as she plunged it into the side of the draheim's body. She used it as a handgrip and hoisted herself onto the beast's back. The monster roared in agony as she yanked the blade free and began scrambling up toward the draheim's neck. She could see Adam up ahead of her. He'd managed to stab his own mount a couple of times, but the thing was now flying inverted, hoping to shake Adam off. Now Adam had to use both hands to hang upside down and keep from falling. Apparently, her own dragon thought this was a good technique because it, too, flipped over and tried to shake Elle free.

Peri watched from the ground as her two friends vaulted into the air and landed on the dragons. She didn't know how successful they'd be at taking down the beasts, but at least they'd keep the draheim from attacking the wolves. Now, it was time for Peri to do what she came to do—kill Volcan. She was just about to flash to the other hill where Volcan stood when she saw something out of the corner of her eye. A small shape was moving away from where the healers stood. She recognized Ciesel. "Adira," she yelled and pointed to Ciesel's retreating form. "Catch that pixie."

"On it," came the reply.

Again, Peri was about to flash when something else caught her attention. It was the bright red tunic of Evanora. She was fighting tooth and nail with Sly and Z. They were trying not to hurt her. She had no such reservations. "Dammit," cursed Peri. She ran to where they fought. With a few muttered words, Peri held up her hands and shot a couple of shimmering lengths of rope from each of them, quickly binding the new witch. The woman cursed and thrashed, but the magical bonds held. "Get her somewhere safe," Peri commanded, then growled in frustration. She needed to get to where the healers stood with Volcan, but she didn't want to leave the rest of the wolves to fight the witches alone.

"We've got this," came Lucian's reply through their bond. Apparently, he'd picked up on her thought. *"Go!"*

She went, flashing to the top of the hill. Just as she appeared, she heard Volcan scream. "Now!" As one, the healers attacked.

HEATHER FOUGHT the urge to go to Kale. She could feel his every thought through the bond as he fought the witches at the bottom of the hill. She almost gasped every time he took a hit. But she knew she had to remain quiet or Volcan would know that he no longer controlled her. Peri had told them to wait until she appeared to strike. The timing had to be perfect. Heather would stand close to Stella and try to lend her strength, but they had all agreed she wouldn't try any aggressive magic. In Peri's words, "the last thing we need is

Hellen Keller tossing fireballs around the battlefield at anything she hears or smells."

Volcan was giving a running commentary on how the battle was progressing. He seemed to be quite pleased. Much as Peri had instructed, he'd told them to hold their positions until Peri appeared. Then, they were to each attack her with all their might. Volcan hadn't given any specific instructions to Heather. Apparently, he trusted her sense of direction, or he simply didn't care what she hit.

"Get ready," he said. "Peri will be here any second." Heather tensed. She wasn't sure she could do this. But she had to. She had to do it for her sisters. She had to do it for her new mate.

He was right. A few seconds later, Peri appeared.

"Now," Volcan yelled. Anna, Stella, and Kara raised their hands and sent out three bolts of pure energy. Heather lent her strength to Stella, and her sister's bolt of power was so strong that she could feel it roll over her.

THE MAGIC never made it to Peri, however. Volcan's eyes widened as all three bolts struck him in the back. He fell forward and landed on his hands and knees. Peri, too, extended a hand and shot a bolt of light at the evil fae. Quickly Volcan raised a hand and blocked Peri's attack, which bounced away harmlessly. Then, Volcan did something none of them expected, especially Peri. He began to chuckle. Peri watched as he rose to his feet.

"Again," said Stella. And the healers shot another bolt of power at the dark fae.

He didn't even try to block them this time. The bolts struck him and rebounded into the dirt. Volcan laughed louder. "Ah, yes," he said. "The surprising but inevitable betrayal. Pathetic, Peri, even for you."

Peri shot another shining orb of power at the fae, but again, Volcan batted it away harmlessly.

"You've always thought much too highly of yourself, Perizada. Do you think I didn't see this coming?"

Peri didn't respond. She just clenched her fists.

"I take it the bad guy isn't writhing on the ground in agony now," Peri heard Heather whisper to Stella.

"Far from it. He looks stronger than ever."

"How are you doing this?" asked Anna.

"How? Easy enough, my little plaything. I created you all. The creator controls the creation. You girls don't do anything without Daddy knowing it. I know you cast your little spell that turned you good, and I know all about your sacrifices. It doesn't matter. I can undo that damage. And I will always be stronger than you. Have you forgotten I have the blood of the original witch-healer flowing through my veins? Jewel's blood flows within me. You can never match her strength."

"Jewel's dead," said Kara.

Volcan cocked his head. "*That* is a mystery even I don't understand."

"What are you talking about?" asked Peri.

"The healer is not dead. I'm not sure what she has done, but her power still courses within me."

"That can't be," said Peri. "I watched her die."

"Still," said Volcan, "she must still be alive. Or I wouldn't be able to do this." He waved a hand, and all four of the healers fell to their knees. They gasped and squealed, trying to get up, but none of them could move. Volcan kept them pinned to the ground as easily as if they were newborn puppies.

"Let them up," said Peri. She took a step forward. Volcan extended a hand, and Peri bounced backward as if she'd hit an invisible brick wall.

"Or what, Perizada? What are you going to do?"

"I'm going to kill you," she ground out.

"You're going to kneel, just like they are," said Volcan.

Peri snorted. In the blink of an eye, Volcan grabbed the closest healer, Kara, and yanked her to her feet. He snatched a dagger from his belt and held the tip to Kara's throat. "Kneel, Peri, or watch this girl bleed."

Peri exhaled. "I'm going to kill you," she said again. But she knelt.

~

DALTON'S HANDS shook as he took Jewel's still face in them. His lips trembled as he leaned down and pressed them to her still-warm mouth. He felt the sob well up in him as he pressed himself closer. As he sat in Peri's home with his dead mate in his arms, he didn't care if the whole world burned down around him. All he cared about was that his Jewel, his Little Dove, was gone. Her body was an empty shell that used to hold the woman who had captivated him, heart and soul.

"Please open your eyes," he whispered, his forehead touching hers. His wolf was whining, needing to be close to her, unable to accept that she was really gone. "Please, my love, please don't leave me."

She didn't move. Her chest didn't rise and fall. Her lips didn't turn up in the shy smile he'd grown to adore. Her hand didn't reach for him and her body didn't curl into his as he wrapped her closer to him.

His shoulders rocked as he wept. With every tear that

fell he felt a piece of himself dying. As he sat there on the floor holding her, feeling the heat seep away from her, he felt himself slipping further from the world of reality. He wanted no part of this life without his Jewel.

He shook harder, and when his wolf could no longer be contained, Dalton threw back his head and howled. The mournful sound would no doubt be heard even beyond the walls of the house and for miles and miles as he poured every ounce of grief into the sound.

As the sound died down, he looked back at his mate. "It wasn't supposed to end like this, Jewel," he told her. "We were supposed to have decades and decades and longer together. I was supposed to drive you crazy with my constant brooding, and you were supposed to bring light and playfulness to my dim existence. We were supposed to be a team up until the very end. This isn't right. This isn't how true mates end up. We are together, always. I'm not supposed to be left here without you." Dalton thought back to life before Jewel, and he knew he wouldn't be able to go back to that existence. He wouldn't be able to live without her.

"Dalton, Beta of the Colorado pack and beloved wolf." The voice was joined with a warm light filling the high fae's living room.

Dalton looked up and saw the Great Luna standing a few feet away. She had tears running down her cheeks as she stared down at Jewel's lifeless body. "You both have sacrificed much," the goddess said. Her voice was full of understanding, as if the same pain Dalton felt was hers as well.

"Why?" he asked. "Why did it have to end this way?"

"Jewel has been faithful. Even though the darkness that has been living inside of her has been fighting for dominion, she has fought back. She knew it would take a great sacrifice to stand against great evil, but even now, it is not enough. Jewel, even with the goodness that lived in her, cannot be the final sacrifice for all. She cannot cover the taint of all those with Volcan's evil in them."

"So, they will fail?" Dalton asked. "She died for nothing?"

The Great Luna shook her head slowly, and her eyes met his. "There is one who is pure. There is one who has no evil because evil cannot live inside of holiness. I can be the sacrifice that will cover it all. The shedding of my blood will wipe out the blackness that has begun to take hold in the healers and those Volcan has turned."

Dalton's mouth dropped open. "You? But, you're ... you're the Great Luna."

"I created you, Dalton. I created my wolves and my healers, and I will never forsake you. For such a time has come that my creations sacrifices are not enough. I will stand in the place of the healers, in place of Jewel."

Then she knelt down beside Jewel and placed a hand on her forehead. "Jewel Stone, my precious one, rise up. Your sacrifice has been rewarded. Rise, child of mine, and join your mate. Stand beside him as we face evil and defeat it."

Dalton stared at Jewel, waiting. He wasn't even breathing, afraid that if he made any movement, he'd somehow screw up what the goddess was doing. Several heartbeats later, Jewel's eyes blinked open.

She gasped in a breath of air as she looked from him to the Great Luna.

"Jewel," Dalton rasped as he tenderly held her.

The goddess placed a hand over each of their hearts and said, "I am restoring the bond that was taken from you. This is my blessing to you for choosing to love one another despite the fact that the supernatural bond that joined you was gone. You are one. I have joined you and nothing can separate you."

She stood and helped Dalton pull Jewel to her feet. Dalton watched in awe as the skin over Jewel's heart knit back together leaving only a thin scar. Then her clothes were replaced by new ones.

Dalton turned to the goddess and fell to his knees. He bowed his head and held his hands up to her. "I can never thank you enough. Your sacrifice will never be forgotten."

JEWEL STOOD in awe of the Great Luna as she touched Dalton's shoulder and closed her eyes. She didn't know what the goddess was doing, but when Dalton stood, there was peace in his eyes that Jewel hadn't ever seen.

"Time is of the essence," the goddess said. "Take my hand. We will arrive in the draheim realm. Dalton, take your wolf form and carry Jewel on your back. I will deal with Volcan. You will be my witnesses. Darkness will not prevail."

FROM THE MOMENT Jewel took the goddess's hand, it was only a second later that they were in the draheim realm. Jewel's eyes widened as she saw what was arrayed before her.

Women she didn't recognize and a host of wolves lay strewn about the battlefield. Two draheim lay dead on their sides. Adam and Elle were close by, both struggling to get to their feet. Peri, Anna, Stella, and Heather knelt before Volcan. He held Kara from behind, a knife at the girl's throat.

She felt a nudge on her hip and turned to find Dalton's

wolf staring at her. He rubbed up against her. *"Climb on, Little Dove."*

"I love you," she said in response, unable to hold it in any longer.

"I love you more."

Jewel wiped a tear away as she climbed up onto his back. They bounded across the field and up the hill. She leaped off of Dalton's back and screamed at Volcan. "Stop!" She wasn't sure what to do next. Should she threaten him, beg him, bargain with him? She just knew she couldn't let him kill her friends.

"Ah, look, my queen. I knew you weren't dead." Volcan indicated Peri kneeling before him. "This whelp of a fae could never take down my Jewel." There was a ferocious growl and Dalton leaped at the fae, his fangs dripping and his eyes red with malice. Volcan merely extended a hand and Dalton fell to the ground, frozen, much as Peri had done in Jezebel's shop weeks ago.

"Join me, Jewel," said Volcan, indicating that she should come to his side.

"Never," she hissed.

"Come to me now, or I'll cut this little healer's throat out and feed the rest of her to Morfran." He pushed the tip of the dagger a little way into Kara's neck to prove his point. A trickle of blood began to run down onto her collarbone.

"Okay." Jewel held up her hands. "Whatever you want. Just let my friends go."

"No, Jewel! Don't!" All of the healers began speaking at once.

"I must," said Jewel. She took a step toward Volcan.

"Jewel, stop." The voice was almost a whisper, but it froze Jewel in her tracks. It was Peri, speaking from where she knelt on the ground.

"I would advise you to keep your mouth shut, Perizada," Volcan spat out at her.

"I would advise you to run as fast and as far as you possibly can," the fae replied. "Go to the dark forest and hide. Seal yourself back in. Do that, and you will live a little longer. Otherwise, you'll be dead in a few minutes."

Volcan laughed, a high-pitched sound.

All of a sudden, there was a loud clap of thunder, and everyone's heads turned. A woman appeared at the base of the hill.

"Told you," said Peri softly.

The woman began walking slowly toward them. As she came closer, several of the watchers gasped. The Great Luna, no longer clad in a white gown but now wearing a plain, brown tunic, approached. Volcan's eyes widened as the goddess headed straight for him, bearing no weapon or threatening stance.

Volcan lowered the dagger and faced the Great Luna. "My power has grown so great that even a goddess realizes she is no match for me!" Volcan's voice boomed over the open field.

Everyone on the field froze as they realized there was a goddess in their midst and she was walking toward the enemy, but she looked completely human. All the glory she usually carried was gone. She appeared as any other woman, except for the compassion that filled her eyes, even as she gazed at Volcan.

"Volcan, I will stand in the place of the healers. My power is beyond anything they will ever have. My blood is yours. You need not seek to have theirs any longer."

Volcan's eyes widened. "You're giving me your blood? How much?" His words were greedy, and the look in his eyes even more so.

"All of it," the Great Luna said clearly. She turned and faced the field and then knelt. Volcan walked around her and taunted her.

"Some goddess you are. The great and powerful is now kneeling at my feet. Your blood will join with my own, and I will be untouchable." He slashed a blade across his palm and then quick as lightening he plunged the same blade into the heart of the Great Luna.

Jewel's stomach clenched as she watched the powerful goddess take the blow that she didn't deserve.

As soon as her blood began to flow, Volcan pressed his cut hand to her chest so her blood would flow into him. The wind began to pick up, and lightning streaked across the sky that had been silent. Thunder clapped and boomed, and Jewel's voice wasn't the only one that rang out as she screamed, "NO!"

The Great Luna's eyes ran over each of them as the wind picked up as if all of nature was outraged at what was unfolding. Volcan threw back his head and laughed, but Jewel was too focused on the goddess to be concerned with the lunatic fae.

Within minutes the storm stilled and the Great Luna spoke. Her voice filled every empty place of the field. "It is finished." Her head fell forward, and her body collapsed to the earth.

Everyone fell to their knees. Jewel felt the darkness inside of her gathering, the taint that Volcan had put inside of her pooling into one place. Her focus was lost as she heard Volcan's maniacal laughter.

Jewel opened her eyes and looked at the high fae who had allowed his own need for power to fully corrupt him. He looked gleeful, but that only lasted for a minute. Then the laughter stopped and his eyes widened.

"What's, what..." he stuttered. "What's happening? What!" He roared and his arms flung out to his sides, his back bowed, and his chin pointed up to the sky. Suddenly light shot out from his body, his arms, hands, legs, everywhere. It just radiated off of him. It grew more and more powerful until finally the ground shook and the light fractured, right along with Volcan himself.

Jewel felt herself fall forward, and when she rose up again, the light was dissipating, and it was no longer so bright she couldn't see. Volcan was gone, and in his place, the Great Luna stood in all her glory. Her white gown shone like the sun, and love radiated off of her.

"My blood has been shed to cover the darkness that lives inside of you," the Great Luna said. "As long as you live in this world, there will be evil and it will tempt you. But I have shed my blood to cover your darkness. Only my light can destroy darkness and evil. The light lives in each of you, if you so choose to accept it. There will be more battles to come. There will be more evil to stand against. Some will be external battles, and some you will fight within your own flesh. Through them all, I am with you.

"Go now and rest for a time. Strengthen your bonds, your packs, and yourselves because soon you all will need to join together across the world to stand as one. My beloved children, I will be with you always."

When she was gone Jewel climbed to her feet with the help of Dalton, who'd phased back to his human form. Thanks to one of the fae, he was at least wearing pants, as were all the other men who'd phased back into their human forms.

"JEWEL," Kara bellowed from across the field and came barreling toward her. The other healers followed, and Peri snagged Heather's hand, dragging her along as she headed for Jewel. Dalton got behind her and placed his hands on her hips, as if he felt like he needed to brace her for impact and maybe he did.

Arms wrapped around her and bodies crashed into her, causing her to be pressed into Dalton's stomach and chest. Jewel felt tears sliding down her cheeks as she held onto the girls who'd become family to her.

"Not to take away from this kick-ass moment," Heather's voice broke through the tears. "But to recap things, Jewel's alive, Volcan killed the Great Luna and then was obliterated, and then said killed goddess came back to life and destroyed the hold Volcan had over us, and boom, here we are? Kale was trying to keep me filled in on things, but it was difficult to hear him at times."

"It sounds so simple and anticlimactic when you put it like that," Stella said. "It really was much more impressive than just 'boom here we are'."

"Of that, I've no doubt," Heather said. "I'm just glad it ended with 'boom here we are', rather than 'damn, there we went'."

Jewel laughed and felt Dalton's arms tighten on her. She was laughing. She was alive and so were all of those that she loved. They'd won. They'd defeated Volcan because of the Great Luna and her love for her creation.

The End

EPILOGUE

"Yes, it was worth it."
~Heather

The battle was done. The enemy, or at least one of them, was defeated. And though there was much to be thankful for, the losses we suffered were painful. Tonight, only hours after Volcan was defeated, we lay Bannan's body to rest.

"I figured you all didn't have anything to wear for such an occasion," Peri said as she flashed into the room. She was holding an armful of black garments.

Jewel walked over and grabbed one for herself and one for Heather. "Here, Heather," she said, touching the blind healer's hand and placing the material against it. "It's a black dress."

"Thank you, Peri," Heather said as she raised the dress in both hands.

"It just slips over your head," Peri told her.

They each dressed in silence and Peri waited, her eyes glassy and staring off into space. It was the most subdued Jewel had ever seen the high fae.

"I think we're ready," Jewel said as she looked at each of her sister healers. They all nodded.

Peri held out her arms. "I don't feel like walking any more than I have to. Touch some skin I'll flash us to the location."

They did as she asked and, in the blink of an eye they were on a beach. It was dark. The night sky was filled with a thousand stars, and the ocean breeze blew warmly across Jewel's face.

Dalton was by her side a minute later. He wrapped an arm around her waist. "You look lovely, Little Dove," he said, his deep voice a gentle caress against her frazzled nerves. Neither of them had wanted to be separated from each other for even a second, but Jewel had needed a few minutes with her friends, who she now considered sisters.

"I missed you," she told him as she looked up into his eyes.

Dalton leaned down and pressed his lips tenderly to hers. "I could feel that through the bond," he said, concern marring his handsome face. "I would have come to you. But I wanted to respect your desire to spend some time with the other girls."

"Thank you," she said. "I know it was hard for you to be away from me as well."

"And now that we are together, forgive me if I don't release you for even a second." He ran the back of his fingers across her cheek, staring at her so reverently Jewel had to remind herself to breathe.

"I won't be leaving your side, so no worries," she replied shamelessly.

"If everyone could please join me and my mate." Kale's voice filled the dark night.

Jewel and her mate headed toward the couple, who were standing beside the still body of Bannan. The former pack member lay on a funeral pyre ready to be sent off into the ocean.

KALE'S tightly controlled emotions began to unravel. His heart was heavy as he looked down at his fallen packmate. Their alpha had already called to verify what he'd felt in the pack bonds when Bannan had died. The pack would be morning right along with Kale, Heather, and the group of people who had come to mean so very much to him.

Once every one had created a half circle around the pyre, Kale looked at each of the members of their unconventional pack. Thad stood next to Jezebel with his arm wrapped tightly around her. Next to them, Elle and Sorin, as well as Adam and Crina, stood hand in hand. Peri and Lucian held the next spot and then the healers were lined one after the other with their mates standing behind each of them, their arms wrapped tightly around the girls' waists. The unmated males came after the mated ones and each stood proud as they met Kale's gaze and bowed their heads briefly to him, in respect for his fallen packmate. The only ones not present were Z, Sly, Evanora, and Adira. The warlocks had felt it was important that they get Evanora home to begin to heal. Adira had expressed her condolences and then told them that she'd had all she could handle of other people for quite a while. But she'd told Peri if the fae needed her help, Peri need only call. Heather stood beside him holding his hand tightly, letting him know she would help comfort him through the pain. She wouldn't leave his side.

"Not going anywhere, my mate," she whispered through the bond. "I love you and I'm so sorry for your loss, for the loss to all of the Canis lupus by the death of Bannan."

"Thank you, my beloved mate," he said softly and mentally caressed her face.

"Thank you for coming to honor the life of Bannan McNair, third to the Irish Pack, friend and loyal protector," Kale said, raising his voice above the ocean waves rolling in. "His time in this life is over. Now, he will travel on to be with the Great Luna. He will be rewarded for the selfless life he has led. Tonight, we light a fire and add our light to his pyre so he can be sent out into the ocean burning as bright in death as he did in life."

Kale stepped forward and took a match from a match box, lit it, and dropped it into the straw that made up the pyre. Heather took the matches and did the same and then one by one each of them lit a match and added it to the pyre. The fae didn't need the matches, the simply used their magic to add their own fire. When it was finished, the males stepped forward and helped Kale push the pyre and Bannan out into the ocean.

The fire blazed bright and Kale threw his head back and howled, sending his friend off with the battle cry of his wolf, and the other wolves joined with him. Peri, Elle, and Adam all three lifted their hands and balls of light shot from their palms straight for Bannan and the glow magnified.

"Rest easy my friend," Kales whispered. "You did well in this life."

∼

For a matter of days I, who have been blind from the day I was born, had been able to see. I witnessed the incredible beauty of nature, the joy of a smile on the face of people I cared for, and the colors that have been described to me my whole life, but I've never truly understood. I saw the man I loved, I saw myself, and I saw the differences in humans that many choose to curse instead of celebrate. What an incredible gift I was given, even if it was just for a short time.

I gave that gift up because I didn't want to be a wicked witch, and I didn't want my friends to be, either. I'd rather be blind than allow evil to rule, no matter the promises of power that were given to us. I'd rather be blind and know that light exists than to have sight and live filled with darkness.

Besides, I don't really need to see. I have a wolf-mate and his sight works just fine. He sees what I cannot. And I see, in my own way, what he cannot. We're a pretty great team. In fact, I offered to put him through my seeing-eye dog training program, but I'm pretty sure his answer was "no thank you." Or at least that's how I interpreted his very rumbly growl.

~

"How mad are you?" Kara asked Nick as they sat on Peri's back porch. Two days had passed since Volcan was obliterated, Jewel had died and come back to life, the Great Luna had shed her blood to save them, and Bannan had been sent off for his time in eternity. They'd all slept for nearly a day and a half and now were taking some time to process everything that had happened.

"You mean about the whole giving up children thing?"
She nodded.
"Children are never a guaranteed outcome in a relation-

ship, Kara," he said as he took her hand in his. "Would I have loved to have had children with you? Yes. But if giving up children means I get to keep you, then I'm more than okay with that."

"Thank you," she said softly.

"Hey." He placed a finger under her chin, raising her face so he could look her in her eyes. "I'm excited about our future, babe. Kids or not, I am in awe of you as my mate. Don't buy into that lie that we have to have kids to be a real family. We're already a family. And we always have the option of adoption. That would be a wonderful way to bring a child into our lives. That would make me just as happy as if we'd had a biological child. Okay?"

Kara nodded. "Okay."

Nick leaned down and pressed his lips to hers. "Very soon we will be bound and married and with our pack, which is the rest of our family. We will face everything together, side by side."

"I love you," Kara told him.

"It's a good thing or it might get really awkward if I was following you everywhere and trying to sleep in your bed."

She laughed. "Awkward is putting it lightly."

"I love you too, baby."

~

"ARE YOU ALRIGHT WITH YOUR DECISION?" Gustavo asked Anna. When he'd sat down on the couch, he'd pulled her into his lap and began running his fingertips up and down her arm. She loved his touch and craved it.

She nodded. "I am. I'm sad, but it was the right sacrifice and I knew it the moment it came to me."

Gustavo pressed a kiss to her forehead. "I know that wasn't easy for you."

"Sacrifices aren't supposed to be easy. If they were, then they wouldn't be sacrifices."

"Very true," Gustavo said with a small smile.

"So what's next?" Anna asked as she laid her head on his shoulder. She took a deep breath and let his scent fill her.

He tilted his head so she could get closer and then nuzzled her back. "Next we go home and see what's happening with our pack and the other packs in the world."

"Home to Spain?"

"Yes. I can't wait to show you my country and introduce you to our pack. They are going to love you," he said, his voice filled with pride as he spoke of his home.

"It will be your home as well, mi amor," he told her, having picked up on her thoughts.

"I'm excited, too," Anna admitted. "I've been stuck in the same town all my life, and now the whole world has been opened to me. I've been alone and, honestly, a little lost. And any place you are, that is where my home is."

"You're not lost anymore. I've found you and I'm not letting you go. You are my world, my sweet Anna. You hold not only the other half of my soul, you also hold my whole heart."

She looked up into his eyes and smiled. "Same," she said, pointing at herself. Then she reached up and cupped his face with her hand. She ran her thumb across his lips, leaned up, and quickly nipped them. "Then take me home, mate. Let's start our life together."

∾

STELLA WAS WRAPPED in Ciro's arms as they stared up at the

moon through the window in the room they were sharing. All the males insisted on sleeping in the same room as their mates, which the girls found hilarious because they were still sleeping on the floor, just not out in a hallway anymore.

"We can stay with one of the other healers if that would make you more comfortable," Ciro said. "I don't want to rush you."

Stella turned to look up at him. "You're not rushing me, Ciro, and I'm ready. I'm not going to let my past keep me from having an amazing present and future. I'm ready to be with you, to be your mate, and to go with you to your pack."

Ciro pressed his lips to her forehead. "You have no idea how much that means to me. You are so incredibly strong, and I am honored to be your mate."

"I'm pretty fond of you myself," she teased. "I am looking forward to getting to spend time with you that maybe doesn't include us fighting off evil or chasing bad guys, at least for a little while."

"I could do with some uninterrupted mate time as well," he agreed. "I will show you my home, and I hope you will love it as much as I do."

"As long as you're there, I know I will love it."

∼

THERE WAS a knock on the door of the bedroom Dalton was sharing with his mate. He pulled it open and reached out his hand to shake Lucian's. Peri stood next to him, and smiled at Dalton.

"We are honored you would ask this of us," Lucian said as they stepped inside.

"Even you?" Dalton asked the high fae. They'd had some pretty tense moments over the past months.

"I've never disliked you, Dalton," Peri told him. "I did what was necessary at the time for the safety and wellbeing of our pack. I would have done it to anyone else that had been in your shoes. Please don't take it personally. I am very happy for you and Jewel and as my mate said, honored you would ask us to be here for you both." She looked around the room. "Speak of your other half, where is she?"

"She's in the bathroom. She doesn't know I planned this."

Peri chuckled. "It's going to suck if she tells you to go pound sand."

Dalton felt a twinge of fear at the thought of his mate denying him.

"Oh man, the look on your face is bad enough to make me want to shoot myself. I was teasing, wolf. She adores you. You have nothing to worry about." Peri reached into her pocket and pulled out something. She held out her hand to him and opened the closed fist. There on her palm was a beautiful golden ring.

"Whoa," Dalton said slowly.

"I figured you hadn't exactly had time to go out and get one, considering what we've been dealing with, the killing and dying and anguish and what not. So I made one for your healer."

"Peri, it's beautiful and I am so honored. Thank you," Dalton said and meant every word. The ring held a stone in the center of a type he didn't recognize. "What is this?" He pointed to it.

"It's a piece of the moonstone."

"The moonstone as in one of the fae stones?" he asked, his eyes going wide.

"The one and only. I told Lucian I wanted to make a ring for Jewel and the moonstone suddenly appeared in my hand. I took that as a pretty big sign I was supposed to take a piece of it. My interpretation is that the Great Luna is very pleased with this union and she is showing her blessing to you. It's a good sign."

"Is everything okay?" Jewel's voice caused Dalton to clamp his fist closed. He put it behind his back as he turned to face his mate.

"Everything is great, Little Dove."

"Hey Peri, Lucian," Jewel said as she stepped up beside Dalton. "What's up?"

Lucian and Peri both smiled. "We have been asked by your mate, to be here," said Lucian. "I think everything will be very clear in a moment."

Jewel's brow drew down as she looked up at Dalton. He dropped to one knee as he held her stare. "Little Dove, I love you. I adore you. I cherish you and I'm honored you are my mate. Will you also give me the great gift of being my wife?" He held the ring out to her and waited.

Tears filled her eyes as she stared at him and then looked at the ring. It only took a few heartbeats before she quickly nodded. "Yes, absolutely yes."

"Fantastic," Peri said and rubbed her hands together. "Lucian, my love, you're up."

Dalton stood and slid the ring onto Jewel's left hand and then took her face in his hands and kissed her reverently. "I love you," he whispered and then pulled back and took her hands in his.

"Peri and I have come to witness the joining of Dalton Black and Jewel Stone in marriage," Lucian began.

Jewels eyes widened and her mouth dropped open. "We're doing this now?"

"Do you want to wait?" Dalton asked.

Jewel seemed to think about it for a minute and then

said, "I feel like I should tell you that fifty percent of all first marriages end in divorce."

Dalton grinned and he was sure his wolf was peeking out through his eyes. "And I feel I should tell you zero percent of *Canis lupus* bondings end in separation. We wolves mate for life. Divorce doesn't exist in our world."

"What if you get tired of me?"

"That's not possible," he told her.

"You have lady bits," Peri cut in. "They never get tired of those."

"Perizada." Lucian growled.

"She's not wrong," Dalton said causing Jewel to giggle.

"And what if you get annoyed with me?" His mate challenged.

"I'll spank you for annoying me and then make love to you to make you get over being angry for spanking you." Dalton's words were blunt, but he needed his mate to understand he would do anything to keep her happy and to keep them together. Even teasing her and enjoying her shocked expression. Life would never be boring with her.

Jewel gasped and Dalton noted the change in her scent.

"Wow," Peri muttered. "Ship just got real."

Dalton growled. "Say yes, Little Dove. Or I will continue to say things that are going to make you put even more pheromones into the air. It's going to get very awkward."

She practically squeaked when she spoke. "Yes."

"Thank the Great Luna," Lucian muttered. "So, then, without further ado. Do you, Dalton, take Jewel to be your wife? Will you love her through peace and war? Will you care for her in times of illness or injury? Will you hold her when she is cold, feed her when she is hungry, offer your comfort when she is in distress, and take her burdens when they are too much to bear? Will you stand beside her forever in this life and in the next?"

"I will," Dalton said without hesitation.

"Jewel Stone, do you take Dalton to be your husband? Will you love and respect him through peace and war? Will you care for him in times of illness or injury? Will you hold him when he is cold, feed him when he is hungry, offer your comfort when he is in distress and take his burdens when they are too much to bear? Will you stand beside him forever in this life and in the next?"

"Absolutely," Jewel said. A huge grin spread across her face as she stepped closer to Dalton.

"By the power given to me on a website that granted me a certificate saying I could legally marry a couple, I now pronounce you man and wife," Lucian finished. "You may kiss your bride."

"But before you do," Peri said quickly. "Congratulations. And goodnight. Let's go, mate. Judging by the look in Dalton's eyes, when their lips touch, clothes are going to be coming off. I'm not staying for all that."

Dalton didn't even turn to see them leave. His eyes were only for his mate, his wife.

"We're married," Jewel said into his mind.

"We are," Dalton said as he wrapped his arms around her and pulled her body tightly to his own. "And now I'm going to kiss my wife."

Jewel tipped her head back so her lips were closer to his and licked her lips.

"Minx," he whispered just before his lips captured hers. He picked her up and she wrapped her legs around his waist. Dalton went straight for their bed.

"You say the word stop and this goes no further," he said through the bond.

"You're my husband, my mate, my best friend," said Jewel. "Why would I tell you to stop?"

"Are you ready for this next step?" he asked as he laid her down on the bed, propped his body over her, and looked down into her eyes. He brushed some stray strands of hair from her face as she stared back at him with lust and love.

"I want you," Jewel said. "I want you in every way and I want you to have me."

Dalton's stomach tightened at her words. "Then I will give my wife what she desires." Their lips met again and Dalton pushed his tongue into her mouth. He groaned as her taste flooded his own. He pressed his body down against her as his hands began a slow, thorough exploration of her body.

Dalton peeled Jewel's shirt over her head, her jeans were next. By the time he'd removed her undergarments, he was so lost in his desire and need of her that he couldn't have told you how is own clothes had been removed.

Jewel's hands skimmed over his back and across his shoulders. He could feel the slight tremor in them and heard the catch in her breath when their chests touched.

"I love the way you feel," he whispered against her ear. "Your skin is like silk." His right hand ran up her calf, then her thigh and her waist. His thumb brushed the underside of her breast and she stopped breathing all together. Dalton didn't move his hand any further up. He stared into her eyes and searched her mind for any signs of distress or fear. All he found was pleasure, passion, and his mate's own voice repeating in her mind *"don't beg, don't beg, don't you dare beg."*

"Little Dove," he crooned. "Tell me what you need? You don't have to beg. I will give it to you."

"I want you to mark me. Hands, teeth, lips, mark me and

make me yours," she said and there wasn't even a tremor in her voice. All he heard was desire.

Dalton's eyes roved over her body. He could see the faint scars on her arms and the scars on her stomach courtesy of Lorrelle and Volcan. They didn't take away from her magnificence. They only made him more in awe of her because those wounds were a testament to her strength.

His lips trailed across her jaw and down her neck to her shoulder. Dalton licked his bite mark once before sinking his teeth into her and marking her again. At the same time, he joined their bodies.

He made love to his mate, showing her how precious she was to him, how desirable and sexy he found her. As he took her, Dalton whispered to her all the things he wanted to share with her. With every moan, sigh, and whispered plea for him not to stop, he felt their bond growing stronger.

Much later, he held her tightly against him, their hearts pounding heavily in their chests as they both tried to catch their breaths. Dalton wanted to say something sweet and loving but he just couldn't speak. To put it bluntly, his Little Dove had rocked his world. In fact, he was pretty sure the world had fallen off its axis.

"Did you know that studies show that doing something for twenty one days in a row will make it become a habit," his mate said, and he could hear the humor in her voice.

"Is that so?"

"It is."

"And are you saying what we just did needs to become a habit?" Dalton bit his lip to keep from laughing.

"Absolutely."

"And what do studies show when you do something several times a day for twenty one days in a row?" he asked, loving how her body moved against his as she laughed.

"Well, if that something is drugs, the outcome is most likely death. If that something is cleaning, the outcome is a creepy obsession with cleanliness. And if that something was what we just did, the outcome would be friendlessness, homelessness, and a sex-induced stupor we might never recover from."

Dalton pulled her up on top of him and nipped at her neck. "I think I'll risk it."

∼

Sly held his mate in his arms as they sat in front of the fire place in their home. She'd been chilled to the bone ever since getting back from the draheim realm three days prior. She hadn't said much and it was breaking his heart that he couldn't fix what had happened to her. Z had tried talking to her, but Evenora only wanted Sly. She didn't like him to leave the room or get too far away from her. So, he simply held her.

"I love you, Evie," he whispered against her hair.

"I love you too," she said through her tears. "I feel broken, Sly. He broke me."

Sly squeezed her tighter, wishing her could somehow get closer to her. "We all get broken at some point in our lives. Volcan broke me when he took you away. But here you are, back in my arms where you belong. We will put each other back together again. We will heal."

"Don't leave me," she said and it sounded like a question. "He said you wouldn't want me anymore. Not after everything he did to me. I can't lose you."

Sly took her face in his hands and made sure she was looking in his eyes before he spoke. "I have loved you since we were children. Do you remember? I use to follow you around practically begging for your attention and you would throw rocks at me and tell me to go eat worms?"

She smiled, though it was small. "You were a smelly boy."

"And now I am a smelly man, but I am your man. And that will never, ever change. Throw rocks at me and I will dodge them. Tell me to eat worms and I will dig them up and smile as I swallow them. Tell me you believe Volcan's lies and that I won't want you anymore and I will spend my life proving you wrong. I. Will. Never. Leave. You."

Tears streamed down her face and she leaned forward pressing her lips to his. "I might ask you again tomorrow," she warned.

"And I will tell you the same thing and then kiss you senseless."

Evanora pressed her forehead to his. "Thank you, Sly. For not giving up. For doing whatever you needed to do to get me back."

"You don't have to thank me, my precious one. I will always come for you. I will always want you and need you."

She yawned and he pulled her down onto the pile of furs he'd laid on the floor. "Sleep, my love. You need rest. Sleep and then when you wake I will make love to you so you will know how much I love you, need you, and desire you no matter what that lying snake told you. Sleep." He pulled the blanket over them and tucked her close to his body. When her breathing evened out and he knew she was asleep, he finally let his own eyes close. Before he drifted off, he whispered into the night, "Please, Great Luna, heal my love, restore her so one day she will smile and laugh again. Remind her of how precious she is, as I will do every minute of every day."

"Vasile needs us," Peri said as she sat in Lucian's lap. They were sitting on a spot at the top of the Carpathian Mountains, where he'd been born. She'd needed to get out of her home and away from the others for just a little while.

"Don't you think maybe you need a few days to yourself?" her mate asked.

Peri knew she did, but she didn't know how to do that. The world was still turning and bad people still needed to be destroyed. And she also didn't want to deal with her emotions after having seen Jewel die, the Great Luna die, and what she had thought was going to be the end of the world as she'd known it. A piece of her had broken inside, and Peri didn't know how to deal with it.

"I can help you," Lucian said, hearing her thoughts. "Let me hold you and bear this for you."

Peri turned her face and burrowed into his chest as she let go of the hurt and fear that had ripped the air from her lungs. She'd watched too many that she loved die. Some had stayed dead and some had been given another chance, but it still hurt. She'd watched a goddess lay down her life and thought evil had won. She'd felt the world crumble around her, and then the ground had shaken, and everything had been okay. She hadn't been able to catch her breath since her time in the draheim realm, and she was still panting. Peri was beginning to wonder if she was finally going mad.

"You're hurting, my love. That's all. It's pain. Let it go. Let yourself mourn. I'll hold you."

"Don't let go," she whispered. "Please, whatever you do, don't let go."

"Never," Lucian promised as he held his mate tightly to his chest. He had no idea what was going to come. He had no clue what they would face tomorrow, but he knew that he would be by her side, or he'd carry her if need be, but he would never leave her to face any of it on her own.

THANK you for reading Wolf of Sight. If you enjoyed it, we would greatly appreciate it if you took time to leave a review.

Thank you so very much!

ACKNOWLEDGMENTS

As usual, there are so many people to thank when it comes to the journey of writing a novel. It takes more than just an author to achieve such an endeavor. First and foremost, I thank my Lord and Savior. He is the ultimate creator, the ultimate being with incredible imagination and I am daily in awe of the world he fashioned together for me to live in. Thank you to my husband, my love, and my best friend, all rolled into one. I couldn't do this without him. Thank you to Jessica for your unending humor and willingness to delve into the scary place that is my mind. Thank you for your friendship. Thank you to my readers. Without you I'm just a chick putting words down on pages, but because of you I've gotten to live my dream. There really is no way for me to show my thanks.

ABOUT THE AUTHOR

Quinn Loftis is a multi-award-winning author of over thirty novels, including the USA Today Bestseller, Fate and Fury. When she isn't creating exciting worlds filled with romantic werewolves, she works as a pediatric nurse and crafts like there's no tomorrow. She is blessed to be married to her best friend for over twenty years and they have three sons, a crazy French bulldog, and a cat that wants to take over the world.

Connect with Quinn

www.quinnloftisbooks.com
lovetoread@quinnloftisbooks.com
www.facebook.com/QuinnLoftisBooks
www.twitter.com/AuthQuinnLoftis
https://www.instagram.com/quinnloftisbooks/
https://www.pinterest.com/quinnloftisbooks/

QUINN'S BOOKSHELF

The Grey Wolves Series

The Gypsy Healer Series

The Elfin Series

The Dream Maker Series

The Clan Hakon Series

Nature Hunters Academy

Sign up for Quinn's newsletter here:
www.quinnloftisbooks.com/newslettersignup

You can also find Quinn writing contemporary romances as her alter ego, Alyson Drake, at www.alysondrake.com.